LEGION
BOOK
SIX

HEIR

A.D. STARRLING

COPYRIGHT

FOREWORD

I am light. I am salvation.
I am rebirth. I am savior.
I belong to Heaven.
P.S. I like bunnies.
- Artemus Steele

PROLOGUE

2033, LIBYAN DESERT

Shooting stars streaked across the night sky, silent streams of light with barely anyone to witness them but endless desert sand. Solomon Weiss paused to admire the celestial bodies as they burned through Earth's atmosphere. A cool breeze ruffled his thawb and danced across his exposed skin from the north, bringing with it the salty taste of the sea.

It never ceased to surprise him how much more beautiful the world looked now that he had lost everything but his damned soul.

Solomon's gaze wandered down to the ridge he was climbing. He made a clicking noise with his tongue and tugged on the reins of the camel. The creature obeyed his command with a low huff. It wasn't long before they reached the summit of the elevation. Solomon pulled the animal to a stop and studied the landscape before him.

Stretching out as far as the eye could see was a dark ocean of sand dunes, barren hills, and rock plains. A jagged line some hundred miles long blocked out the low-lying stars to the west. Though he should not have been able to see the lights of the closest town at the base of the mountain range, Solomon's otherworldly eyes detected their presence nonetheless.

He wondered if the child had seen them too.

It took him another hour to reach the cave where the boy had sought shelter for the night. Solomon climbed off the camel and looped the creature's reins loosely around a boulder. He stilled and concentrated.

A steady thumping reached his unearthly ears, too fast and thready for his liking.

Solomon frowned and took the water gourd and a bag of dry raisins from the camel's saddle. He followed the sound of the boy's heartbeat into the dark crevice carved into the rockface before him.

The child had crawled into the farthest corner of the cave, where water had dripped down through cracks and fissures in the cliff to form a shallow pool. The puddle was only four inches wide and an inch deep, not enough to quench the boy's raging thirst. He lay on his front, his thin body shuddering with shallow, labored breaths, as if the very air hurt his lungs. His tousled, black hair obscured his eyes where it had fallen across his face, and his lips were cracked and bleeding.

Solomon knelt on the ground and gently rolled the child onto his back before lifting him onto his lap. He cradled his head with one hand and brought the water gourd to his mouth. A trickle of liquid fell between the boy's dry lips.

It took a moment for him to realize what was happening. The first thing he did was lick his lips and swallow. The second thing he did was grasp Solomon's wrist with a speed and strength that surprised him, even though he had half expected it.

He knew the child was only semi-conscious. The boy tugged the gourd close to him and took giant gulps of the water falling across his parched lips.

He finally blinked, his long lashes gritty with desert sand. Dark pupils contracted and dilated as they focused on Solomon. He froze when he registered Solomon's unworldly identity.

Solomon heard an alien heart start to beat somewhere inside the child.

Thump.

He masked a grimace. *Well, it's not as if I wasn't expecting this either.*

He took a deep breath and suppressed his aura.

Thump-thump.

The boy trembled, as if in pain.

But Solomon knew better. It wasn't discomfort that was making the boy shiver in his hold. It was the furious excitement of the beast who was awakening inside his frail body.

Thump-thump. Thump-thump.

Golden light gleamed in the boy's dark eyes.

The beast's stormy gaze scorched Solomon's face as she beheld him for the first time.

Solomon gazed steadily back at the creature. "I have to say, you haven't exactly done a great job of looking after your host."

Irritation filled the beast's gaze, dampening her blood-lust. A sibilant hiss escaped the boy's throat.

"Who are you to tell me what to do and not to do with my host?!"

"Ah," Solomon said wryly. "She speaks."

He took some raisins from the bag and offered them to the boy.

The beast blinked.

The boy took a cautious sniff of the food before taking a careful mouthful between his lips. His teeth grazed Solomon's palm as he swallowed the rest with ravenous gusto.

Solomon rose, the boy's limp form in his arms, and headed for the exit. Though the boy's eyes were open and his beast had spoken to Solomon, he was not truly conscious still.

"Where are you taking my host?" the beast demanded haughtily as Solomon came out of the cave and took long strides toward the camel.

"Somewhere he has a better chance of survival."

The camel grunted in faint alarm as Solomon drew near. It could sense the nature of the creature in Solomon's arms.

I can't say I blame it.

"We are doing just fine," the beast said in a disgruntled tone. *"Now, put us down."*

Solomon stopped in his tracks. "Alright."

He let go of the boy.

The child thudded onto the ground next to one of the camel's saucer-shaped feet and bounced once. The camel startled and backed away.

The beast hissed in rage. *"How dare you hurt my host?!"*

"You said to put you down."

"I did not mean for you to drop him so callously!"

Solomon squatted and stared calmly at the mythical creature glaring at him. "I don't want to hurt your host, beast. I want to help him."

Golden eyes narrowed with suspicion. *"Why would you*

come to our aid? I know what you are. Your kind wants nothing more than to kill us."

Solomon smiled faintly and rocked back on his heels. "So, my glamor isn't working on you, huh?"

The beast sniffed. *"No, monster who walks in the form of man."*

A surprisingly comfortable silence fell between them.

"I can sense your intent is genuine," the beast finally said reluctantly. *"But why would you want to help him? Help* us?"

"To atone for my sins and the sins of my kind," Solomon admitted quietly. "To stop what is coming."

The beast observed him for a moment. *"And how do you intend to do that?"*

"By protecting you. And by guiding your host."

"You mean to serve us?"

"Yes."

"And use your powers to do good?" the beast asked insistently.

"Always."

The beast was quiet for a long time. A shudder ran through the boy's body. His eyes flared with brightness.

"Then, I accept. On behalf of my host and myself. But heed my words. If you betray us, if you so much as look at the boy the wrong way, I will kill you."

CHAPTER ONE

SERENA STIRRED AND OPENED HER EYES.

Soft light streamed through the bay windows behind the four-poster bed in Drake's bedroom. She glanced at the antique clock on the wall and saw that it was still early.

A muscular arm tightened slightly around her waist. Serena looked over her shoulder at the man tucked up close to her. A tender smile stretched her lips.

Drake's eyelashes rested softly against his cheeks as he slept, the stubble on his handsome face dark against his skin.

As a super soldier, Serena could survive days without sleeping. Yet, she and Nate had gotten into the habit of sleeping almost every night since they started living at Artemus's mansion. Serena's smile turned wry as she clocked the fresh hickey on Drake's shoulder. Besides, there were plenty more reasons for her and Nate to need to rest up these days.

Drake blinked fuzzily. Serena watched awareness wash across his face. She loved watching Drake sleep. She loved it even more when he woke up. Not that she would ever admit this to him.

Drake's mouth split in a sexy smile that made her heart skip a beat. "'Morning."

His husky voice danced down her spine. Serena congratulated herself on not immediately jumping the man. "Hey."

Drake rolled her over and hugged her body close to his. "What're you up to today?"

"Gideon has a new mission for me and Nate. He's sending us details this morning."

Serena bit back a sound of appreciation as Drake slipped his leg between her thighs. She could feel sexual tension coiling between them, as it always did when they were in each other's company these days.

Serena wondered whether this hunger would ever abate. Whether this wild desire they felt for one another would ever disappear one day.

She chastised herself inwardly the next moment.

She knew better than to make plans for the future. Super soldiers did not get a happily ever after.

Drake didn't miss her attempt to mask her arousal. His hand drifted down her back and curved over her butt. He angled her hips closer. Serena stifled a moan as she felt the evidence of his desire against her belly.

Drake smirked. "Does this mean a trip?"

Serena dipped her chin and tried to ignore the way he was drawing patterns on her bare skin with his fingers, his touch feather-light. "Probably. It's about those strange earthquakes we've been having lately."

Lines furrowed Drake's brow. He stilled. There had been a series of earthquakes reported recently across the four continents.

His frown deepened. "Since when did super soldiers get involved in seismology?"

"Since the U.S. government requested our assistance."

Unease darkened Drake's eyes. "Wait. Does this have anything to do with Ba'al?"

Serena swallowed a sigh. She knew Drake was still unnerved by what had happened during their last battle with the demonic organization. He hadn't been able to fight alongside them at full throttle like he normally would have. The fact that his father's influence on him was growing stronger with every encounter with Ba'al was a source of concern for all of them, especially his twin.

It had only been a handful of days since Elton LeBlanc had revealed what Karl had told him during the brief time the two brothers had shared a few weeks ago. The older LeBlanc had been revived along with a horde of other dead people across Chicago, a side effect of the awakening of the latest Guardian to join their ranks.

All of them had been troubled by Karl's dictate that Artemus not follow Drake if the dark angel were to fall to Hell, Artemus and Serena more so than anyone because of their intimate connection to him. This combined with a similar warning that Otis and Sebastian had since unearthed in Otis's mother's journals made it clear that Drake's eventual downfall was not just a possibility but, in all likelihood, fated to happen, whether they liked it or not.

Serena shook off the dark misgivings dancing through her subconscious and lifted a hand to Drake's face.

"We don't know if Ba'al is behind those earthquakes yet." She smoothed the furrows on his forehead. "But they have been happening close to recent demonic sightings. The Immortals are sending a team of experts to assist us."

Drake looked unconvinced by her reassurances. "One of us should go with you. Just in case there's trouble."

Serena started counting on her fingers. "Sebastian and Otis leave for Rome today. Daniel is joining them for his vacation. Callie and Haruki are heading out on business trips next week. That just leaves you, Artemus, Leah, and the rabbit to guard the fort."

"You forgot the undead chicken."

Serena grimaced. "Gertrude's affiliations are still unclear. She chased the hellhound around the estate the other day. For all we know, she's on the demons' side."

Drake sighed. "I wouldn't put it past Smokey to have provoked her. You know how territorial he gets." He arched an eyebrow. "And does the fort need guarding? Theia's barrier is more than strong enough to—"

Serena pressed her lips to his. "You know what I mean."

She gasped as Drake grabbed her and moved onto his back. She settled atop him, their legs tangling and their naked bodies kissing from their chests to their groins.

"I do," Drake admitted in a disgruntled tone. "Now, how about I collect in advance? Since I'm not gonna see you for God knows how long."

Serena rose into a sitting position and straddled Drake's hips. She wriggled her lower body and grinned when the movement earned her a heartfelt groan. Drake's fingers bit into her waist, passion bringing a flush of color to his face and chest.

"I didn't know we were doing retainers," Serena drawled.

"We are now. So, how about we get down and dirty for the next..." he glanced at the clock, "two hours or so?"

Serena grinned. "You sure you can go that long, cowboy?"

"We've gone longer than that before," the dark angel said with smug confidence. He tucked his hands behind his head and bucked his hips slightly. Serena bit her lip. "Also, correct me if I'm wrong, but you're the one riding me right now."

Serena leaned down and kissed him slow and deep, the way he liked it. She captured his lower lip between her teeth and sucked on it before letting go with a wet pop.

"Giddy-up," she murmured sultrily.

Drake's eyes blazed with lust.

IT WAS GONE EIGHT A.M. BY THE TIME THEY MADE THEIR way downstairs.

Serena grabbed a carton of orange juice out of the refrigerator and looked over at Nate where he was removing a loaf of bread from the oven.

"Why does Goldilocks look like he's about to cry into his cornflakes?"

She indicated the kitchen table, where a morose-looking Artemus was munching on his breakfast, Smokey on his lap and Daniel reading the paper next to them.

Artemus flashed her a warning look.

Nate took off his oven gloves and saw to the eggs frying in the skillet on the range. "He lost a game of chess to Sebastian last night."

Daniel turned a page.

"Which means Sebastian gets his room for three months when he comes back from Rome," the priest said, without looking up from the article he was reading.

Drake headed over to the coffee machine. "You played chess with the Englishman?"

"Yeah," Artemus muttered.

Serena raised an eyebrow as she passed Drake their cups. "The guy who's been playing the game for nearly two hundred years?"

"And who also happens to be the Sphinx," Drake added.

Daniel smiled faintly, his gaze still on the paper.

Artemus narrowed his eyes at them. "What are you guys getting at?"

Bacon crumbs fell on his lap as Smokey crunched down on the strip of bacon Daniel had just passed him under the table. Artemus gave the priest and the rabbit an irritated look.

"Your stupidity knows no bounds," Serena said.

"Hey!" Artemus protested. "I resent that!"

Callie entered the kitchen. "You resent what?"

"He lost a game of chess and his room to Sebastian," Nate explained.

Callie kissed her boyfriend and gave Artemus a look of pity. "Are you an idiot? You know my brother is an expert at chess."

"I may have been under the influence last night," Artemus admitted grudgingly.

"You mean you got *drunk* and played chess?" Drake said drily.

Serena shook her head slowly. "You naïve, little fool."

"Gambling *and* drinking," Daniel muttered. "Your father would be most disappointed."

Artemus scowled. "Michael is hardly a saint."

Callie helped Nate carry their breakfast over to the

table. "Is something bothering you?" she asked Artemus. She pursed her lips. "Is it Haruki?"

Artemus blinked, nonplussed. "Why the hell would I be worrying about the Dragon?"

"Leah did steal him from you," Drake said, poker-faced.

"He's right," Callie said in a sympathetic voice. "Your spouse has cruelly abandoned you for a younger paramour."

Artemus's eyebrows met in the midline. "I couldn't give a rat's ass what those two do together!"

"Strong words for a guy who just lost his wife to another woman," Serena said.

Before Artemus could utter another word, said wife appeared with said woman.

Leah greeted them with a somewhat shy smile. "Good morning."

Even though she'd moved in a couple of weeks ago, she was still getting used to living with them. Compared to the four-bedroom house she'd shared with her detective father, the mansion was immense and full of strange and other-worldly tenants, not to mention cranky ones. Though Jeremiah Chase remained unhappy about the situation, he had eventually capitulated in the face of Leah's pleas and his mother-in-law's assurances that the young woman would be safer at the LeBlanc mansion.

Drake smiled lazily at the Yakuza heir and the art student. "We were just talking about you two."

"You were?" Haruki said suspiciously.

"Yeah," Serena said with a grin.

Haruki glanced at Artemus's stormy expression and grimaced. "Let me guess. You guys were taunting Goldilocks again."

No one missed the way he served Leah some orange juice and guided her to the table.

"He makes it so easy," Drake said.

Artemus flipped the finger at his twin.

"I must say, that is rather rude for this time in the morning," Sebastian said coolly as he entered the kitchen. He paused and studied Artemus with a jaundiced air. "I see from your grim countenance that you are regretting your actions last night."

"You have no idea how badly," Artemus muttered. "You and the witch had better not defile my bed."

Callie blinked. "Oh. So, *that's* what you're worried about."

Sebastian was currently dating Naomi Wagner, Leah's first cousin once removed and a witch who had helped them fight the demons who had hoped to use Leah to open a gate to Hell under one of the city's oldest museums. A human who carried the blood of the demon Azazel, she was a member of the Nolans, an influential family of witches and sorcerers who ruled over those of their kind who lived in the city and its surrounding suburbs. Barbara Nolan, the High Priestess of the coven, was Leah's maternal grandmother.

Sebastian drew himself to his full height.

"What I do or do not do with Naomi is no one's business but mine," he declared haughtily.

"From all appearances, you are doing her, alright," Serena drawled.

Haruki sighed. Leah blushed. Sebastian frowned.

"So, you're all packed up and ready for Rome?" Haruki asked the Englishman.

Sebastian took a seat at the table. "Yes. We have exhausted the existing information in my personal library.

It will be interesting to see if the Vatican holds any clues about the new symbols on Otis's hand."

Three more inverted Vs had appeared on Otis's right palm during their latest conflict with Ba'al, forming a four-pointed star with the one that had originally materialized when his powers first manifested in Salem. They had made his defensive barrier visible and had granted him even more power than he had previously possessed, so much so he had managed to seal away the demon goddess Astarte without killing her.

Otis and Sebastian were convinced Rome held the answers they were seeking. When Daniel had heard about their travel plans, he had made arrangements to take some leave so he could visit Persephone.

"It's gonna be quiet without you guys around," Drake said.

"Haru and I don't leave for another week." Callie linked her hand with Nate's and gave the hulking super soldier a mournful look. "Although, I don't know what I'm going to do with myself without my Pookie Bear."

Nate flushed under their stares.

Pookie Bear? Drake mouthed silently to Serena, his expression amused.

She kicked him under the table.

Artemus's cell rang. He fished it out of the back pocket of his jeans and frowned at the number on the screen.

"You really should get a new phone," Callie said.

"I don't need a new phone," Artemus muttered as he took the call. "Hey, Elton. What's up?"

He listened for a moment, surprise slowly widening his eyes.

CHAPTER TWO

Isabelle Mueller inspected Artemus's outfit with a lazy smile. "Looking good there, Goldilocks."

Artemus sighed. "Coming from you, that sounds like an insult."

He fiddled awkwardly with his bow tie and studied the glitzy crowd filling the auction house ballroom.

"She's right," Mark Daniels said. "You clean up pretty nice, man."

"I think your boyfriend is hitting on me," Artemus told Isabelle.

"I can't exactly blame him," the Immortal drawled, her eyes twinkling. "You make for a mighty fine—"

"There you are!" someone exclaimed from the main floor.

Artemus turned and spied the couple striding toward him. He descended the shallow flight of steps to greet them.

"Congratulations on your engagement." Artemus pressed a warm kiss to Helen Tempest's cheeks and shook

Elton's hand. "We would have brought a gift if this wasn't such short notice."

Elton tugged him close for a hearty hug. "Forget the gift. I'm just glad you could make it. I've been busy with work and got worried when Helen told me she hadn't received your RVSP."

"I'm so sorry," Helen said apologetically. "I could have sworn we sent an invite to the mansion. I really don't understand how it could have gotten lost."

A faint jingle reached Artemus's ears. He turned and eyed the rabbit hopping inside the ballroom ahead of Callie and Haruki, a silver bell tied around his neck.

"I have an idea," Artemus said darkly.

Smokey avoided his stare and did his best to look cute.

"Awww!" Helen's expression melted when she saw the outfit the Rex rabbit wore. "How sweet! He's wearing a tux."

She leaned down and lifted Smokey into her arms.

Callie bit her lip worriedly. The rest of them blanched.

"Why are you looking at me like that?" Helen said, puzzled.

Smokey huffed and went limp in her arms, a sure sign he wasn't intending to attack or maim.

Artemus decided now was not the best time to reveal to the retired college professor that she was currently cuddling the three-headed hellhound Cerberus.

"Nothing. I'm just surprised he's letting you hold him. He can be a bit feral at times."

A crimson light danced in the rabbit's eyes. Luckily, Helen was the one member of their party who failed to see the unholy phenomenon.

Elton peered past Callie and Haruki. "Where are Drake and Leah?"

"Leah has an exam tonight," Haruki said apologetically. "She said she's going to make popcorn and watch a movie with Gertrude when she gets home. Drake decided to stay back and watch over them."

Elton's eyes glazed over slightly. "The chicken is still around?"

"Yeah." Artemus grimaced. "Leah and Drake are about the only people Gertrude tolerates. Must be a kinship thing."

Elton's unintelligible grunt earned him a curious stare from his fiancée.

A frail voice rose behind Artemus, distracting them all. "Would this young man be the person you wanted to introduce me to, Elton?"

An elderly lady wearing a throatful of pearl necklaces and the kind of evening wear Sebastian would have approved of squinted at them with rheumy eyes, her walking stick striking the tiled floor with forceful taps as she approached.

"Mrs. Kaufman, I'm so glad you could join us this evening," Elton said in a smooth, business voice. "And to answer your question, yes. This is Artemus Steele, the person I told you about. Artemus, this is Esther Kaufman, an old client of mine."

Artemus greeted the woman with a polite murmur, already wary about where this was going.

"Esther wants someone to look at some of her antiques," Elton said. "I told her you're the best man for the job."

He smiled at Artemus, a warning look in his eyes.

"Really?" Artemus said thinly. He turned to the old woman. "Elton does exaggerate. His other valuers are pretty good too."

Esther beamed. "Somehow, I doubt that. I can tell he's right. Plus, you sure are eye candy." She reached up and pinched Artemus's cheek. "Why, if I were fifty years younger, I would gobble you up like the hot piece of ass that you are."

Smokey's eyes rounded. Artemus made a choking noise. Elton gaped. Callie and Helen turned away slightly, shoulders shaking with silent laughter. Only Haruki, Isabelle, and Mark managed to keep a straight face.

"Now, how about you get me a drink, young man?"

Esther hooked her arm through Artemus's elbow and guided him onto the main floor. Artemus glanced over his shoulder as he was dragged toward the bar.

Help me! he mouthed.

Callie grinned. "You go, you little firecracker."

"Good luck, Casanova," Isabelle called out.

Artemus scowled at them.

It was another half hour before he got rid of the elderly widow and that was only after he agreed to her visiting him at his antique shop. By this point, the beginning of a headache was drilling at Artemus's temples.

"You should go easy on the alcohol," Haruki said as he came up behind him.

Artemus turned. He couldn't help but catch the admiring looks the Yakuza heir received as he joined him. Haruki was used to these kinds of glamorous parties and seemed unaffected by the female attention he was drawing.

Artemus, on the other hand, would rather poke his eye out than voluntarily attend a function. This fact never ceased to aggravate Elton, considering Artemus was the principle reason his auction house was so successful in the first place. Artemus's reputation and presence at the high-stake private auctions Elton held once a month were a beacon that drew many people with deep pockets and considerable political influence from all over the world.

The auction house didn't just sell rare goods. It was also a networking scene for the individuals and organizations the Vatican was recruiting for its fight against Ba'al.

It was at one of these events that he and Smokey had first met Callie and Drake.

Artemus downed his champagne, made a face when the alcohol burned his throat, and placed the empty flute on a passing waiter's tray.

"Trust me, you'd be drinking too if you just had your butt groped by someone who could be your grandmother."

Haruki grimaced. "She groped your butt?"

"I think I have bruises."

They stood in silence for a while, the chatter of the crowd a steady drone around them.

"What's bothering you?" Haruki finally said.

Artemus glanced at him. "What makes you think something's bothering me?"

Haruki's expression grew pinched. "We've all noticed it. And we think it's about more than just what Karl said to Elton."

"Yeah, well, what Karl said to Elton is enough to give anyone acid. But you're right. There's something else." Artemus hesitated. "It's about the girl I told you about. The one I've been dreaming about since I was a kid."

Haruki brightened up slightly. "You mean the one in your hentai dreams?"

Artemus narrowed his eyes.

"Sorry," Haruki mumbled. "Go on."

"The last time I saw her was three months ago," Artemus admitted in a low voice.

Haruki arched an eyebrow. "Is that so unusual?"

"Yes. I've dreamt about her every week since the night I first met Smokey and my marks appeared."

Haruki studied him curiously. "So, you think the fact that you haven't seen her since—"

"Since before we went to Rome," Artemus confessed.

Lines marred Haruki's brow. "You think something's wrong? Just because you haven't dreamt of her? That's a bit far-fetched, don't you think?"

"I just feel that something bad is going to happen," Artemus said stubbornly.

Haruki sighed. "Something bad always happens to us. We're fighting an organization of demons who want to raise Hell on Earth."

"I mean something worse than that." Artemus finally voiced the fear that had been growing inside him for the last few weeks. "I feel like I'm going to lose one of you soon."

Surprise flashed on Haruki's face. His expression softened. "Look, I know you're worried about what might happen to Drake. We'll just have to do our damnedest to make sure that what Karl said doesn't come to pass."

Artemus blew out a heavy sigh. "Thanks. Still, I can't stop worrying about—"

He froze. Haruki grew still beside him.

They looked across the ballroom to where Callie had stopped talking to Elton, Helen, and a few of their guests, Smokey in her arms. Her eyes widened as she turned her head mechanically and met their gazes, the hellhound's eyes flashing crimson.

They could all feel it.

Something was coming. Something powerful. Something demonic.

The chandeliers swayed and clinked above them. The ground started to shake.

CHAPTER THREE

ARTEMUS AND HARUKI BOLTED ACROSS THE FLOOR toward Callie, Smokey, and Elton, sidestepping the frozen guests in their paths with ease.

"*Get everyone out of here!*" Artemus yelled in Isabelle and Mark's direction.

A chandelier crashed on Artemus's right, peppering him with glittering shards. More followed, the sounds of the crystals exploding drowned out by the panicked screams of the crowd as they came to life and stampeded toward the exit.

Artemus knew they had but moments before whatever was drawing close got there. He scanned the ballroom for rifts as he ran over the increasingly unsteady ground, wondering where the demon would appear, and saw none.

Shit! Where is he?!

"This demon feels stronger than a commander!" Haruki said.

His juzu bracelet transformed into a flaming, holy sword as he kept pace with Artemus. Silver scales exploded across his skin. His pupils narrowed to glowing, vertical slits that burned with a fiery light.

Artemus clenched his jaw. "I know!"

He reached under his tuxedo and yanked his switchblade from the sheath strapped to his lower back. Cracks formed on the tiled floor as the tremors intensified, a spiderweb of jagged, dark lines. They expanded and raced up the walls and several of the marble Corinthian columns holding up the ceiling.

Elton was pleading with Helen when Artemus and Haruki reached their group. "Please, go with Shamus!"

Artemus looked over at the hulking figure of Elton's bodyguard closing in on them from the direction of the foyer, a modified Beretta in hand and his face full of tension.

"We have a Code Black!" Shamus barked into the smartband on his wrist as he approached at a dead run. "I repeat, this is a Code Black!"

Artemus knew the gun the Vatican agent and former world-heavyweight boxing champion was holding was loaded with silver-leaded bullets impregnated with Holy Water, as were the weapons carried by the rest of Elton's security team. Though the bullets couldn't instantly kill a demon, they could hurt them and slow them down.

"No! Not without you!" Helen retorted.

Only Elton, Helen, Callie, and Smokey remained, their other guests having joined the growing stream of people fleeing the ballroom.

Callie removed her heels, ripped the sides of her gown from the mid-thigh down, and unleashed the golden staff hidden inside the ivory cane she carried everywhere with her, her eyes glowing with an emerald light. Smokey's fur stood on end where he crouched on the floor beside her, his eyes glowing scarlet and his body trembling as he controlled his transformation.

There were still some two dozen souls trying to squeeze through the doorway that led to the main entrance of the building and the terrace doors opening out onto the rear garden. Enough eyes for Artemus and the divine beasts not to show their full forms yet.

Elton's face hardened as the last of the guests finally deserted the ballroom. He drew his gun from the holster under his jacket, a muscle jumping in his jawline. Helen's eyes widened.

"Do as I say, Helen," Elton ordered in a steely voice. "I can't fight if you're here."

Confusion replaced the shock on Helen's face. "What do you mean, fight?!" She glanced around dazedly, color leeching out of her cheeks as her gaze landed on their weapons. "This is an earthquake! We need to get out of the building before it collapses!"

As if to prove her point, a large chunk of plaster crashed down some twenty feet from where they stood.

"Take her!" Elton snapped at Shamus.

The bodyguard nodded, murmured an apologetic "Sorry, ma'am," to Helen, and looped an arm around her waist. Helen gasped as Shamus lifted her as if she weighed nothing and headed resolutely for the main door.

"Stop!" Helen shrieked. "*Put me down, Shamus!*"

A mixture of relief and remorse flooded Elton's face. He turned to Artemus. "What the hell is going on? I can't see a rift! How is this thing even doing—?"

The earthquake stopped with a suddenness that made Callie gasp.

The hairs rose on the back of Artemus's neck. An eerie silence descended upon the gloom-filled ballroom, most of the lighting having gone out with the shattered chande-liers. Shamus stood frozen halfway to the door, Helen in his hold.

Artemus's gaze gravitated to them.

"There," Haruki said in a low, tense voice.

Callie's attention was also riveted to the ground beneath Shamus's feet. Artemus swallowed. He could feel the corrupt energy growing there. They had but seconds left to act.

"Smokey, *go!*" Artemus shouted.

Smokey went into full three-headed Cerberus mode at the same time Artemus transformed. They shot across the ballroom, Haruki and Callie close on their tails in beast form and Elton's startled shout ringing dimly in Artemus's ears.

The floor cracked beneath Shamus. It caved with Arte-mus's next heartbeat, forming a gaping hole that would swallow the agent and the woman in his arms.

Smokey smashed into the couple and carried them clear of the growing void.

Artemus swooped down and caught Shamus's arm as he sailed across the ballroom. He beat his wings and moved, eager to get away from the being he could sense rising from the abyss.

Something shot past him as he spun in the air and retreated from the bottomless crater that now occupied the center of the ballroom, Michael's flaming sword in one hand and Shamus and Helen dangling limply from the other.

The ceiling exploded as whatever had soared out of the ground kept on climbing, the stars becoming visible as the auction house roof collapsed in its wake a couple of seconds later.

Artemus landed on the ground next to an intact, marble column, Shamus and Helen settling beside him. Helen's eyes were giant saucers in her ashen face. She stared dazedly at his wings and armor.

"Get behind the pillar," Artemus ordered grimly. "And stay close to the ground."

Shamus nodded and dragged Helen around the column. Artemus could tell from the bodyguard's uneasy expression that he knew his weapon would be useless in the face of this enemy.

"Elton, stay back!" Artemus barked, his knuckles whitening on his sword.

Divine flames danced on the blade and the gauntlet on his right hand, courtesy of the ring he had inherited in Rome from Daniel's key.

"I can help!" Elton shouted.

"For once in your goddamn life, will you do as you're—!"

The attack came with a swiftness that shocked Artemus.

Something that felt like a giant, invisible blade dropped from the sky and tore across the ballroom. It carved through half a dozen marble columns and the walls and sliced crimson lines into the hellhound and the Chimera's flanks.

Though the sheer force of the assault sent Artemus and Haruki skidding backward across the floor, it did not penetrate the Dragon's scales nor Artemus's divine armor.

Blood dripped down Callie's dress as she glared at the yawning hole in the ceiling. She glanced at Smokey, the giant snake sprouting from her tailbone and the hundreds of others making up her mane writhing and hissing in fury at the injuries she had sustained.

"Are you okay, brother?" the Chimera growled.

I am fine, sister.

Acid saliva dripped from the hellhound's massive jowls and a low, continuous growl ripped from his three throats as he followed Callie's gaze, the wounds on his body oozing scarlet trickles that burned holes into the tiles beneath his giant paws.

Get ready. He is coming.

Smoke curled at the corners of Haruki's mouth and wafted from his nostrils as the Dragon's divine fire bloomed in his stomach and worked its way up his chest and throat, the passage of the flames accompanied by an orange glow under his tuxedo. Power bloomed inside Artemus as he called upon the core of heavenly energy inside his own body.

The bond that tied them glowed brightly inside their minds and souls, a golden leyline of divine energy that amplified their strength the more divine beasts joined their ranks.

A shape descended from the starlit heavens, its outline blurring as it rocked to a stop some fifteen feet above what had once been the ballroom's floor, but which was now a mess of concrete, marble, and plaster ringing a jagged chasm.

Artemus's eyes widened as he finally made out the figure that had manifested its presence in such a catastrophic fashion.

The apparition looked like an angel. He bore wings, had glittering skin and pale hair, and wore armor like Artemus, except everything was a uniform gray. In his right hand was what appeared to be a divine broadsword. It was dull and lackluster, without the flames that commonly marked Artemus and the other Guardians' weapons as heavenly instruments.

But for all his unusual appearance, it was the creature's eyes that captured Artemus's attention the most and made his stomach twist with alarm. They were black from edge to edge, with pinpoint, crimson pupils.

Smokey's enraged hiss echoed in Artemus's mind.

The Nephilim have risen!

CHAPTER FOUR

THE MICROWAVE DINGED. DRAKE TOOK OUT THE BOWL of popcorn and headed into the TV room. Leah sat on the main couch, Gertrude beside her. The Guardian had the remote in one hand and was channel surfing. Drake took the seat on the other side of her and eyed the chicken.

"You know Artemus gets pissy about Gertrude being on the couch, right?"

A low cluck rose from the undead chicken at the sound of her name. She inched closer to Leah and settled against her thigh.

"Yeah, well, what Artemus doesn't know won't hurt him," Leah muttered, her gaze on the TV screen. "What's your poison? *Night of the Living Dead* or *Frankenstein?*"

Drake grimaced and opened a bottle of beer. "Are those the only choices?"

"They are the only choices I'm willing to entertain," Leah said bluntly.

"Wow. I forgot how much of a pain in the ass teenagers are." Drake glanced at Gertrude. "Considering present company, *Night of the Living Dead* seems appropriate."

Leah narrowed her eyes. "I'm a young woman, not a teenager."

She put the movie on and grabbed the bottle of beer on the coffee table.

"With emphasis on the young." Drake eyed Leah's drink. "I don't think Jeremiah would approve of you drinking."

Leah rolled her eyes. "It's been a shitty day. I swear Naomi made that test deliberately harder just for me. And Dad knows I have the occasional beer. Besides, I doubt you were a saint when you were my age."

"You are correct," Drake drawled. "Speaking of which. It's a Friday night. Shouldn't you be out painting the town red with your friends?"

"I'm not really into the party scene."

Drake raised an eyebrow. "Does Haruki know he's hooking up with an extreme introvert?"

Leah gave him a dark look and reached for the popcorn. "That's rich coming from the guy spending his Friday night with a teenage girl and a dead chicken."

They were thirty minutes into the movie when they realized they had made the wrong choice. Gertrude had relocated to the coffee table and was watching the screen with avid concentration. Every time an undead died, she squawked and launched herself threateningly at the screen.

"Gertrude is ruining movie night," Drake muttered.

Leah leaned over and picked up the chicken. She cradled the fowl in her arms, one hand stroking ruffled feathers in soothing motions.

"There, there, Gertie. It's not real. They're just actors." Leah became aware of Drake's leaden stare. "What?"

Drake shook his head lightly. "There's a first time for

everything." He rose and headed out of the room. "Want another beer?"

"Sure."

Drake had his hand on the refrigerator door when he felt it. He stiffened, his gaze swiveling to the windows overlooking the backyard. His pulse accelerated at the ominous echo that had just bounced across his bond with Artemus and Smokey.

Leah appeared, a subdued Gertrude waddling at her feet.

"What is that?" she said uneasily.

"You feel it too?"

"Yes." Leah nodded and fisted a hand over her heart. "The others. Something's happened to them, hasn't it?!"

The ties that bound Drake to his twin and the hellhound trembled with a trace of pain. He stormed to the back door and headed out into the yard.

"Take me with you!" Leah called out behind him as he transformed into his dark angel form.

"I can't. I'm gonna fly there!"

Drake shot up into the night, his dark sword in hand and his rune-covered shield braced against his left arm. The mansion shrank below him, Leah a diminishing figure where she stood staring up at him.

THE NEPHIL'S PUNCH LANDED WITH A FORCE THAT would have shattered a normal man's bones. Artemus grunted as he shot across the ballroom and crashed violently into a wall. Blood filled his mouth and his left cheek tingled from the impact of the Nephil's fist.

That's gonna bruise.

Artemus wiped an angry hand across his crimson-stained lips and glared at the gray angel staring him down, the monster's expression as cold as the moon.

How the hell is this guy so strong?!

Callie's golden scepter flashed through the air and pierced the Nephil's right wing. Black blood oozed out of the gaping wound, falling in glittering drops among the pale feathers fluttering down into the abyss beneath the monster. The Nephil turned his attention to her, his injury closing as fast as it had formed.

His body blurred as he moved.

Callie inhaled deeply before unleashing a sonic roar that made the remaining chandeliers suspended from the intact pieces of ceiling tremble and whine.

The monster slowed fractionally in the grip of the sound storm.

Artemus pushed away from the wall and pelted toward the Nephil, his holy sword raised, the flames on the blade burning bright. Beneath him, Haruki and Smokey converged on Callie's location from opposite directions.

Callie's weapon returned to her hands a heartbeat before the Nephil reached her. Sparks exploded as the monster's sword clashed with the scepter, the blade's tip stopping an inch from Callie's left eye. The Chimera's feet skidded backward under the sheer brute force of the attack. She snarled and dug her heels in, her claws tracing grooves in the ground as she resisted her attacker.

Callie drew her head back, opened her mouth, and let loose a river of fire.

Haruki's flames joined hers, the Dragon's roar bouncing off the walls of the ballroom.

Smokey leapt into the air and closed the jaws of his middle head on the Nephil's arm, the beasts' divine flames washing harmlessly across his hide. He carried the monster across the room and smashed into a marble column. The Corinthian pillar exploded under the impact, raining pale shards of debris upon them.

Smokey rose, shook his three heads lightly, and turned to face the enemy, his eyes aglow with divine light. The Nephil climbed to his feet, his skin unmarked. He studied the hellhound with an expressionless face. His body blurred once more.

It took a second for Artemus to register Smokey's faint grunt and feel the echo of pain that danced across their connection.

Horror widened Callie's eyes. Her scream filled Artemus's ears the next instant. "*Noooo!*"

Artemus wasn't aware he'd moved until he locked swords with the Nephil. Behind him, Haruki and Callie rushed to Smokey's side as the hellhound blinked and staggered sideways, crimson blood flowing thickly from the stab wound in his breast.

The dark foreboding that had gnawed at Artemus's consciousness for weeks swept over him as he looked over his shoulder and met the hellhound's golden gazes.

"Don't you dare die on me!" Artemus roared.

Smokey blinked. *It is only a flesh wound.*

Relief flooded Artemus as he sensed Smokey's undiminished lifeforce. He turned his attention to the enemy once more, the rage burning through his heart racing along his veins and filling him with strength. Divine flames exploded on Michael's sword, so pale and bright they were almost blinding.

"Let's dance, asshole!" Artemus snarled at the Nephil.

Light flared in the gloom of the ballroom as their swords clashed repeatedly, their fight soon taking them into the air. A cold wind buffeted Artemus's wings as he and the Nephil rose above the sprawling, brownstone mansion. Artemus glanced down at the auction house. A frown knotted his brow.

There were still many guests gathered around the building, figures milling about in confusion in the aftermath of what most of them probably believed to have been a natural disaster. Even though he was high above them, Artemus made out the frantic voices of Elton's security team urging them to get away from the area.

Air shifted on his left. Artemus blocked the Nephil's blade an inch from his head, his arms straining as he resisted the forceful strike. He cursed himself for his brief distraction.

I really should concentrate on this guy for now!

The monster watched him across the crossed blades, his expression still vacant. Artemus clenched his teeth.

It's as if he doesn't have any feelings. The demons who attack us normally show some emotion, even if it's just rage. Artemus scowled. *In fact, he has the same look as those super soldiers from Rome.*

The next attack came out of nowhere and punched the breath from Artemus's lungs. He wheezed as he flew backward through the darkness.

The Nephil lowered his knee and moved.

Sharpness sliced across Artemus's face. Blood bloomed hotly on his left cheek. He blinked and saw the Nephil's broadsword heading inexorably for his neck.

Something blocked the monster's blade a hairbreadth from Artemus's flesh.

It was a dark, serrated blade with crimson flames flickering on its jagged teeth. Artemus's heart pounded erratically as he followed the sword to its owner.

Drake hovered in the air next to him, his face a fearsome mask. He glared at the Nephil, his crimson-gold eyes telling Artemus he was not yet under Samyaza's influence.

The Nephil flapped his wings and withdrew some twenty feet.

"Who is this guy?" Drake growled.

"Smokey said the Nephilim have risen," Artemus replied bitterly.

Drake exchanged a frown with him. "As in the offspring of fallen angels and human women?"

"Yeah." Artemus fingered the cut on his face. "He's strong. Stronger than a demon commander. He—" Artemus faltered and swallowed convulsively, "—he stabbed Smokey."

Drake stilled.

"The pooch is hurt?" he said in a deadly voice.

Artemus dipped his chin, frustration and the pain of his failure eating at him.

Drake's body flickered.

Artemus's stomach lurched.

The Nephil was forced backward some ten feet by the sheer violence of Drake's assault. He raised his broadsword and parried the dark angel's savage strikes, his expression impassive still in the face of his attacker's rage.

Alarm twisted Artemus's chest as he felt the demonic power inside Drake escalate. "Drake, stop!"

His twin paid him no heed, his attention focused on defeating the Nephil, his fury a red cord tightening across their bond. Artemus extended his wings and shot toward his brother, intent on stopping his descent into darkness at all costs.

He staggered to a halt in mid-air seconds before he reached the dark angel.

What the—?!

Artemus's gaze dropped to the mansion.

He could sense another energy building there. One that dimly echoed the corrupt power radiating from the Nephil and from Drake's soul.

Shit. Demons!

A shape grew beneath Artemus. One made of dark blue bodies, a hundred black wings, and as many ochre-colored eyes. He gritted his teeth, gripped his blade, and braced himself for the onslaught that was to come.

Except it never did.

The demon horde flew past him, silent but for their rustling wings, their focus on something else entirely.

The Nephil opened its mouth when it saw them. The high-pitched, ululating sound that left his lips made Artemus's ears vibrate and his bones tremble.

The noise ripped through several of the demons, their bodies falling through the air before crumbling to fiery ash. More appeared in their wake.

Drake moved back as the horde swarmed the Nephil, his expression startled. The cobalt-colored demons kept multiplying until they surrounded the monster in a globe of darkness.

Another sonic scream reached Artemus.

Bright cinders bloomed in the night as the demons closest to the center of the black sphere exploded into nothingness.

Still they kept coming, their numbers legion.

Artemus's heart thundered against his ribs as he watched the demons' sheer weight drag the Nephil toward the ground. He and Drake followed the group as they fell through the mansion's broken roof and into the ballroom.

A final screech escaped the Nephil as he was forced back into the abyss whence he'd come.

It faded into silence as the demons drove the creature into the depths of the Earth, their departure as shocking and as sudden as their appearance had been.

CHAPTER FIVE

"Jesus Christ, Artemus," Jeremiah Chase said darkly. "Could you guys have been any more conspicuous?"

Artemus grimaced. "Yeah, well, there were extenuating circumstances."

He watched the video streaming on the mobile device in the detective's hand with a degree of unease. It belonged to one of the guests at Elton's party. The woman had managed to record part of the battle that had taken place in the sky above the auction house from where she'd taken refuge in the gardens.

Though the angels' and the Nephil's movements were too fast for the human eye to follow, the presence of their wings and their fiery swords could just about be made out.

"I've got more of them, boss."

Jeremiah and Artemus twisted on their heels. They stood in the main foyer of the auction house, the giant, crystal chandelier suspended from the inlaid mosaic ceiling miraculously untouched above them. The golden light it radiated washed across the pimpled face of the young man with reddish hair strolling toward them, a boxful of bagged and labeled mobile devices and smart-bands in hand.

Hugo Shaw was a novice detective and Jeremiah's temporary partner pending Tony Goodman's return to active duty. Goodman had been gravely injured by a demon several weeks ago and was still recovering from his wounds. Had Naomi not been there to heal him on the day of the attack, he would more than likely have died before he got to hospital.

"I told you to call me Jeremiah," Leah's father said with a frown. He studied the contents of the box. "Is this everything?"

Shaw glanced between Jeremiah and Artemus, evidently curious as to their relationship. "Yes, I believe so. I've got a list of all the guests who were at the party tonight from Mr. LeBlanc."

"Great job." Jeremiah studied the officers scurrying through the building. "Let them know we'll be interviewing them starting tomorrow. I shall personally take care of Mr. Steele and his companions' interrogations."

Artemus tried not to wince at Jeremiah's last word.

Disquiet filled Shaw's eyes. "I should be there too, sir."

"Jeremiah."

"Sir, Jeremiah." Shaw's Adam's Apple bobbed in his scrawny throat as he squared his shoulders. "It's against protocol for detectives to carry out interviews on their own."

Admiration darted through Artemus. Jeremiah's new partner had guts, especially considering the senior detective looked ready to shoot someone at the slightest provocation.

"Your subordinate is correct, Chase," someone said behind them.

Artemus turned. A dark-haired man with hazel eyes was approaching them from the direction of the main entrance.

"Great," Jeremiah said under his breath. "Just what I need right now." He directed a frown at Shaw. "Did you call him?"

"No, sir!" Shaw mumbled hastily. "I mean, Jeremiah, sir."

"Who is this guy?" Artemus murmured.

The newcomer's gaze switched to Artemus.

"He's—" Jeremiah started.

"Franklin Milton," the other man interrupted smoothly. "I'm the Deputy Special Agent in charge of the Chicago FBI Field Office. Mr. Steele, I presume?"

He put out his hand.

Artemus shook it reluctantly. "You presume correctly." He observed the other man with an inscrutable expression. "Do I know you, Agent Milton?"

Milton's mouth stretched in a thin smile that did not quite reach his eyes. "I'm afraid I haven't had the honor of making your acquaintance before now, Mr. Steele. But your reputation does precede you."

Artemus narrowed his eyes. "My reputation?"

Milton shrugged. "As an antique valuer, of course. I have an interest in antiques myself."

"What brings you here, Agent Milton?" Jeremiah asked in a guarded tone that Artemus didn't like one bit.

"Why, I would have thought the reason was clear, Detective Chase."

Jeremiah's eyes narrowed to slits. "Humor me."

Milton indicated the auction house with a vague motion of his hand. "It's evident this was some kind of terror attack. As such, investigating this incident falls under my jurisdiction." He pointed at the box Shaw held. "I believe that's technically my evidence."

Disquiet filled Artemus at the FBI agent's statement.

"There's a strong probability this was a natural phenomenon," Jeremiah argued. "What the guests have reported so far indicates this place experienced some kind of quake."

Milton observed the detective steadily. "What's currently being streamed on the local news channels doesn't look like any kind of earthquake I've ever seen before."

Jeremiah scowled. "What?!"

He removed his cell from his pocket and tapped the screen.

Artemus's stomach dropped when he saw the video being played on one of the city's main news stations.

"It's evident someone or something was behind this attack," Milton said. "Although there haven't been any fatalities, several of Mr. LeBlanc's guests have suffered injuries. And some of them are pretty powerful people."

Artemus cursed silently.

"I shall personally be interrogating Mr. Steele and his friends at the local FBI office," Milton continued, his gaze moving to Artemus. "I hope they may be able to cast some light on the identity of the person responsible for what happened here tonight."

A muscle jumped in Jeremiah's cheek. Artemus knew from his grim expression that there was little he could do to stop the FBI agent from taking over the investigation.

"I would be grateful if you and your companions could refrain from leaving the city in the next few days," Milton told Artemus, his tone still mild. "It would be a shame if you missed your appointments."

Artemus tried not to let his irritation show. "Sure. Now, if you'll excuse me, I need to see if my friends are okay."

He headed for the stairs, conscious of the policemen and the FBI agent's gazes on his back.

There was a lot he still needed to digest about what had taken place tonight. A dozen questions stormed Artemus's mind as he navigated the corridors leading to his destination. Of them, there were two he wanted some urgent answers to.

Why had a Nephil, an entity whose existence they had not been aware of until tonight, made a sudden appearance at the auction house and attacked them? And, more importantly, who were the blue demons who had come to their aid and ended the battle as quickly as it had started?

Restlessness raised butterflies in his stomach. He needed to get back to the mansion and soon. Callie, Haruki, and Drake had left the auction house moments after the fight had ended, taking a wounded Smokey with them. The hellhound had still been bleeding when Callie had swaddled him in his rabbit form in Haruki's jacket.

Heated words reached Artemus's ears as he approached Elton's office. He slowed and sighed.

But first, I need to help Elton sort out this mess.

He knocked and opened the door.

"You're an agent of the Vatican?" Helen was saying stiffly where she sat on the couch. "What the hell does that even mean, Elton?!"

Elton met Artemus's gaze warily. Artemus closed the door and leaned back against it. The only other person in the room beside them was Isabelle. The Immortal stood by the window, her tense gaze on the street outside.

"I can't go into the details, Helen," Elton told his fiancée. "I'm bound by the vow I made to the Holy See."

Helen's fingers clenched around the tumbler of Scotch in her hand. "You're about to make a vow to me too, Elton. One that is even more sacred."

A painful expression darted across Elton's face.

"Tell her," Artemus said quietly.

His old friend and mentor looked at him as if he'd lost his mind. Isabelle glanced at Artemus, her expression similarly surprised. Helen blinked, as if registering his presence for the first time.

"She's not going to be able to forget what she saw tonight," Artemus told Elton. "So, you might as well come clean. About everything. Or else your marriage will end before it can even begin."

Silence descended inside the room. Helen studied Artemus with a look that was part fear and part awe.

"Who are you, really? What I saw tonight. Was—" she paused and swallowed, her voice trembling slightly, "—was any of that real?"

"I am the son of the archangel Michael and the goddess Theia. I also have a human mother. Her name was Alice." Artemus raked a hand through his hair. "And yes, everything that happened tonight was real. What you saw was but a glimpse of the fight Elton and Isabelle have been engaged in for a long time. I only got involved recently."

Helen's eyes rounded. "You—you are the son of an angel?! And a goddess?!"

"Archangel," Elton murmured.

"One with a sick sense of humor," Isabelle added drily.

Artemus swallowed a sigh. Considering Michael had led the Heavenly Army that had defeated Satanael and his followers and cast them into Hell, the archangel's attitude left a lot to be desired. Still, Artemus couldn't help but feel that Michael had not revealed his real self to him yet.

"What fight are you talking about?" Helen mumbled.

"The fight to save mankind from Hell's dark intentions," Artemus said laconically. "The End of Days. Or, as others call it, the Apocalypse."

The color drained from Helen's face.

"Wow," Isabelle murmured. "You could have eased her in a bit more gently. You know, started with the Bible and shit."

"She deserves to know the truth," Artemus grumbled. "Besides, she's going to be even more shocked when she finds out how old you really are."

Isabelle narrowed her eyes at him before looking over at Elton. "Permission to shoot him?"

Elton sighed. "Permission denied."

Helen rose and went over to the liquor cabinet. Elton's expression turned cautious as he watched her pour more Scotch into her glass.

"Honey, maybe you should go easy on—"

"Shut up, Elton!" Helen snapped.

Elton sucked in air. Artemus swallowed a smile.

Though Helen Tempest came across as a pleasant and demure woman most of the time, he hadn't failed to notice the core of steel she possessed. He suspected it was what had attracted Elton to her in the first place.

Helen downed half the glass and wiped her mouth on the back of her knuckles, her hands the steadiest they'd been since Artemus entered the room.

Her eyes narrowed to slits as she observed them. "Now, how about you all start at the beginning."

CHAPTER SIX

A CHILLY WIND SANG THROUGH THE VALLEYS surrounding the terraced elevation the village straddled. Goosebumps broke out on Serena's skin as the breeze danced across her exposed flesh. The nanorobots inside her body gradually adjusted her core temperature to compensate for the sudden coldness. She looked up from the corpse she was inspecting and stared out into the darkness that shrouded what she could see of the Vilcabamba mountain range.

Though faint, the smell of blood and gore still tainted the air above the small settlement located a few miles from Choquequirao, a world-renowned Incan site in the Cusco region of southern Peru. The Immortals had retrieved several bodies from the banks of the Apurimac River, which the village overlooked. Some had been tourists who'd been unlucky enough to be around at the time the earthquake struck.

Serena frowned.

It had become inherently clear to her and the team who had been assigned to investigate this disaster that the tremors that had damaged the village and killed most of its inhabitants had not been a natural phenomenon. Although the country was used to earthquakes, what with being positioned in a seismic zone over two tectonic plates, the death toll from one of this magnitude should have been minor.

It should not have wiped out two hundred of the souls who once lived there.

Serena frowned. *Gideon's right. There's something real fishy going on here.*

"You found anything?" someone called out behind her.

Serena twisted on her heels and eyed the man walking up the slope. Zachary Jackson's face was pale under the starlight bathing the mountain. Though not a seismologist, the Harvard archeology professor had been dispatched by the Immortals to accompany the group assigned to investigate what had happened to the village. With his knowledge of the local area and his sharp mind, Jackson was the kind of man who would spot clues the super soldiers and the Immortals could easily miss.

"No." Serena studied the mutilated remains before her. "Every corpse I've inspected so far bears the same wounds. Whoever did this appears to have killed them and drained them of all their blood."

"Shit." Jackson rubbed the back of his neck, his expression tired. "It's the same as India and Africa. What the hell could be doing this?"

Serena straightened and dusted her hands. "You considered vampires?"

Jackson blinked. It took him a moment to realize she was yanking his chain.

"Ha ha," he muttered. "You're just as bad as Alexa."

Serena smiled faintly at the mention of Alexa King.

Jackson's wife was one of a family of incredible Immortals who had freed Serena, Nate, and hundreds of other super soldier children from the grim prison where they had been artificially created twenty-two years ago, bred to serve as an army of killing machines.

King and Jackson had helped them out again in Rome a couple months back, when Paimon, a powerful demon and sub-Prince of Hell, had threatened to bring about the Apocalypse that Ba'al so wished to visit upon the Earth. Their kindness and the sacrifices they had been willing to make to help out Artemus and their group had gone some way toward dampening the bitterness Serena still harbored toward the Immortal societies.

"How's your son and daughter? And Alexa?" Serena asked out of genuine interest.

"They're good, thanks. Mila is sailing through her PhD and Caspian's fighting skills are improving all the time. Alexa is busy troubleshooting for the Immortals, as always."

Serena smiled faintly. "So, your daughter got your brains and your son your wife's brawn, huh?"

Jackson's mouth tilted in an answering smile. "Yes, although Alexa is determined that Caspian gets an education too. She never fails to trot out the story of how she was my bodyguard when we first met, but it was because of me that we ultimately solved the mysteries of our first mission." He grimaced. "Although she does spend rather a lot of time telling them how she kicked my ass before we got together."

Serena chuckled. She stilled a moment later, her gaze swiveling to a cluster of trees some fifty feet to her left. She glanced at her smartband, snatched her gun from the holster on her thigh, and moved protectively in front of Jackson.

"Who goes there?" Serena barked. "Identify yourself!"

The GPS location of each member of their team was a red dot on the screen of her smartband, courtesy of the tracking device they all carried on their uniforms. Only she and Jackson were in this area of the village right now.

For a moment, the only sounds that reached her were the wind whistling in the trees and the animal noises from the rainforest.

A voice came from the darkness, calm and steady. "Easy there. I don't want to die from friendly fire."

Jackson drew a sharp breath behind Serena. "Conrad?!"

He moved around her.

Serena startled. *Wait, does he mean—?!*

The figure of a man materialized from the shadows beneath the treeline. He closed the distance to them at a leisurely pace, his features becoming clearer as he approached through the tall grass. Serena's heart thumped as she looked upon a face she hadn't seen in nearly a decade.

Conrad Greene looked the same as the last time their paths had crossed, when he'd visited her adoptive father's house on one of his missions for the Immortal Council.

Her gaze dropped to the dark lines making up the black, Aesculapian snake birthmark entwined around Greene's left forearm. She knew without looking that his silver-gilded staff would be strapped to his back. The weapon was never far from Greene's grasp.

"What are you doing here?" Jackson met Greene halfway and engulfed him in a hearty embrace. "Victor didn't tell me he'd assigned you this mission too."

Greene hugged him back, a wry smile curving his lips.

"He didn't. A little bird told me I might be needed here tonight."

Jackson raised an eyebrow. "A little bird, huh?"

"Yeah." Greene locked eyes with Serena. "It's good to see you again."

"It's good to see you too," Serena murmured.

"You should visit your father. He misses you."

Serena stiffened at the Immortal's words. King had told her and Nate the same thing in Rome. An old, familiar anger swirled through her as she frowned at him.

"You know as well as I do why we've kept our distance from him all these years. Our presence in his life would make his position in the Immortal societies untenable."

"He doesn't give a damn about his position." Greene's gray-blue eyes bore into Serena's face. "He cares about you and Nate. Like he cared about Ben, when he was still alive. Besides, you underestimate him and the influence he wields. He has a lot of powerful friends. They would have backed him wholeheartedly against any resistance some factions of the Immortal societies would have offered in an attempt to control you and your kind."

Surprise shot through Serena. She could tell Greene meant what he'd just said. And she knew he was one of the Immortals who would have supported her father.

"Now, take me to the survivors," Greene said. "I might be able to help heal their wounds."

Footsteps rose in the gloom behind them. Serena turned and saw Nate approaching. The super soldier's eyes widened slightly when he saw Greene.

Unease stirred inside Serena at Nate's agitated expression. "What's wrong?"

"Callie just called. Something happened in Chicago."

CHAPTER SEVEN

THE DREAM BEGAN AS IT NORMALLY DID. WITH HIM standing on a foggy plain.

It wasn't long before she appeared, her chestnut hair framing her beautiful face with shiny curls. Her soulful, blue eyes glimmered with secrets as she walked toward him, her bare feet causing the mist to dance around her legs.

Artemus's heart skipped several beats as he gazed upon the woman he had loved for as long as he could remember. Though they had never met, he felt like he was the one person in the world who knew her the best. Like they were meant to be together in this lifetime and many more to come.

Like they were soulmates bound by a destiny that was still unclear to him.

The air shimmered as she approached the intangible barrier that always separated them. Artemus stiffened when she raised a hand and shattered it with a gentle touch.

The sound of the ocean reached his ears. A warm, salty breeze washed across his face. Then, she was standing in front of him, her head tilting slightly as she gazed up at him.

"How—?" Artemus started.

She raised a finger to his lips and stayed his words.

Artemus let out a shaky breath at her touch. Her skin felt hot against his mouth. Desire sparked along his veins.

Her eyes darkened with the same hunger building in his blood. She cradled his face in her hands, rose on her tip toes, and brought her lips to his ear.

"I'm sorry, Artemus," she whispered.

Artemus shivered, her voice raising goosebumps on his skin.

She drew back slightly and stroked his cheeks with her thumbs, her feather-light touch fanning the passion raging through him. Her eyes bore into his, searching for something only she knew. Then, she kissed him.

Heat bloomed inside Artemus's soul as she molded their lips together. With it came a flood of images, same as the last time she had appeared before him. Just as had happened then, he couldn't make out any of them but for the last one.

He froze as the final vision rose before his inner eye.

ARTEMUS SHOT UPRIGHT IN HIS BED, THE SCREAM a dying sound in his throat. It took a moment for him to register the sweat beading his face and soaking his pajama top.

Something stirred next to him. Limpid eyes glittered in the gloom.

"Sorry, buddy," Artemus mumbled, heart still racing like a freight train. "I didn't mean to wake you."

His hand trembled as he reached out and gently stroked Smokey's head, the remnant of the dream still with him.

A pained sound escaped the rabbit.

Artemus frowned. He leaned over the nightstand, switched the lamp on, and turned to examine the hellhound. Alarm twisted his gut when he saw the blood soaking through the bandages around Smokey's chest. The pillow the rabbit lay on was drenched crimson.

How?! His wound had almost closed!

A soft knock came at the door. Callie's anxious voice traveled faintly through the woodwork.

"Artemus? Is everything okay? I—I felt something from Smokey just now."

She walked in just as he rounded the bed and picked the rabbit up in his arms. Callie inhaled sharply when she saw the bloodied dressings.

"He's bleeding again." Artemus couldn't help the panic lacing his words. "Why is he bleeding? His wound should be almost healed by now!"

"Let me take a look at him," Callie said shakily.

Artemus sat on the edge of the bed, Smokey's limp form a heavy weight on his lap. Footsteps came from the corridor outside his bedroom. Drake, Haruki, and Leah appeared in the pale glow of the night lamp.

"What's happening?" Leah's knuckles whitened where she gripped her nightshirt. "I can feel this prickling in my chest."

Callie's fingers shook as she peeled away the bandages covering her brother's body. "It's coming from Smokey."

Artemus clenched his teeth at the sight of the gaping wound in the hellhound's flesh. The edges had started to darken, as if turning gangrenous. Blood oozed out between them in a steady trickle.

"Why hasn't he healed?" Haruki said, his voice full of anger and distress.

The hellhound's pain was a raw, burning ache twisting along the bond that tied all of them.

Tears glimmered on Callie's eyelashes. "I don't know."

She rose and collected fresh bandages from the stack she had piled earlier on Artemus's dresser. A faint whimper escaped Smokey as she applied a wad of gauze to the cut.

"I'm sorry, brother."

She pressed a tender kiss to the rabbit's brow, her tears soaking into his fur. He butted his head gently against her cheek in a move meant to reassure.

"You lied, you stupid rabbit." Artemus blinked away the moistness blurring his own vision. "You said it was only a flesh wound."

Smokey's voice echoed in his mind and heart, his words heavy with pain and remorse. *I am sorry. I truly thought it was so.*

"Naomi," Leah mumbled. "Let me call her!"

Hope burst into life inside Artemus at the mention of the witch. "Yes!"

Dawn was breaking across the city when Naomi's classic convertible pulled up outside the mansion in a screech of brakes. Artemus opened the front door and watched her climb out of her car, impatience tightening his limbs.

"Where is he?" she said briskly.

A white cat leapt out of the vehicle and dashed past her. Gemini darted up the stairs and bolted inside the mansion as if Hell itself were on her tail.

The witch's familiar had grown pretty close to Smokey in the last few weeks.

Naomi climbed the steps to the porch at a slower pace, her anxious gaze scanning his face. "You look terrible."

"He's in the TV room. And thanks."

∼

NAOMI FOLLOWED ARTEMUS THROUGH THE HOUSE. SHE tensed when she entered the place where they had all gathered. She had seen Artemus and the other Guardians fight on a few occasions. She had never felt what she was feeling from them right now.

Fear. It filled the very air around her, making it heavy and hard to breathe.

Callie looked up from where she sat on the couch. Drake paced the floor in front of the windows, his expression strained and his fingers clenching and unclenching by his sides, as if he wanted to wring someone's neck. Haruki and Leah hovered behind Callie, their faces pale.

Naomi greeted them with a soft "Hey," before focusing on the rabbit lying on a cushion next to Callie. Gemini was crouched beside Smokey and was carefully licking the hellhound's ears, her anxiety thrumming through to Naomi.

"Can I have some space?" the witch said.

For a moment, she thought Callie would refuse. The Chimera took a shaky breath and relinquished her seat.

Naomi knelt in front of Smokey and undid the bloodstained dressing on his chest. A frown knotted her brow as she inspected the wound carved in his flesh. It was thin but deep, as if made by some kind of blade. Leah hadn't given her any details about how the hellhound had sustained the injury when she'd called.

Naomi placed her hand on the cut and drew on the power of the demon who had gifted her race with magic. The fallen archangel's dark energy surged inside her soul, tempered by the light of his mate, the first witch. The jade bracelet on her right wrist lit up with a green glow, as did the dichromatic eyes of the cat.

Tissue started to knit and mend under her touch,

millimeter by slow millimeter. Smokey shuddered as the wound started to close.

Sweat broke out on Naomi's forehead minutes later. Her pulse stuttered when she felt what lay deep within the hellhound's body. Gemini's pants reached her ears dimly, as did Leah's alarmed voice.

"Naomi?"

Naomi didn't realize she'd closed her eyes until she opened them again. She blinked when she met Gemini's strained gaze, the cat's breathing coming hard and fast, a direct side effect of the amount of power they had just used to try and cure the hellhound's injury.

Naomi gritted her teeth, her frustration echoed in her familiar.

This was as much as they could do. This was the limit of their powers.

"It's done."

"Thank you," Callie breathed.

She and the others gazed at Smokey's restored flesh, their faces full of gratitude and dread slowly fading from their eyes.

Smokey already looked brighter.

"Don't thank me yet," Naomi warned.

She climbed to her feet, her legs unsteady. She felt like she'd just run a marathon.

"What do you mean?" Artemus said.

"I may have repaired the visible wound, but there is still something inside his body. Something I can't reach." Naomi frowned. "Whatever it is, it's in his bones. And it's resistant to my magic." She hesitated. "I fear the wound will open again."

There were sharply indrawn breaths all around her.

"What is it?" Drake fisted his hands so hard his fingers

blanched. "Is it some kind of poison?!"

Naomi thought about the strange blemish she'd detected inside the hellhound. "Something like that, yes. If I had to describe it, it feels like a stain. Or a curse."

"Artemus?" Callie said in a deathly still voice. "Your cheek. It's bleeding again."

Artemus startled and raised a hand to his face. His fingers came away bloodied.

Consternation filled Naomi as she observed the oozing cut on his left cheek. "Were you hurt by the same weapon that injured Smokey?"

Artemus hesitated before swallowing and bobbing his head.

Drake stared at his twin, ashen faced.

Naomi clenched her jaw and raised a hand to Artemus's cheek. Gemini's eyes shone a bright green as the witch called upon the familiar's powers once more.

"That kind of tingles," Artemus mumbled.

"Just shut up and let her do her thing!" Drake snapped.

Relief flashed through Naomi as she worked on Artemus's wound. She wasn't sure if it was because he was born of an archangel and a goddess, but the blemish had stayed localized in the area where it had been borne and hadn't seeped in farther. She suspected it would eventually have healed itself, so strong was the divine energy she could sense coursing through Artemus's body.

"There." Naomi lowered her hand. "It's gone." She narrowed her eyes at them. "Now, how about you guys tell me what happened."

Artemus froze. It took Naomi a moment to realize it wasn't her request that had rendered him so still. The others were similarly motionless around her.

Gemini let out a soft, questioning meow.

The sound seemed to galvanize the two angels and the Guardians into action. Surprise jolted Naomi as they reached for their weapons.

"What's going on?"

"Something just came through the barrier," Artemus said in a hard voice.

CHAPTER EIGHT

T HEY GATHERED IN THE FOYER, C ALLIE CLUTCHING Smokey protectively in her arms.

"How many people can you sense?" Naomi said nervously.

Artemus frowned. "Two."

One of the beings who had crossed Theia's barrier definitely gave off a demonic vibe. The other felt oddly familiar.

"Wait," Haruki mumbled after a moment. "Is—is one of them a *divine beast?*!"

Callie drew a sharp breath. "You're right. That's the energy signature of a Guardian!"

Drake gripped his sword tightly. "What the hell is a divine beast doing with a demon? And why would another Guardian show up here? I don't recall Otis or Sebastian mentioning another gate in Chicago."

"They didn't," Artemus said grimly.

He stiffened when he sensed the two strange presences approach the mansion.

Wood creaked as someone climbed the porch steps. A

shadow moved across the frosted glass on the left side of the entrance. Artemus blinked.

"Is it me or is whoever it is awfully short?" Leah mumbled.

Someone knocked on the door. They all jumped. Smokey let out a low growl.

The hellhound was evidently feeling better.

Artemus glared at the main entrance to the mansion, his knuckles whitening on his sword. *Let's get this over with.*

He steeled himself, crossed the foyer, and yanked the door open. He slammed it shut a second later.

"*Who is it?!*" Callie hissed.

Artemus swallowed. "It's a kid."

Leaden silence rose behind him.

"A kid?" Drake said, suspicious. "Why did you close the door on him?"

"It's a creepy kid," Artemus mumbled.

"What is wrong with you?" Naomi marched past him, opened the door, and slammed it shut. "Shit," she said, pale-faced.

Drake rolled his eyes at both of them and went to open the door again. "Seriously, what's so—*holy crap!*"

He banged it closed and stumbled back into the foyer.

The knock came again with a bit more force. A sibilant, female voice followed. "*Excuse me, but that was rude. My host is a most charming child. Now, open the damn door.*"

"Who is that?" Naomi mumbled.

"I think that's the beast's voice," Haruki hazarded.

"*Of course, it is I, you foolish Dragon,*" the voice said contemptuously. "*Now, are you opening this door or am I going to have to kick it down?*"

Artemus hesitated before walking over to the entrance once more. Whoever this new Guardian was, she was bossy and cranky. Still, he didn't feel he had any choice but to let her and her host in.

The boy glared up at him when he opened the door, outrage painted across his face. At around four feet, he just about reached Artemus's chest. His inky hair flopped across his forehead, accentuating his fair skin and dark eyes.

"*Let us in,*" the boy's beast ordered.

He glanced to his right.

Artemus blinked. He'd forgotten all about the demon. He followed the boy's gaze to the man leaning against one of the ornate, metal, Victorian posts holding up the porch roof, his arms folded across his chest and his ankles crossed in a relaxed pose.

Piercing green eyes focused steadily on Artemus.

Shit. Was he standing there the whole time?!

The man tucked his hands into the pockets of his long coat and smiled faintly, as if he'd read Artemus's thoughts. "Don't feel bad. I'm an expert at masking my presence."

"Really?" Artemus said between clenched teeth. "How the hell did you get through the barrier?"

"*Must we have this conversation outside?*" the boy's beast hissed. "*It is cold out here.*"

The demon sighed, removed his coat, and strolled over to the boy. He dropped the garment on the kid's scrawny shoulders. "There. Is that better?"

The boy gave the demon an irritated look. "*I was trying to guilt the angel into letting us in.*"

He clasped the lapels of the coat and drew them close. A shiver shook his tiny frame.

"Sure," the demon drawled, his expression amused.

He and the boy became aware of a battery of hot stares.

"He's not that scary," Callie volunteered from where she huddled behind Artemus, her gaze on the boy.

"*Why, thank you, Chimera,*" the beast said graciously. "*My Jacob is quite cute.*"

"I wouldn't go that far," Drake muttered.

The kid scowled.

"That's a bit mean, isn't it?" Leah protested. "I mean, sure, he looks like that freaky kid out of that movie we watched the other week—"

"You mean *The Omen?*" Haruki grimaced. "Nate said Gertrude couldn't sleep for days."

"Hey, should you guys really be insulting a Guardian?!" Naomi hissed out the corner of her mouth.

Gemini let out a wary meow.

"Are they always like this?" the demon asked Artemus.

"Pretty much." Artemus frowned. "You haven't answered my question."

"You mean about the barrier?" The demon shrugged. "It's simple. It let me in."

"What?" Drake scowled. "Why?!"

"Because I am not your enemy."

∽

SOLOMON WATCHED SURPRISE DAWN ON ARTEMUS STEELE and his companions' faces.

He bit back a sigh and glanced warily at the sky. Though he was certain he and Jacob hadn't been followed, he could sense the presence of Ba'al's demons in the city.

Theia and Michael's protective shields meant that Hell's attention could not focus on the estate or Artemus's antique shop for any useful length of time, nor could Ba'al easily pinpoint the location of those who lived in the

mansion or in the apartment above the shop. It was as if
the two sites and their residents blurred out of the fiends'
sights whenever they tried to concentrate on them.

It was one of the reasons Solomon had chosen to bring
Jacob here.

"Now, how about we take this inside?" he suggested in
a mild tone. "Although Jacob and his Guardian are
pretending they aren't cold, they really are freezing."

For a moment, the demon thought Artemus wouldn't
move. Michael's son finally shifted, his expression still
suspicious. The others backed away across the foyer, their
faces just as unenthusiastic.

Solomon followed Jacob inside the house and closed
the door.

He knew the moment the divine beast inside Jacob
relinquished her hold on her host. A shudder shook the
boy. His figure seemed to shrink as he became aware of his
surroundings. He grabbed Solomon's leg and huddled
behind him, wary eyes wide as he stared unblinkingly at
Artemus and his companions.

"It's okay, Jacob." Solomon laid a light hand on the
boy's head. "They won't hurt you."

Jacob looked unconvinced. He went still.

Solomon braced himself, senses on high alert. But it
wasn't danger that had turned Jacob to stone.

Solomon followed the boy's gaze. "Oh." The demon
grimaced at the Chimera. "You might want to hold the
hellhound higher."

Callie Stone blinked. "What do you mean?"

A boyish squeal erupted across the foyer. "*Bunny!*"

Jacob darted across the floor, lifted the startled Rex
rabbit out of Callie's grasp, and squeezed him tightly
against his chest. The rabbit wheezed, his eyes bulging.

"Hmm," Artemus said, clearly conflicted in the face of Jacob's childish delight.

"Not so tight, Jacob," Solomon admonished gently.

The white cat standing by Callie's feet let out an alarmed sound.

"Sorry," the boy mumbled distractedly, his face buried in Smokey's fur. He looked down at the cat. "Hello, Kitty."

The feline went willingly into his arms when he bent down and scooped her up.

Solomon frowned at what he sensed inside the rabbit. "Did the Nephil's sword injure him?"

Artemus blinked, as if coming out of a daze. Lines furrowed his brow. "How do you know about the Nephilim?"

"And who the hell are you?!" Drake spat out.

Solomon ignored their questions and approached Jacob.

"Will you allow me to take a look at your wound?" he asked the hellhound in the boy's arms.

Smokey's nose twitched as he stared at him. His gaze flashed a crimson warning.

"Come now, old friend," Solomon murmured. "Your eyes see past my glamor. You know I bear no malice toward you or your companions."

Smokey hesitated for a moment before letting out a low huff. He hopped into Solomon's arms.

Artemus and Drake clenched their fists, their weapons still drawn.

Solomon turned a blind eye to their scowls and placed a hand on the hellhound's breast. He traced the recently healed wound with his fingertips before glancing at the witch. "You did a good job, child of Azazel."

Naomi Wagner blinked.

Solomon focused his attention on the hellhound's injury. It took him but a moment to identify the poisonous stain buried in the beast's bones and isolate the corruption with bands of his own energy. The rabbit shivered in his hold.

Artemus took a threatening step toward Solomon. "What did you just do to—?"

Smokey looked at the angel and his equally aggrieved twin.

Whatever passed between them made Artemus and Drake stop in their tracks, although it did little to temper the murderous light in their eyes.

Smokey met Solomon's gaze once more. The rabbit huffed again and bumped his head affectionately against the demon's chest.

Sadness filled Solomon as the hellhound's sorrow and heartfelt apology echoed through his mind. "I know. I am sorry too, Cerberus. About everything."

Callie let out a frustrated sound and threw her arms up in the air. "Will someone explain what the heck is going on here?!"

CHAPTER NINE

"MY NAME IS SOLOMON WEISS." THE DEMON PAUSED. "Or, rather, that is the name I have chosen to assume in this human form." His face softened as he looked at the boy eating cookies next to him. "And this is Jacob. Jacob Schroeder."

Jacob grew still as he became the focus of their stares, one hand clenching around the glass of cold milk on the table. Crumbs had fallen onto his shirt and a trace of chocolate chip clung to the corner of his mouth. Smokey was gobbling up the stray fragments of cookie on the boy's lap.

Though the kid appeared, to all intents and purposes, to be harmless, Drake could sense the latent power inside him. The Guardian who inhabited his soul was currently quiet, having apparently chosen to lie low while the demon did all the explaining.

"Do you know the identity of the divine beast Jacob carries?" Callie asked curiously.

"No. But I have my suspicions." Solomon's expression turned dry. "She said something about a grand reveal."

"Funny how they all like to do that," Artemus said glumly.

Smokey huffed, his expression abashed. Callie, Haruki, and Leah glanced guilty at one another.

Jacob's eyes brightened as Leah fished more cookies out of a jar and placed them on his plate.

"Thank you," he mumbled shyly.

"You're welcome," Leah replied with a smile.

"You shouldn't eat all of them," Solomon told Jacob in a mild voice. "You know you'll get stomachache after."

Jacob hesitated before letting go of the cookie he'd already grabbed. He sighed and sipped his milk with the mournful expression of a child who had been denied life's greatest pleasure.

Drake exchanged a cautious glance with Artemus.

They didn't know what to make of the demon and the Guardian currently sitting in their kitchen like it was a sunny Sunday afternoon and the pair had come over for coffee and cake. Though they could feel the corrupt energy that lay at the core of Solomon's soul, the demon had done nothing to warrant them attacking him thus far. As for the Guardian, why she had chosen to accept a demon as her companion was something they couldn't fathom.

"I know you have a lot of questions. So, I'll start with what you need to know," Solomon said. "My true name is Sariel. I am the twentieth Leader of the Watchers, or the Grigori as you also know them."

Drake startled. "You are the one who was known as the Prince of God?"

A mournful light glinted in the demon's eyes at his old name. "Correct."

Callie drew a sharp breath. Haruki narrowed his eyes.

"Is a Leader the same as a Prince of Hell?" Leah asked, puzzled.

"The ones who fell from Heaven during the Holy War numbered many," Solomon explained. "In addition to the princes who make up The Council of Hell, twenty powerful demons called Leaders commanded the legion of cursed angels, each with an army subservient to them. The Second Leader is Samyaza, Drake's father."

Drake clenched his jaw at the mention of the demon who had sired him.

Artemus narrowed his eyes at Solomon. "So, you are one of the seven archangels possessed of primordial powers, huh?" He clocked Drake's surprised glance and shrugged. "I've been catching up on my reading."

"Yes," Solomon said sedately. "I, along with my brothers Uriel, Michael, Raphael, Gabriel, Ramiel, and Raguel, once formed the highest level of the First Sphere of Heaven."

Haruki frowned. "First Sphere of Heaven?"

Surprise dawned in Solomon's eyes. He scanned their faces. "Hasn't Michael explained any of this to you?"

"The less said about my father, the better," Artemus grumbled.

Solomon rubbed the back of his neck. "I see he hasn't changed. Uriel and I used to chase him all over Eden so he would do his duties." The demon made a face. "That guy is the definition of work shy." He sighed. "The First Sphere of Heaven is the highest hierarchy of divine servants. It belongs to the seven archangels and the seraph who stands closest to God."

"Wait." Artemus stared at Solomon. "Do you mean Otis?!"

Solomon nodded. "I do indeed mean Mr. Boone. The

First Sphere is also inhabited by Cherubim and Elders, celestial beings with their own roles and duties. The Second and Third Spheres of Heaven are the domain of other divine entities, in descending order of hierarchy."

Drake's mind raced as he listened to Solomon. *How could an archangel become a demon?!*

He voiced the question.

Solomon's expression turned melancholic once more as he met Drake's curious gaze. "The Morning Star can be quite persuasive."

"You mean Satanael?" Drake said.

"Yes. I was not the only powerful angel who was swayed by his words." Solomon paused. "Nor am I the only one who regrets following him to Earth."

"Astarte said the same thing when we fought her a few weeks ago." Doubt clouded Artemus's voice. "She said not all demons were allied with Ba'al."

"She was right," Solomon said. "There are those in Hell who will not bear arms alongside Satanael and his brethren at the End of Days." His gaze grew guarded. "As to whether they will choose to side with you is a question I cannot answer."

A contemplative silence befell them.

"How did you meet Jacob?" Leah said curiously.

"And why are you here, in Chicago?" Naomi added, her expression vigilant.

Drake could tell the witch still had reservations about the demon's sudden appearance and intentions. If Solomon noticed her qualms, he paid them no heed.

"I found Jacob six years ago, in the Libyan Desert. He looked to be about three years old at the time." Solomon laid a gentle hand on Jacob's head. "I traced his first appearance to the Argolid Peninsula, in Southern Greece, a few months before I came upon him. He has no memories of who he is or where he was born. As for his beast, she remains as full of mysteries as the day we first met."

A golden light gleamed in Jacob's eyes for a moment.

Solomon's voice grew steely. "The reason why we came to Chicago is because the Nephilim are awakening. Which means the sixth gate of Hell will soon be revealed."

"The sixth gate?" Artemus frowned, his questioning gaze shifting briefly to Jacob. "You mean the kid's gate?"

"Yes."

"What do you know about the Nephilim?" Callie said uneasily.

"They are the offspring of the Grigori and the human women they slept with when they first came to Earth." Lines wrinkled Solomon's brow. "In Earth's religion and mythology, they are often described as giants who feast on the blood and flesh of humans. The giant part is exaggerated." His frown deepened. "The bit about feeding on humans isn't."

CHAPTER TEN

ARTEMUS'S STOMACH CLENCHED AT THE DEMON'S WORDS.

"To be more precise, they thrive on human blood," Solomon added with a moue of distaste. "It is what feeds their corrupt souls."

Haruki grimaced. "So, they are like—vampires?"

Solomon sighed. "Not quite. You most definitely can't repulse them with garlic or slay them with a stake to the heart."

Artemus digested the demon's warning with growing unease. A thought came to his mind then. "What did you do to Smokey's wound?"

Smokey looked up from Jacob's lap, his nose twitching. Artemus was relieved to see that the hellhound's appetite had returned.

"I sealed away the Nephil's curse, which remained in his bones," Solomon said. "If allowed to spread, it will slowly kill him."

"Can you get rid of it?" Drake asked roughly.

Solomon hesitated. "Not completely. The only thing

that can release the curse is the death of the Nephil who caused it."

"Why did the monster we fought last night look like an angel?" Haruki asked, troubled. "And how is he so strong?"

Solomon's expression turned regretful. "Although the humans who now walk the Earth do not possess divine energy, the first males and females made in the image of God retained remnants of the powers of celestial beings." He looked at Naomi. "Your kind knows this better than anyone."

"You mean the first witch?" Naomi asked tensely. "The one Azazel chose to be his queen?"

"Indeed. The Nephilim's strength stems from the combined powers of the First Sons of God and the First Daughters of Men. It was only after their fathers fell to Hell that the Nephilim turned savage and became a danger to humanity. Though they did not take on the hateful appearance God cursed upon his Fallen Sons, their white wings and fair skin all turned a lackluster gray and their eyes took on the crimson light of their bloodlust." Solomon stared into space, as if seeing memories he would rather not revisit. "They were banished to Tartarus, where they should have remained until the End of Days. Except someone is raising them again."

Disquiet filled Artemus at the demon's words. "Do you know who that person is?"

Solomon shook his head, frustration dancing briefly across his features. "I do not, unfortunately. But he must be a powerful demon indeed. Likely a Prince of Hell. My fiends did not detect any trace of his corruption when they dragged the Nephil back into the Earth."

Callie sucked in air. Surprise widened Drake and Haruki's eyes.

"Wait," Artemus said in a dazed voice. "Those blue demons who got rid of the Nephil last night? They were *yours?!*"

"Yes." Solomon raked a hand through his hair, his expression uncomfortable. "Like I told you, every Grigori Leader and every Prince of Hell commands an army of demons who pledge their allegiance to them. When I escaped Hell to atone for my sins, I took my troops with me."

"Why didn't they kill him?" Drake asked grimly. "Your demons. Why didn't they kill that Nephil?"

Solomon frowned. "They are not strong enough to do that. They returned him to the depths from which he came and forced him back into slumber. They will not be able to hold him there for long, though."

"How many demons do you have at your command?" Leah asked, pale-faced.

Solomon grimaced. "I would rather not say. For the most part, they walk this Earth in human form and try to live within and blend in with human societies as best they can. They do not commit the atrocities visited upon humans by Ba'al's demons and only answer my call when I need them."

Callie studied Solomon with something akin to sympathy. "You look after them."

Solomon did not deny her claim.

"It is my fault that they fell from Heaven," he murmured awkwardly.

Artemus fisted his hands where they rested on the countertop he leaned against. "These Nephilim. Do you have some kind of headcount for them?"

He saw the worried look Drake cast his way. A single Nephil had almost overpowered them last night.

Artemus did not dare imagine what a few of them could do.

"One hundred."

Artemus's mouth went dry.

"That's how many Nephilim were born to the fallen angels before they were cast to Hell," Solomon said gravely.

Artemus knew the demon was not lying.

"Shit," Drake whispered.

A low growl rumbled out of Smokey. Callie and Haruki shared an anxious look.

Leah studied them nervously. "Are they really that powerful?"

"Yes." Callie frowned. "I doubt we could handle more than a handful of them, even with Sebastian and Daniel."

"What about Otis?" Naomi asked.

Artemus could see the alarm throbbing through the Guardians reflected on the witch's troubled face.

"She's right. Otis is still an unknown quantity." Drake looked at Artemus, a trace of hope in his voice. "His powers are still evolving."

"The seraph is indeed all-mighty," Solomon said with a nod. "There is a strong chance he will be able to defeat a Nephil single-handedly. But not a hundred of them at once."

The hope that had burst to life on Drake's face died a sudden death.

"We still don't know what Jacob can do," Haruki said.

The boy startled at the mention of his name.

Artemus observed the kid with a frown. "You're right. His Guardian may be able to defeat the Nephilim."

Jacob grabbed hold of Solomon's arm and shifted closer to the demon, his dark eyes full of apprehension.

A pained look flitted across Solomon's face. He wrapped his other arm around the kid and gave him a hug. "It's okay, Jacob. We've talked about this." The demon's tone grew sad. "When the time comes, your beast will tell you what you must do."

The boy buried his face in the demon's chest and clung to him with his small fists.

"I don't wanna," he mumbled. "It's scary."

Guilt shot through Artemus at the way Jacob's voice shook.

"Dammit!" Callie barked, her frustration plain to see. "Are we that powerless that we have to leave this on the shoulders of Otis and this poor kid?!"

Her words cut through all of them.

"No." Artemus's voice hardened. "We're not just going to leave this to them. We will fight, as we always do." He narrowed his eyes at Drake and the Guardians. "Together."

Warmth blossomed inside him the next instant, the bond he shared with the divine beasts, Smokey, and Drake a bright band vibrating through his soul as they affirmed their commitment to one another.

"Oh." Jacob blinked and pulled back from Solomon. He touched his chest with hesitant fingers. "What was that? It...it tingled."

"That was but a trace of what you will come to share with them when you awaken," Solomon said gently.

He indicated Artemus and the others. The apprehension faded a little from the boy's eyes.

The sound of the front door thudding open reached them. Artemus stiffened before relaxing slightly. He recognized the energy of the pair who had just entered the mansion.

Serena and Nate stormed into the kitchen a moment later.

Serena walked up to Drake and clutched his face in her hands, her expression strained. "Are you okay?"

"What are you doing here?" Drake said, surprised.

Callie rose from her chair and walked into Nate's welcoming embrace.

"I didn't know you were coming," she breathed against his chest, relief lacing her voice. "I thought you two were still busy with your mission."

"We told Gideon something came up," Nate said grimly.

"Besides, he said an earthquake struck Chicago last night," Serena added with a frown. "One that bore the same seismological signature as the event he sent us to investigate in Peru. He wanted us to look into it before we go to Europe."

"Why? What's happening in Europe?" Drake said stiffly.

"More earthquakes, I suspect," Solomon muttered pensively before Serena could answer. "So, *that's* how he's raising the Nephilim."

Artemus stared, understanding dawning inside him. "You mean those weird earthquakes on the news? Those are all because of Nephilim?!"

Serena narrowed her eyes. "What are you talking about?" She cocked a thumb at Solomon and Jacob. "And who's the new guy and the creepy kid?"

CHAPTER ELEVEN

"Mr. Hunter." Agent Milton smiled. "Thank you for coming in."

Drake studied the man seated at the table with a neutral expression. The door to the interview room closed behind him, the FBI agent who'd taken his details and brought him to Milton disappearing without a word.

Drake noted the discreet cameras in the corners of the ceiling. *No doubt there's one behind that glass window too.*

Though he hadn't done anything recently that would warrant a giant, red target on his back by law enforcement standards, he still felt twitchy at having to answer the FBI's questions.

The summons had come late that morning, shortly after Serena and Nate had left Chicago to board a private jet that would take them and the Immortals working with Gideon across the Atlantic to Southern Europe.

The short time Drake had had with Serena had been filled with tense discussions, with Artemus bringing the super soldiers up to speed on what had happened the night before and who Solomon and Jacob were. Though the identities of the demon and the child had surprised Serena and Nate, that of the Nephilim had had them sharing a shocked look. That was when the super soldiers had revealed the details of their secret mission to South America.

It had become apparent to the governments of the countries where the unusual quakes had been happening that something far more sinister was going on than just some random, seismological anomalies. Gideon, the Vatican, and the Immortals had been called in to assist the investigations behind the scenes once it had become clear the phenomena were of supernatural origin.

Solomon's expression had grown hard when Serena had spoken of the mangled human remains that had littered the streets of the village at the center of the incident in Peru and the bloodless state of the corpses. It was a scene repeated across all the quake sites to date, with the affected human settlements characterized by how remote they were in their geographical locations and the attacks taking place at night.

Nate had explained how those who had survived were now sick with a mysterious disease.

"Conrad thinks it's some kind of poison," Serena had said. "He's managed to contain it to an extent, but he hasn't been able to cure the villagers he's seen to date."

Artemus and Solomon had exchanged a frown.

"Sounds like it's the same stuff that made Smokey sick," Callie had muttered with a scowl.

"Who's Conrad?" Drake had asked.

Serena's expression had grown guarded. "He's an Immortal."

"He was with Alexa King, the day we were freed from our prison in Greenland," Nate had added in a low voice.

Solomon had raised an eyebrow at that. "Uriel's child was with you in South America?"

They'd all looked at him blankly then.

The demon had registered their puzzlement with a sigh. "Ah. I see you do not yet know the truth of the Immortals. They are of Uriel's bloodline, just as Artemus is of Michael's lineage and Drake Samyaza's."

"Wait," Artemus had blurted out. "Are you saying the Immortals are descendants of Uriel? As in, the archangel?!"

Solomon had shrugged at his stunned expression. "In a fashion, yes. Though he did not mate with a human female to make it so. His method was more...unorthodox."

"So, that's what we felt from King in Rome," Artemus had muttered as he glanced at the rest of them. "It *was* divine energy."

Milton cleared his throat. "It was remiss of you to have left the premises of a crime without making your presence and identity known to the police, Mr. Hunter."

Drake focused his attention on the man who'd just spoken. He understood now why Artemus had disliked the agent at first sight. Milton looked like the kind of guy who would shoot first and ask questions later. It was also clear he liked playing by his own rules.

The FBI agent's assertion that the attack on Elton's auction house had been a terrorist act was still to be been borne out by any physical evidence. Chicago CSI and the FBI crime scene investigators had found no traces of explosives or guns having been discharged at the location. All they had so far were blurry videos of strange shapes in the sky and the testimonies of several dozen guests who'd still looked to be in a state of shock when they'd been interviewed.

Drake knew this because he and Artemus had had

Serena and Nate hack into the Chicago PD and FBI's databases before they'd left the mansion that morning.

"Was it?"

Milton arched an eyebrow at Drake's question. "Was it what, Mr. Hunter?"

Drake leaned back in the chair and folded his arms loosely across his chest, his posture deliberately insolent. "The scene of a crime? So far, I have failed to see much that would make me believe it was anything but an unfortunate, natural disaster. Much like what has been taking place in other parts of the world lately."

Milton studied him for a moment. "How about you leave the investigating to the experts, Mr. Hunter?" He turned on the digital recorder on the table, his tone now cool. "Now, tell me what happened at the auction house."

By the time the FBI agent had finished grilling him, a headache was pounding at Drake's temples. Nausea churned his stomach as he made to rise from the table. All he'd had that morning was two servings of the shitty coffee Milton had offered him.

Sweat broke out on his brow as he pushed himself up onto his feet. A wave of dizziness swept over him. Drake blinked and swayed, black spots blotting his vision.

What the—?!

"Are you okay?"

Milton's concerned voice reached Drake dimly through the dull ringing in his ears. The agent braced a hand against his back.

"Yeah," Drake mumbled.

Shit. Was it something I ate last night?

He blinked sweat from his eyes, his pulse racing. He felt strangely feverish all of a sudden.

"If that's everything, I'll take my leave."

"Of course. I'll see you to the entrance." Milton frowned. "You look like you could do with some fresh air."

By the time they reached the steps fronting the building that housed the local FBI field office, Drake had started to shiver. Milton bade him goodbye and went back inside, his expression troubled as he cast a final, backward glance at him.

Drake waited until the man had disappeared before fishing his cell out of his jeans and calling Artemus.

His brother answered on the third ring. "Hey. You done?"

"Yeah. He wants to see you in an hour." Drake swallowed and fought down another wave of nausea. The cold air wasn't making him feel any better. "Where are you?"

"At the antique shop. Solomon and Jacob wanted to see the place."

"Callie and the others?"

"They're at the mansion with Smokey." Artemus paused. "Are you okay? You sound a bit strange."

Drake wiped a hand across his brow and stared at the moistness soaking his skin. "I don't know. I don't feel so good."

"What's wrong?" Artemus said, alarmed. "Are you still at the FBI headquarters? I'll come get you."

"Don't. I'm not far from your place. I'll be over soon."

Artemus's protest died off when Drake ended the call. Acid burned the back of his throat. The effort of having to speak had left him drained. He headed over to where he'd parked his bike, his limbs heavy and his skin prickling as if a thousand needles were dancing across his flesh.

CHAPTER TWELVE

"BE CAREFUL WITH THAT, JACOB," SOLOMON SAID.

Jacob hesitated, his fingers stopping shy of touching the brass astrolabe that had caught his eye. He lowered his hand and dropped back down on his heels.

Artemus removed the antique from the display shelf and placed it on a thick, velvet cloth on the shop's main counter.

He brought over a wooden stool. "Here."

Jacob's eyes rounded as Artemus grabbed him under the arms and lifted him easily onto the seat. He stiffened, his panicked gaze swinging to Solomon.

Artemus saw their exchange and frowned. "What?"

A rueful sigh escaped Solomon. "He's not used to being touched by strangers. I'm probably at fault for that."

"Oh." Artemus lifted his hands hastily off Jacob. He grimaced and scratched his head. "I didn't know. Sorry, kid."

Jacob blinked at his apology.

"It's okay," he mumbled awkwardly.

He gazed at the astrolabe, hoping to hide his embarrassment. He'd felt oddly safe in Artemus's hold. As safe as he would have felt if it had been Solomon touching him.

Artemus pretended he hadn't noticed his reddening ears and went on to explain how the instrument worked, his voice light and patient. Jacob absorbed it all, like he always did any new thing he came across. But something kept distracting him.

Artemus did not miss the furtive glances Jacob cast his way. "What is it? Do I have something on my face?"

Jacob shook his head. "No. It's not that." He hesitated. "You're just...pretty, is all."

A choked sound escaped Solomon where he was perusing the contents of a display cabinet a few feet away, his back to them. His shoulders trembled slightly.

Artemus flashed a frown at the demon before gazing at Jacob. "Look, I know you mean that as a compliment, but men like to be called things like, oh, I don't know, handsome. Or good-looking. Pretty is for girls."

Jacob stared. "Like Callie and Leah? And the cat lady?"

Artemus winced. "Don't call Naomi cat lady to her face. She'll hex you."

Jacob blinked. An involuntarily giggle escaped him the next instant. The sound shocked him as much as it did Artemus and Solomon.

"You should do that more often," Artemus said once his surprise faded.

"Do what?"

"Smile. It suits you."

"He's right," Solomon concurred, his green eyes warm.

"Oh. Okay."

Jacob attempted to do as they suggested, the corners of his mouth lifting uncomfortably. The angel and the demon stared before exchanging a look.

"We should work on that smile," Artemus said briskly.

"Yes," Solomon muttered.

Jacob sagged on the stool. "It was creepy, wasn't it?"

He startled when Artemus ruffled his hair lightly.

"Hey, don't take what the others said yesterday to heart," Artemus said gruffly. "They didn't mean it."

"But you said I was creepy too," Jacob pointed out morosely.

Artemus made a face. "I was wrong. First impressions aren't always accurate." He brightened slightly. "Do you want some hot chocolate?"

Jacob perked up. "Yes, please."

"Give me a minute. I'm sure Otis has a tin of the stuff in his apartment. One that doesn't have weed in it."

Artemus disappeared toward the back of the shop.

"What's weed?" Jacob asked Solomon curiously.

The demon sighed. "Something little kids shouldn't have. Remind me to taste that hot chocolate before you drink it."

Jacob climbed off the stool and wandered over to another display cabinet.

He hadn't been sure what to make of things when Solomon had announced that they were to leave their farm in Carolina and come to Chicago. In the years since he'd first met the demon, Jacob had had many a home, in dozens of countries. It had taken him a while to realize that Solomon was running from something. Or someone.

He had been six years old when he'd discovered the reason why they never settled in any one place for any length of time.

Their enemy had come upon them quite by accident, in the Australian outback. Jacob and Solomon had been traveling through the area at the time, on their way to visit an old friend of Solomon's.

Though Jacob had been able to sense and see the aura of corruption demon-possessed humans projected for as long as he could remember, that was the first time he'd seen a fully transformed demon in the flesh.

It was also the one and only occasion he'd witnessed Solomon's true form.

When their vehicle had been surrounded by a group of figures with ochre eyes in the middle of nowhere one night, Jacob had climbed into the back of their rental car and hidden in the trunk, just like Solomon had instructed him to do.

Solomon had tried to negotiate their safe passage at first, his tone calm and steady as he stepped out of the car and started to talk with the hostile group. They'd attacked before he'd finished his sentence, their bodies transforming into hideous shapes that had had Jacob gasping in fear, even as the otherworldly creature inside him had stirred with excitement.

The battle had been short-lived. As he'd watched the demons' bloodied carcasses fall to the ground, their expressions frozen in rictuses of shock, Jacob's supernatural eyes had perceived the blistering fast movements of the man who had felled them with his bare hands.

Except Solomon had not looked like the Solomon Jacob knew and loved.

"Are you afraid of me?" Solomon had said forlornly after the fight had ended and Jacob had appeared before him.

Jacob had clasped Solomon's clawed hand and looked up into the demon's sad, crimson gaze. "No. I am not afraid of you."

What he'd read on the demon's face in that moment had had a warm glow of emotion blossoming inside Jacob's chest. He'd known the feeling was not his only, but was shared by the beast who lived beneath his skin. Though both Solomon and the creature were as old as time, they had formed a strange kinship since that fateful night the demon had rescued Jacob in the desert in North Africa, all those years ago.

"Here you go."

Artemus's voice broke through Jacob's thoughts. The angel appeared, three steaming mugs in hand.

"What?" he said somewhat belligerently in the face of Solomon's expression. "I checked. This doesn't have weed in it."

Solomon smiled. "I'm more surprised by the fact you made me a drink."

"Yeah, well, some habits are hard to kill," Artemus muttered. "Besides, Karl would have had my guts for garters if I were a shitty host to you two."

Jacob accepted the mug Artemus handed to him. "Who's Karl?"

A strange emotion lit Artemus's eyes for an instant. "He was the guy who used to own this shop. And the man I considered to be my father."

"Oh," Jacob mumbled. "Like me and Solomon."

Surprise flared on Artemus's face.

Solomon stared at Jacob, as if his words had stunned him too. "I—" The demon paused and swallowed. "I didn't know you thought of me as your father."

Jacob's heart twisted with sudden guilt. "I'm—I'm sorry," he said, panicking. "Was it wrong of me to—?"

Solomon strode across the room, took Jacob's mug from his hand, and closed his arms around him. "Don't apologize. It is I who should be saying sorry." His voice turned grave. "I am deeply honored that you think of me so, Jacob."

Happiness filled Jacob as Solomon pressed a tender kiss to his head. He hugged Solomon back just as tightly.

The shrill ring of Artemus's cell made him jump.

Artemus took the phone out of the pocket of his chinos. Relief flashed in his eyes when he looked at the caller ID. He took the call.

"Hey. You done?" Artemus listened for a moment. "At the antique shop. Solomon and Jacob wanted to see the place." He paused, a faint frown marring his brow. "They're at the mansion with Smokey. Are you okay? You sound a bit strange." Artemus stiffened. "What's wrong? Are you still at the FBI headquarters? I'll come get you." He scowled. "Hey, don't hang up!" Artemus swore. "Drake?!"

He lowered the cell and glared at it.

"What's wrong?" Solomon said.

"That was Drake. He just—"

The shop door jingled open behind them.

Thump.

Jacob blinked.

CHAPTER THIRTEEN

ARTEMUS TURNED, HIS TWIN'S TROUBLED VOICE STILL dancing through his mind. An elderly woman had entered the shop. Surprise shot through him.

"Mrs. Kaufman. I wasn't expecting to see you."

Esther Kaufman's eyes glittered sharply as she studied Artemus. A young man in a chauffeur's uniform and a cap came in behind her, a medium-sized, wooden chest with wrought-iron fittings in his hands. The strained expression on his face and the way his arms looked like they were about to be ripped out of his shoulder sockets indicated that the item was heavy.

"Why, don't tell me you forgot about our appointment," Esther said breezily, blithely ignoring her chauffeur's grunt of effort. She looked curiously at Solomon and Jacob. "Hello. Are you friends of Mr. Steele?"

Solomon smiled at her politely. "Yes, after a fashion."

He glanced at Jacob, a faint frown wrinkling his brow.

The kid had gone deathly pale. He clung to the demon and stared at Esther as if he'd seen a ghost.

An uneasy feeling swept over Artemus at the

Guardian's fearful expression. He focused his attention on the old woman. It only took a moment for him to ascertain that there was no demonic aura above her head or that of her chauffeur.

"To be honest, I kinda did," Artemus murmured in reply to her question, wondering what had spooked the kid so. "Besides, I would have thought you'd still be recovering after what happened last night."

"Oh, piffle." Esther waved a frilly, gloved hand dismissively. "Young man, if I had to take a nap after every little adventure that happened to me, I might as well just stay in bed."

"Well, *I'd* rather be in bed," the chauffeur muttered behind her. "That stuff last night was batshit crazy."

"What was that, Albert?" Esther poked the young man in the midriff with her walking stick, her tone shrill. "Are you giving me lip?"

"No, I am not, Mrs. Kaufman," the chauffeur replied in a tired voice. "And my name is Chad. Albert was my uncle's name."

"May his soul rest in peace," they both mumbled at the same time.

"I prefer Albert," Esther stated. "Chad is too newfangled for my taste." She ignored the chauffeur's pained expression and turned to Artemus. "I brought the antiques I wanted you to take a look at."

She gestured impatiently at Chad.

The chauffeur huffed and puffed as he headed over to the closest counter. A groan left him when he hoisted the antique trunk onto it. The box landed on the worktop with a dull thud.

Artemus stared. He could tell that the item and whatever it contained were several hundred years old. His legs carried him across the shop before he was even aware he'd moved.

There was something else. Something...strange. It was inside the box. And it was drawing Artemus like a beacon.

"I found this chest recently, in a house I inherited from Ariadna, my dearly departed sister," Esther explained as Artemus stopped in front of the casket. "It seems she bought it at an auction a few months before she passed away." The old woman frowned. "It's the damnedest thing, really. We couldn't find an invoice or even an inventory for the item. When I spoke to the New York auction house where Ariadna's butler swore she'd purchased it from, they had no recollection of ever having had the box in their possession in the first place."

Artemus froze, one hand hovering above the latch. He stared blindly at the wooden chest, alarm bells ringing at the back of his mind.

The story Esther had just recounted bore a startling similarity to several odd tales he'd heard in the last year. Tales that had to do with the divine beasts and their keys.

The hairs rose on his arms as a weak energy pulse washed over his skin. Though faint, Artemus knew it had come from whatever object inside the box that was resonating with his powers. Another wave blasted over him a heartbeat later, this one much stronger than the first. His gaze found Jacob.

The second pulse had come from the kid.

A shudder shook Jacob. His eyes glazed over, as if he were seeing something no one else could see. Perspiration exploded across his brow. His knuckles whitened where he'd fisted his hands on Solomon's jacket.

Solomon grew as still as stone beside him, his eyes turning glassy.

The demon's pupils flashed with a crimson light.
Artemus scowled. *Shit.*

THUMP-THUMP.

Sweat beaded Jacob's face as he fought down the sick feeling twisting his belly. He didn't know what was happening to him. Why he suddenly felt as if he'd eaten something bad. Something rotten.

Thump-thump. Thump-thump.

The creature inside him stirred.

Fear threatened to overwhelm him. A whimper tumbled from his lips when he sensed the beast behind his eyes, her existence a heavy weight in his mind.

Of all the things that frightened Jacob in this world, none did so more than the monster who dwelled within his body. Though the creature had never done anything to harm him and Solomon had been at pains to explain her origins and divine mission, Jacob could not help the dread that squeezed his chest whenever he felt her presence.

It had taken him a while to fathom why he was so afraid of the being who had laid claim to his soul. His long-held suspicion was turning into a conviction given what he could sense from her in this moment.

He was going to lose himself to the beast. And he feared, once he did, that there would be no coming back. That he would forget who he had once been. That his memories of his life with Solomon would be no more.

Thump-thump. Thump-thump. Thump-thump.

"No," Jacob mumbled. "Please. Stop!"

Solomon shivered.

The old lady who'd brought the wooden chest stared at Jacob, clearly puzzled.

"Is he okay?" she asked Artemus. "He looks like he's gonna be sick."

"Yeah, well, he's not the only one." A muscle jumped in Artemus's jawline. His wary gaze remained locked on Solomon. "Chad, take Mrs. Kaufman and leave. Right now!"

The chauffeur's legs remained rooted to the floor. He was looking past Artemus at the demon, terror slowly leaching the color from his face. The old lady's eyes widened as she followed his horrified gaze.

Jacob looked up at the man he was clinging to, wondering what had frightened them so. His stomach dropped. A hiss sounded inside his head, the beast's surprise throbbing through him.

Solomon's eyes were glowing with the red light that heralded his demonic transformation. But it wasn't his crimson gaze that made Jacob's blood pound erratically in his veins.

The demon's expression was strangely detached, as if he were not really there.

Artemus snatched a knife from his boot. The weapon transformed into a pale, double-edged sword. Even though he was shaking in terror, Jacob couldn't help but stare at it. The blade looked familiar, for some reason. And it was echoing with the unearthly power swelling inside his small body.

Artemus took a step toward Solomon, a determined frown knotting his brow. Jacob suddenly found himself standing in front of the demon, his arms spread wide in a defensive gesture.

"*No,*" the beast said through his lips. "*He is not your enemy.*"

"His aura says otherwise!" Artemus snapped.

The beast hissed at the angel. "*That is because we are awakening, you damn fool!*"

CHAPTER FOURTEEN

DARKNESS SWALLOWED SOLOMON. UNHOLY SCREAMS echoed in his head, each sound drilling into his brain with the sharpness of a thousand blades. At the back of his mind, in the small part of his consciousness he kept protected at all times, the place where he had been able to preserve his true self whilst in Hell, Solomon had a vague idea what was happening to him. And it scared him like little else could.

It was as he had suspected all along. His meeting with Jacob in the desert that night had not been an accident, but the grim hands of Fate and the Devil's will at work.

A voice reached him then. That of a fiend he had not heard in thousands of years. It was as cold and as mocking as the last time Solomon had perceived it.

"*At long last,*" the demon sneered. "*Your work is almost done, Sariel. Now, be a good archangel and open up your soul. Your Jacob needs you.*"

Rage burned through Solomon at the devil's words.

"How dare you say his name?!" he growled.

The heat of his anger was overshadowed by the black

incandescence that exploded inside his chest. He gasped and clutched at his dark heart. Horror flooded him when he glimpsed the abyss threatening to burst open inside his body.

"*No!*"

Something throbbed inside his soul. A point of brightness where none should have existed. He blinked.

The spark grew until it formed a pulsing, golden sphere the size of his hand.

The radiance swallowed the shadows that had engulfed him and drowned out the storm raging in his ears. Murmurs came to him dimly. The black veil obscuring his vision started to clear.

Solomon's stomach lurched at the sight of the tiny figure standing in front of him, arms wide open as if to shield him.

"Jacob?" he mumbled.

Hold fast, demon. It is not yet time.

Solomon drew a sharp breath as the voice of the divine beast who dwelled inside Jacob reverberated in his mind, muting the hellish shrieks of the demons from the Underworld.

Artemus's hazy shape took form. The angel stood facing Jacob, his father's holy blade in his hand, his expression murderous as he stared over the boy's head at Solomon.

Solomon could hardly blame him. *No doubt he thinks I'm about to transform and kill everyone within sight!*

Jacob glanced wildly at Solomon over his shoulder. "It's okay, Father. I'll—I'll protect you!"

Tears shimmered in the boy's eyes and he shook so hard his teeth clattered.

Pain squeezed Solomon's entire being. Before he could

tell Jacob to stand down, something detonated on the counter behind Artemus, the blast as noiseless as it was powerful.

The old woman yelled out in surprise. Her chauffeur unfroze and closed his arms protectively around her as he pushed her to the floor.

Debris filled the air, the fragments expanding on an explosive wave before slowing and contracting slightly, as if time itself had stopped and reversed for an instant.

Rising in the midst of what was once the wooden chest, glowing with the light of Heaven itself, was a bronze key with a snake wrapped around its body.

JACOB STARED UNBLINKINGLY AT THE OBJECT LEVITATING a few feet from where he stood. The world slowly faded around him. Solomon. Artemus. The shop. Everything disappeared until there was only him, his beast, and the artifact rotating on its axis.

It called to him, the energy it emitted pulsing with a beat that matched his heart and that of the creature inside him. Jacob could sense the beast's wonder where she was poised behind his eyes, her attention riveted to the key hovering in the air ahead of them. They raised their right hand, unbidden.

The artifact gravitated past a shocked Artemus and landed in Jacob's waiting palm. The metal kissed his skin. Heat bloomed inside him, a fierce and righteous, holy fever that made his very bones vibrate.

Control it, child. Do not let it transform fully yet.

Jacob startled at the beast's calm instructions. The creature appeared to have come to her senses. He realized then that the fear he had always harbored toward the monster was no more.

"What—what is this?!"

It is our key. And a conduit for our powers.

As if in response to the divine beast's words, the object shifted into a smooth, silver staff as tall as Jacob. He stared at it, stunned.

Solomon's voice jolted him out of his state of shock. "Jacob?"

Jacob whirled around. His eyes widened.

Solomon's features were a rictus of agony. He was bent over, his body shuddering with every gulping breath he drew, his hands gripping his chest as if he were trying to stop something from ripping him apart.

"Do not let the gate open," the demon commanded hoarsely. His crimson gaze shifted past Jacob to Artemus. "Kill me if you must, but the gate. Must. Not. *OPEN!*"

Terror swamped Jacob when he saw a sphere of darkness trying to free itself from Solomon's hold, the evil tendrils squeezing through the gaps between the demon's white-knuckled fingers and sniffing the air with cold-blooded hunger.

He knew instinctively that Hell awaited behind it.

Sigils burst into life on the surface of the staff in his hand.

～

DREAD FORMED A HEAVY PIT IN ARTEMUS'S STOMACH AS he stared from the globe of corruption throbbing over Solomon's heart to the runes covering the holy weapon in Jacob's grasp. A memory came to him.

He recalled what had happened under the museum

several weeks back, when he and the others had fought Ba'al. How Jeremiah Chase and the corpses of the undead who had risen across the city had been absorbed by Leah's gate.

Otis said some of the gates of Hell would likely require human sacrifices! But what if some require more than human ones?!

"Goddammit!" He glared accusingly at the demon. "You're Jacob's gate?!"

Solomon nodded, anguish etched in every line of his face. "I wasn't certain. Not until this moment!"

The demon looked old all of a sudden, as if the years of his long and wretched existence had finally caught up with him. His true form fluttered wildly under his skin as it tried to break through.

Artemus clenched his jaw. He had an inkling what it was costing Solomon to hold back his transformation. And damn if that didn't make him admire the demon more.

"How do we stop it?"

Solomon blinked at Artemus's question.

His gaze shifted to Jacob. "Lend him your strength!"

Surprise shot through Artemus. He kind of had an idea what the demon was asking him to do.

"Is that really going to work?" he said skeptically.

A groan left Solomon, the sound filled with suffering. Dark horns started to sprout from his forehead. Still, he clung on, his resolve unwavering and his grip unfaltering as he held Hell's gate at bay.

"Father!" Jacob shouted miserably.

"It's okay, child." Solomon focused on Artemus, his face shiny with perspiration. "Please! There is nothing to lose and everything to gain by trying!"

Artemus knew they had only seconds left to act. He decided to put his trust in the demon and closed the distance to Jacob, hoping he wasn't making a huge mistake.

Here goes nothing.

Artemus took a deep breath and did what he had done to Drake in L.A., when the dark angel had lost control of his powers during their fight with the demon prince Asmodee. He laid a hand on Jacob's chest and cast the divine energy that filled his soul through his fingertips and into the boy, hoping it would do what it had done to Drake. Which was bring him back to his senses.

Jacob gasped, his body jerking as if struck by a bolt of electricity. Artemus blinked as half a dozen ethereal shapes took form around Jacob, framing his head and body like a halo. For a moment, he thought he glimpsed the nature of the divine beast who dwelled inside the kid.

Jacob's pupils brightened to gold.

"*Thank you, Son of Michael,*" the beast growled through his lips.

"Er, sure. Anytime."

Jacob closed his eyes, a heavy frown marring his brow. Artemus felt the kid's powers surge. The weapon in Jacob's grasp shrank back into a key once more.

Solomon choked and wheezed as he tried to catch his breath. He swayed where he stood, sweat dripping down his face. The throbbing darkness over his heart dissipated into nothingness.

Deafening silence descended on the shop in the aftermath.

"What the heck was that?!" Esther screeched, startling them all.

Chad climbed unsteadily to his feet and helped the old lady up, his face pale.

"Something you shouldn't have seen," Artemus told her

grimly. He eyed Solomon darkly. "Care to tell me why you didn't bother to mention that you thought you might be the kid's gate?!"

Solomon leaned a heavy hand against the counter, evidently still weak from what had just transpired. "Like I said, I wasn't sure. Until now, that is."

A hiss escaped Jacob at the same time the air became heavy with corruption.

"Oh, for Christ's sake!" Artemus scowled. "What the hell is it now?!"

"It's Ba'al," Solomon said numbly. "They know we're here. The gate must have drawn them!"

Shadows engulfed the shop. Artemus looked out of the window fronting the facade.

The daylight outside was fading fast.

CHAPTER FIFTEEN

THE WIND WHIPPED AT DRAKE'S CLOTHES AS HE CLUNG to the superbike, the blacktop roads he was navigating zooming past at breakneck speed. Horns honked in his wake and the disgruntled shouts of the drivers he cut off faded in the distance behind him.

He'd probably violated a dozen traffic regulations in as many minutes.

The dreadful feeling that had nearly overcome him when he'd been at the FBI headquarters had started to fade, though the weird prickling persisted. He didn't know what had caused him to feel so ill or why the strange sensation throbbing through his soul lingered still.

Something had changed inside him. Something he hadn't been aware of until today. A single thought domi-nated Drake's mind in the midst of his confusion.

He needed to be with Artemus.

He was half a mile from the antique shop when he felt it.

Drake cursed and tapped the brake handle. The super-bike screeched as it decelerated abruptly, the front tire burning dark threads into the asphalt while the back wheel rose off the ground. He veered to the side and rocked to a stop in the middle of the road, the machine's gyroscopic, self-balancing system stopping it from crashing over.

Drake took his visor off and stared at the dark, writhing cloud above the rooftops ahead. He didn't need his otherworldly senses to know that he was looking at hundreds of demonic manifestations.

The stink of Hell was so strong it was affecting the people on the streets.

A man bent over and threw up on Drake's right. A woman swayed and collapsed farther up the curb. Startled cries and yells rendered the air as the midday crowd began to scatter, panic sending them crashing into one another in their haste to get away.

The demon inside Drake was roused when he sensed the evil energy of his brethren, his insidious hiss echoing in Drake's mind while his dark excitement seeped into Drake's veins.

Drake gritted his teeth, focused on the lasso of divine power his goddess mother had gifted him with, and pushed the devil back behind the walls that held him prisoner. The fiend screeched in rage. Drake ignored the sound, started the bike, and headed toward the corrupt shadows amassed above the antique shop.

ARTEMUS GRIPPED HIS SWORD TIGHTLY WHERE HE STOOD outside his store, his pulse racing. He studied the horde of demons battering the divine barrier Michael and Sebastian had erected around the building with a heavy frown. Their sulfurous eyes glowed with hate and their talons scraped and sparked across the shimmering, ethereal wall shielding the area.

"Is that going to hold?" Solomon said.

"I don't know." A muscle jumped in Artemus's cheek. "Paimon managed to break through the one outside the Vatican, somehow."

He lowered his gaze to the bodies littering the street.

The people who had been in the vicinity of the shop at the time the demons appeared had fainted, their human senses unable to tolerate the vile pressure thickening the air.

"We should get them somewhere safe," Artemus said grimly. "My workshop should do. It's full of iron."

"Are those—are those demons?!" someone mumbled behind them.

Artemus looked over his shoulder. To his surprise, Esther and Chad were still standing, albeit with some difficulty. They were holding each other up where they huddled in the shop's doorway, a pale-faced Jacob at their side.

Those two are made of sterner stuff than I gave them credit for.

Esther glanced at Artemus while Chad gagged beside her. "What's going on, Artemus?"

"It would take too long to explain. You should get—"

A thunderous crack wrenched the air and drowned out the rest of his warning. The malevolent energy filling the street intensified. Alarm blasted through Artemus at the sight of the small fracture in the barrier above him.

He looked over at Chad, urgency rendering his tone harsh. "Can you help us carry these people inside?!"

Chad hesitated before nodding. He left Esther with Jacob and joined Artemus and Solomon as they started retrieving the unconscious bystanders. More breaches started to materialize in the divine barrier when they came back outside. The muted shrieks of the demons grew louder.

"This would go much faster if we were both in our true forms!" Solomon shouted.

They had only cleared a third of the street and had another eight bodies to move.

Artemus gave Solomon a wary look. "I thought you didn't want to change into your demon form. Isn't that why you were fighting so hard not to transform earlier?"

Lines furrowed Solomon's brow. "I was not myself then. Hell's gate was trying to take over my body."

"So, what, you're saying you can control it?" Artemus said dubiously. "Your bloodlust, I mean?"

Solomon's eyes gleamed with a flash of red. "Yes. I've been doing it for hundreds of years. Besides, I am no longer at the mercy of the hateful emotions of those trapped in Hell. My connection with Satanael's will ended when I escaped."

Surprise jolted Artemus at his words. *Wait. Does that mean the same thing could happen to Drake too? Could he severe his link with Samyaza?!*

"We're running out of time," Solomon warned.

As if to prove him right, one of the demons started to squeeze through a fissure in the barrier. The shield ripped at his left arm and leg, shearing his limbs clear from his body. Still he came, his monstrous face full of loathing.

Artemus clenched his jaw. Solomon was right. They were out of time.

He reached inside his soul and brought forth the powers gifted to him by his archangel father and his goddess mother. His skin brightened to silver. Armor materialized out of thin air and covered his body from his neck down, the metal glowing with a sheen that formed a golden halo around him. His senses sharpened a hundredfold at the same time the blade in his hand morphed into a giant broadsword brimming with Heaven's flames, courtesy of the fiery gauntlet on his right hand.

Chad gaped. He stumbled backward as Solomon's body swelled into his demon form, rising some eight feet in height and casting a shadow across him.

Black horns sprouted from Solomon's forehead, the edges tipped with flames. His pupils became pinpoint beams of scarlet. His fingers and nails lengthened to deadly talons.

A horrified noise left Chad. Solomon ignored it and reached out to his left. A rift tore the air next to his claws. Artemus blinked.

Unlike the corrupt energy that Ba'al's crimson, dimensional tears projected, this one emitted a pale light full of warmth. It wasn't quite what one of Sebastian's divine rifts looked like, but it wasn't far off it either. Solomon pushed his hand inside the crevice and removed a broadsword from within it.

Artemus's eyes widened.

The weapon looked like Drake's demonic blade. Except it was pale and swarming with Heaven's fire.

Artemus's ears popped. He looked up just as the barrier protecting the shop and the surrounding area shattered. The demons descended upon them in a mantle of darkness and hellish screams, their ochre eyes ablaze with hatred.

CHAPTER SIXTEEN

Drake beat his wings and rose, a scowl furrowing his brow.

What the hell is going on?!

The divine dome protecting the antique shop had collapsed just as he'd abandoned his bike some five hundred feet from its location. He'd changed into his dark angel form and made his way rapidly over to the building, only to find the place quasi-invisible, so thick was the flock of demons swarming it. Drake's stomach had churned with trepidation as he'd started felling the fiends.

Artemus was still inside the shop. He could tell from their bond.

But however many demons Drake disposed of, more kept appearing. It was as if something had drawn them to the area. He clenched his jaw.

The only phenomenon that had had a similar effect on Ba'al's demons in the past had been the opening of a gate.

He caught odd glimpses of the building below him from where he floated some hundred feet in the air. The entrance and front window had been smashed in and demons crawled along the walls and rooftop of the shop, their numbers legion.

Though Drake had attacked them, they had not reciprocated in kind. They remained wholly focused on the shop.

This observation did nothing but fill him with dread. The same dread that had coursed through him back at the FBI field office.

Something told Drake the two events were connected, somehow.

It took him another five minutes to break through the mob packed around the antique store. The wall of demons closed behind him as he made his way inside. He shot past the broken shelves and display cabinets littering the interior and followed the bright cord that linked him to Artemus through to the back.

Drake's skin itched uncomfortably as he entered the smithy, the devil inside him making a sound of pain when it sensed iron. His reaction to the metal was growing stronger the more Samyaza tried to possess his soul.

He came to an abrupt halt in mid-air and landed smoothly on the floor, his eyes trying to make sense of the chaos around him. A pale shape shot toward him, startling him.

Artemus collided with Drake and hugged him tightly. "Thank God!"

Drake blinked as his twin's wings folded protectively around their bodies. He hesitated before embracing his brother back just as strongly, gripped by the same need to connect that Artemus was experiencing.

The last time they'd felt this way was a few months ago, in the gardens surrounding the Vatican. It was the night they'd met their mothers, Alice and Theia, and learned the truth of their conception and birth.

Drake drew back slightly. "What happened?"

Artemus let go of him reluctantly, as if he feared their parting. "Esther brought a box of antiques to the shop."

His brother indicated an old woman sitting by the forge.

Though her face was pale, she was watching them with keen interest. A young man in a chauffeur's uniform hovered over her, his eyes full of equal fear and determination. Jacob stood close by, apprehension painted across his ashen features. Bunched together around them and the forge were some two dozen unconscious men and women.

"The chest contained Jacob's key," Artemus said. "The artifact resonated with him and his gate."

Drake froze. "What? His gate is here too?!"

"Yes," someone said behind Artemus.

Drake looked past his brother to the demon hovering by the exit.

The back door of the workshop had been ripped off its hinges. Fiends swarmed the alley that ran behind the building, their angry hisses and shrieks filling the air. They faltered on the threshold.

There was too much iron inside the smithy for their liking.

Solomon gazed at Drake steadily from where he floated near the doorway, his dark wings beating the air gently and a pale broadsword in his right hand. Drake registered the weapon's resemblance to his own with a faint jolt of surprise.

"Where is it?" He looked around the workshop. "Where's the gate?"

Artemus jerked his head at Solomon. "You're looking at it."

Drake shot a bewildered glance at his brother.

"Solomon is Jacob's gate," Artemus explained in a troubled voice.

His twin's words sent bone-deep fear stabbing through Drake's heart. Samyaza's evil cackle echoed faintly in his ears. Before he could make sense of any of it, a deafening noise ripped through the room.

The ceiling imploded, revealing the jagged opening the demons had torn through the shop's rooftop and Otis's smashed-up apartment. Debris clouded the air as chunks of plaster, wood, and glass rained down toward them and the humans around the forge.

Before Drake or Artemus could move to intercept the deadly fragments and shards, a sudden windstorm swept across the chamber. It gathered the rubble some eight feet from the ground and sent it flying back in the direction of the demons crawling across what remained of the building's top half.

Drake followed his brother's shocked gaze to the boy who stood in the center of the localized hurricane swirling inside the workshop. Jacob's pupils glowed a solid gold as he spun the silver staff in his hands rapidly above his head. The weapon blurred, its insanely fast rotation dragging the air currents to form a tornado-like funnel.

Unlike Leah, who could command thunder and lightning, the kid appeared to be using the laws of physics to create the tempest protecting the innocent victims around him.

"Is that his key?!" Drake shouted above the fury of the storm.

"Yeah!" Artemus frowned and looked over at Solomon.

"But the gate isn't opening like it did before." He glanced at Jacob, confused. "How is he doing that?!"

Jacob glanced at him and his beast spoke. "*Sariel has stalled time in a parallel plane of existence.*"

"What?" Drake mumbled.

"*He is using his elemental powers to stop the sixth gate from opening in Hell's dimension.*"

Drake and Artemus stared at the demon.

A stillness had come over Solomon where he levitated in mid-air. His eyes were closed and his brow was furrowed, as if he were concentrating on something. The pressure inside the workshop dropped. Crimson-tinged rifts tore open all around them.

"Shit!" Drake stretched his wings and rose as more demons poured inside the chamber. "Are you sure about that, kid?!"

Artemus clenched his jaw and climbed beside him, his expression similarly skeptical.

The hairs lifted on the back of Drake's neck. The air in the chamber grew even thicker with corruption, stirring the demon within him anew. But there was something strange about the fresh darkness he could sense throbbing around them.

Drake exchanged a startled look with Artemus. "Wait. Doesn't this feel like what happened at the auction house last night?"

As if to prove him right, Solomon's guttural words reached them.

"*Come to me, brothers.*"

Scores of pale rifts materialized around them. Ba'al's demons screeched in alarm as a swarm of ochre-eyed fiends with dark blue skin blasted out of the new dimensional tears.

Just as had happened with the Nephil, Solomon's demons did not attack Artemus and Drake, but focused their assault on Ba'al instead. Ghastly sounds filled the air as Ba'al's fiends fought back.

"Why don't we lend them a hand?" Artemus said grimly.

His brother's divine powers echoed with Drake's own energy as he tucked his wings and darted into the melee, his pale broadsword shimmering with Heaven's fire. Drake clamped down on the sudden bloodlust boiling up inside him and joined his twin.

With every demon he killed, Drake felt his control slowly slip away. By the time Ba'al's last fiend fell, he was barely holding on to his consciousness, the evil within clawing at what remained of his sanity.

The protective storm Jacob had created to shield them started to abate. A heavy stillness descended after it dissipated.

Drake trembled as he shrank back into his human form. He landed on unsteady legs and sank to his knees, his knuckles white around his knife. The sickening feeling that had gripped him at the FBI field office was back. And it was ten times worse than before.

His stomach clenched with sudden violence. Drake retched and threw up.

"Drake!" Artemus's alarmed voice reached him indistinctly, as if his twin were addressing him through a roomful of water. "What's wrong?!"

Artemus grabbed his shoulder. His touch seared Drake's flesh.

Redness pulsed across Drake's vision. It was followed by a sea of crimson dots. The prickling sensation that had stung his skin before returned a hundred-fold.

Dim shouts rose somewhere behind Artemus.

Drake blinked and looked blearily past his brother, the act of lifting his head so taxing he felt his skull would topple to the ground at any moment.

Hazy shapes blurred where the smithy's back door once stood.

Drake thought he recognized Callie and Haruki's voices, and Leah's in the background.

A dark form bolted between them. Smokey's rumbling whine echoed inside his soul. He sensed the hellhound's weight next to his body and felt the rasp of a hot tongue on his face.

"What the—?!"

Artemus's horrified mumble danced in Drake's ears at the same time fire scorched his body in dozens of places, drawing a gasp of pain from his lips. Drake gritted his teeth and blinked sweat from his eyes.

It took a moment for him to make out what had unnerved his brother so.

Symbols glowed on the backs of his hands and his exposed forearms where none had been before. Drake knew without looking that the fiery lines scorching his flesh under his clothes were a reflection of the same sigils.

They bore an uncanny resemblance to the runes that manifested on his shield when his watch transformed and those that had appeared on the Guardians' keys before they fully awakened, the arcane shapes forming a language unknown to man.

Understanding blasted through Drake with the force of a bullet. Terror followed, a sea of despair that threatened to swallow him whole.

He knew then what he was. And he realized why he felt the way he did toward Artemus and Smokey. Why it had always seemed as if his bond with them was stronger and more special than the one he shared with the other divine beasts.

He had always imagined it was because the three of them were brothers, not just of blood but bonded by their kindred spirits. A bark of delirious laughter left his throat at that thought. It came out a choked sound.

So, that's *what Samyaza is after!*

The demon who had sired him sneered deep inside his soul, his hatred a visceral manifestation that slowly ate away at Drake's life force.

Drake could see it plainly now. All that had happened had been to prepare him for his wretched fate. To make him ready for the ungodly task he had been brought into this world to accomplish.

The floor came up to meet him. Shadows started to encroach on his vision.

A pair of strong arms closed around him and lifted him into a desperate embrace. Drake blinked and made out Artemus's ashen features above him. His twin shouted something at him as he held him close to his chest.

"It's okay," Drake mumbled. "It doesn't hurt so bad."

The shadows multiplied. His world imploded into darkness.

CHAPTER SEVENTEEN

CALLIE HESITATED BEFORE KNOCKING ON THE BEDROOM door. She opened it and entered the dimly lit room beyond, a tray of food in hand.

Twilight filtered through the bay windows opposite the door. It cast pale fingers on the unconscious man in the four-poster bed dominating the space and the three figures in the room with him.

Callie balanced the tray in one hand and reached out to flick the main light on.

Neither Artemus nor Solomon stirred from their respective positions on the chair by the bed and the one by the window. Only Smokey lifted his head where he lay atop the bedsheets next to Drake, his nose twitching a sad welcome.

The Nephil's poison had started to seep into the hellhound's bloodstream again. The effects were becoming visible, his eyes having lost their customary vibrance and his healthy fur growing lackluster.

Callie's heart twisted at the grief she could sense from

Artemus and Smokey through the bond that linked them. She didn't know what to do to help them. And that maddened her, just as it was driving Haruki and Leah crazy too.

"I brought you guys some food."

"Thanks," Artemus said laconically, his gaze locked on his brother's face.

The marks that had appeared on Drake's skin back at the workshop had disappeared after he'd fainted. Even though several hours had passed since the incident at Artemus's antique store, he still hadn't regained consciousness.

Callie, Haruki, Leah, and Smokey had been in the mansion's kitchen when they'd sensed a faint wave of corruption coming from the direction of the city. It hadn't taken long for them to figure out that Artemus was under attack, since Smokey had been with them and had sensed the angel's agitation keenly.

The scene of destruction they had come upon when they'd reached the antique store had shocked all of them. It was Smokey who'd guided them to the back of what remained of the building, Haruki and Leah taking care of the few stray demons they'd crossed paths with.

The failure of the divine barrier aside, it was the revelation of what had triggered Ba'al's attack that had rocked Callie and the other Guardians to the core. Solomon had explained everything after they'd returned to the LeBlanc estate, Artemus too distracted by Drake's state to bother to utter more than a handful of words to them before he'd carried his brother upstairs to his room.

Elton and other agents of the Vatican organization headed by Persephone were taking care of the incident at the antique shop. The official story was that there had been a gas leak, with a resulting unfortunate explosion that miraculously resulted in no fatalities. The people Artemus had saved from the street outside the shop had had no recollection of what had happened to them when they'd woken up in hospital that afternoon. As for Mrs. Kaufman and her chauffeur, they had been surprisingly cooperative with Elton's request not to talk about what they'd witnessed.

It was clear that most of the city's officials were not buying the story being sold to them, as evidenced by Jeremiah's tense phone call to Leah that afternoon. Leah had kept the true details of the incident to a minimum when she'd spoken with her father. Like the rest of them, she didn't want to involve him in matters concerning Ba'al any more than was necessary, for his own safety more than anything else.

Callie put the tray on the nightstand and perched on the edge of the bed. Drake's face was relaxed and looked surprisingly youthful, his chest rising and falling slowly with his breaths. If she hadn't known any better, she would have thought he was in a deep sleep.

"Did you know?"

Callie looked up at Artemus's question.

Drake's twin was staring at Solomon, his face inscrutable. "Did you know that Drake is a key?"

Solomon remained silent where he stood staring out at the falling dusk.

Callie drew a sharp breath at the sight of the rage that flashed in the depths of Artemus's eyes. She looked down and bit her lip as she observed his nails digging into his clenched palms.

She reached out and clutched Artemus's hands. "Stop it."

He glared at her. A faint whimper escaped Smokey. He glanced between them, his anxiety throbbing across their bond.

"I know you're upset," Callie murmured. "But taking your anger out on us won't achieve anything. It won't—" she paused and swallowed, "—it won't change what's happened to Drake."

A vein throbbed in Artemus's temple as he continued glowering at her.

"No."

Artemus's head snapped around, his attention shifting to Solomon once more.

Solomon had turned and was looking at him steadily. "I didn't know your brother is a key. Just as I wasn't certain of being Jacob's gate, until today. Or that the blade Drake possesses is Samyaza's sword."

Shock blasted through Artemus. *Wait. Drake's sword belongs to Samyaza?!*

There was movement in the doorway. Jacob rushed inside the room ahead of Haruki and Leah. He launched himself at Solomon, his face crumpling with fresh tears. The demon caught him and hoisted him up into his arms.

"Sshh," he crooned as the boy buried his face in the crook of his neck. "It is alright, child. This isn't your fault."

Sobs shook Jacob. Callie's throat clogged up, her breath hitching as she fought back tears. Though Jacob's connection with them was still weak, they could feel the bone-deep sorrow storming his small body.

Solomon's fate as a gate could only end one way. And that was the demon's destruction, be it at the hands of Hell or the warriors of Heaven.

"Will he die?"

Artemus's stilted question jolted Callie and the other Guardians. Smokey raised his head stiffly.

"Will Drake die, if he is a key?" Artemus asked Solomon, his voice oddly detached.

The demon sighed, his hand moving gently up and down Jacob's back in soothing strokes. "I'm afraid I don't know the answer to that question."

Silence befell them.

"If Drake is a key," Haruki said hesitantly, "then that means he has a Guardian, and that Guardian has a gate, doesn't it?"

"Indeed it does," Solomon replied, his eyes on Artemus.

"Do you know where they are?" Leah asked, her voice laced with hope. "Maybe if we could locate them, we could help Drake."

Solomon was silent for some time.

"I suspect Drake is the key to the seventh gate," the demon said finally. "It is Hell's main exit and the one prophesied to open at the End of Days." He frowned. "No one but Satanael knows its location. Besides, if I am correct in my assumptions, that doorway exists on an interdimensional fracture between our two worlds."

Haruki blinked in surprise. "What do you mean, inter-dimensional?"

"Are you saying that Earth and Hell exist in alternate universes?" Leah mumbled hoarsely.

"Not so much alternate as beneath and to the side." Another sigh left the demon at their confused expressions. "The reason the Bible mentions Hell and Tartarus as existing beneath the Earth is because, in a sense, they do. Earth's core is made of iron. And iron can lock the barriers between dimensions. Hence why every fairy tale involving man's travel to another world invariably involves falling inside a hole in the ground or going through some kind of dark gateway."

Callie's heart raced as she digested Solomon's words. She knew what he'd just said was the truth. After everything that had happened in the last twenty-four hours, she trusted the demon. How could she not, when his love for Jacob was so plain to see?

Artemus narrowed his eyes. "Jacob's beast said you'd stalled time, back at the shop. She said you used elemental powers to stop your gate from opening. What did she mean by that?"

"All archangels possess power over the elements, each to a varying degree. Mine was one of the strongest in Heaven, hence why the title Prince of God was bestowed upon me. Freezing time between dimensions is one of my abilities." Solomon made a face. "Unfortunately, what I did today may result in some unforeseen repercussions."

"What do you mean?" Callie said.

"I'll know for sure in a few hours," Solomon replied evasively.

Haruki raked his hair with a hand, his face troubled. "Okay, so interdimensional doorways aside, do you know who Drake's Guardian is?"

Smokey keened softly.

Callie stared at her brother, her heart clenching in the face of his tangible anguish. He looked at her then, his despair throbbing across their bond. A bolt of intuition flashed through her. Her eyes rounded.

No! It can't be!

Haruki froze, his gaze gravitating mechanically to the

rabbit and Artemus. Leah raised a trembling hand to her mouth as the truth echoed within her too.

"It's the two of us, isn't it?" Artemus said in a leaden tone. "Smokey and me. We are the Guardians of the seventh gate." His gaze moved to his twin, his voice breaking as it dropped to a whisper. "And Drake is our key."

CHAPTER EIGHTEEN

DRAKE FLOATED IN A COLD, DARK VOID. HIS HEART *thudded dully inside his chest, sending a steady pulse to his ears that drowned out the deafening silence around him. How long he'd drifted in that endless, black limbo, he didn't know.*

He had a vague recollection of having been in Artemus's shop and Ba'al's demons attacking. Something had happened to him there. Something terrible. Yet, however much he tried to grasp at the threads of his memories, he couldn't fathom what it was.

The sensation came in a faint wave at first.

A gentle breeze danced across his invisible flesh from behind. It grew in strength and speed until it became a chilly wind that raised goosebumps on skin he could not see. Soon, a gale was buffeting his body.

That was when Drake realized he was falling. Fear brought a gasp to his lips.

The storm wrapped around him and spun him around. His eyes stung as the updraft lashed at his face. He blinked.

Something had flickered in the shadows beneath him.

A point of light.

It came again, gradually growing in size.

Drake stiffened as it split into a pair of crimson eyes.

The demon's form slowly materialized out of the gloom, his dark wings beating powerfully as he climbed, an enormous, black broadsword trailing inky flames in his wake.

There was something strange about the creature.

Something Drake had never seen on another fiend.

The demon's skin was covered with symbols, the runes a bright vermilion against his corrupt flesh.

Terror wrapped icy fingers around Drake's heart.

His every instinct told him he didn't want to see this demon's face.

He scrunched his eyes tightly shut as he continued to fall, wishing this nightmare would end. But, to his horror, he could still see despite the fact that his eyelids were closed.

See the demon grow closer.

See the fiend's mouth part on an evil smile.

See his own face appear beneath him, his features a hideous mask covering the monster's skull, the black sword rising to stab him in the heart.

A scream echoed in Drake's ears as he jackknifed upright.

Artemus jumped in the chair next to the bed, his eyes instantly alert as they slammed open from sleep. The fur rose on Smokey's hide where he'd landed beside Drake, a menacing growl rumbling from his throat.

Drake's heart thundered against his ribs as he gasped and panted, one hand clutching his chest while the other grasped the bedsheet with white knuckles, the nightmare leaching the warmth from his body. It took him a moment to realize that he was the one who'd just shouted out in horror.

Artemus rose and came over. "Are you okay?!"

Drake sagged when his brother sat on the bed and closed his arms around him. He hugged his twin back and buried his face in his shoulder, a shudder running through him.

"No," he mumbled shakily.

Artemus stiffened at his blunt reply.

The bedroom door crashed open. Drake looked up blearily. Callie, Haruki, and Leah stormed inside the room, their weapons in hand. Solomon trailed slowly in their wake.

Drake blinked.

"Er, no offense, but I'd rather not die at the hands of the Mismatched Pajama Squad," he said with a weak grimace. He squinted at Solomon. "Is that Sebastian's peignoir?"

The demon shrugged.

Callie looked down at her oversized T-shirt, her shoulders visibly relaxing.

"Nate usually does the laundry," she said, as if this explained everything.

The tension in the room faded.

Callie came over and perched on the edge of the bed, her expression anxious. "How are you feeling?"

"Like shit." Drake murmured.

He caught the troubled glances the rest of them exchanged.

"You know, don't you?" Solomon said quietly.

Drake met the demon's gaze steadily. "You mean about what I am? Yes. I'm a key." He looked at Artemus and Smokey, feeling surprisingly calm. "And they are my Guardians."

Artemus's eyes darkened with emotion. "I'll find a way to fix this. I will!"

Drake's heart clenched at the desperation in his twin's voice. "I know."

Smokey huffed and bumped his head against Drake's leg.

Something grumbled loudly in the silence.

Everyone stared at Drake.

He grimaced and rubbed his stomach. "Sorry."

"I'll make you something," Artemus said briskly.

He rose and headed for the door. Smokey leapt down from the bed and went after him.

"Maybe I should supervise," Callie said. "The last time you cooked, you nearly burned the house down."

"That was an accident," Artemus snapped. "Besides, how do you think I survived before you guys came along?"

"Takeout," Haruki said with a confident nod.

"Dry bread and water?" Leah hazarded.

"Ha ha," Artemus muttered darkly.

Solomon stayed back while the rest of them headed for the kitchen. Drake couldn't help but feel it was because the demon wanted to tell him something. Solomon watched him for a moment before crossing the room to stand by the windows.

"It suits you," Drake said.

"What does?"

"The peignoir."

The demon looked down at the borrowed dressing gown with a dry expression. "It's not something I would buy myself, but it does the job."

A strangely comfortable silence fell between them.

"So, you're a gate and I'm a key, huh?" Drake drawled, keeping his tone light.

Solomon observed him steadily. "You seem to have come to terms with that fact."

Drake shrugged. "I don't really have a choice, do I?"

"We always have a choice." Solomon looked out into the night. "It's what we choose to do with it that determines who we are and what we stand for."

Drake couldn't help the faint hope that burst into life inside him then. "So, you're saying there's a way to avoid our fate?"

"No." Solomon's eyes gleamed mysteriously as he glanced at Drake. "But we can make it count for something."

A wave of exhaustion washed over Drake.

"Look, it's been a long day," he said with a sigh. "Can you bypass the deep and enigmatic exposition and get to the point?"

"Don't let your brother fall to Hell."

Drake's stomach twisted at the demon's blunt words.

"It is what will bring about the alternative End of Days that Satanael so wishes to visit upon the Earth," Solomon continued, his tone grave. "If he gets his hands on the key *and* the Guardians to the seventh gate, there will be no stopping him."

Drake's pulse raced as the meaning behind the demon's statement sank in.

He swallowed convulsively. "So, you're saying that my fall to Hell is inevitable?"

"Yes."

Drake felt the blood drain from his face. Solomon blew out a weary sigh.

"Artemus will try to follow you, regardless of the consequences of his actions," the demon continued quietly. "He is your Guardian, after all. And he won't be able to help it.

The instinct to protect you is built into the very marrow of his being. And, needless to say, Cerberus will be right behind him."

Drake stared at his hands. They were rock steady, which was shocking considering what he'd just learned. "So, all I have to do is stop them from following me when I fall?"

"It won't be as easy as you're making it sound, but, essentially, yes."

Drake looked up at the demon. "What will happen to you?"

Solomon gazed out into the night once more. "There are only three gates we know of left in this world. Callie and Haruki's. And Jacob's. Otis destroyed the others and no one knows the location of the seventh gate bar Satanael." He paused. "If we want to avoid the Apocalypse Hell's Council wants to bring about, then we need to get rid of them all."

Drake's eyes widened. "That means killing you."

"I have had a long existence," Solomon said wryly. "I would welcome the rest."

"Jacob wouldn't."

Solomon's eyes darkened. "He will get over it. Especially now that he has Artemus and the other Guardians."

Bickering voices rose in the corridor. Artemus and the others appeared, an argument in full flow. Despite the despair twisting his heart, Drake couldn't help but smile faintly as he gazed at them.

He wanted to imprint this memory in his mind. Somehow, he suspected this would be the last time he would see his brother and their friends so carefree.

Drake ate the overdone cheese sandwich his twin had made him and occasionally interjected as the argument progressed. It was late by the time they left his bedroom. He insisted on Artemus going back to his own room in the opposite wing of the mansion and watched as his brother reluctantly took his leave. His twin's expression remained troubled to the very end, as did the hellhound's.

Drake waited until the mansion was asleep once more before he got out of bed and wrote a note to Artemus and the others. He opened the window of his bedroom, changed into his angel form, and took flight just as the sky started to pale to the east.

He needed to think.

And there was only one place he wanted to be to do so.

CHAPTER NINETEEN

A DARK FOREBODING DANCED THROUGH JEREMIAH AS HE studied the sky above the Federal Plaza, in downtown Chicago. The excited murmur of a crowd filled the square, ahead of the mayor's expected public address.

Jeremiah knew the buzz around him had more to do with the unexplained astronomical event the city was currently experiencing than with the pre-election campaign talk the city's elected head would be giving imminently.

A gray light bathed Chicago, an effect of the total solar eclipse it had awakened to that morning. The shocking event had dominated national and international news for the last few hours and the internet was alive with theories as to how NASA and other space agencies could have overlooked such a major celestial phenomenon.

From Jeremiah's quick search that morning, the next solar eclipse was not due for another two months and was meant to be a partial one. A total eclipse would not occur for another eight months. Or so the scientists had predicted.

"That's so spooky," someone murmured behind Jeremiah.

He turned and eyed Shaw. The younger detective looked nervous as he crossed the north end of the plaza, where the truck housing the command unit of the task force overseeing security at the event was stationed. Though the Loop didn't fall under Jeremiah and Shaw's jurisdiction, their district commander had insisted a pair of detectives be dispatched to the mayor's guard detail.

Jeremiah was certain this was a political move to score points with the city's head honcho ahead of the local elections. He'd made it clear to his precinct chief in no uncertain terms that he didn't appreciate being used as a pawn in their commander's dirty games. He'd received the promise of a round of drinks and a steak dinner at one of the best restaurants in town from his overtaxed superior in return for his bitter diatribe.

"The sky isn't the only alarming thing about this whole affair." Jeremiah frowned at the iconic high rises encircling the square. "I don't know why this guy didn't just do a televised address. It wouldn't have required so many of us to be mobilized to watch over his ass."

The commander of the task force glanced over with a frown from where she stood talking to a bunch of cops some fifteen feet away.

Shaw caught the exchange and swallowed. "Are you thinking snipers, boss?"

Jeremiah decided to overlook the rookie detective's use of the honorific he'd banned two days ago. "Snipers. Extremists. Aliens. Take your pick."

Shaw's eyes rounded. "You believe in aliens?"

Jeremiah sighed. "No, I don't. But I believe in good and

evil. Right now, my spider sense is telling me some evil shit might be about to go down."

He stifled a grimace and rubbed the back of his neck. He could hardly tell Shaw about the extraordinary circumstances he'd found himself in a few weeks past, when he'd been absorbed inside a gate of Hell commanded by his daughter. What had become apparent since that time was that he had gained something akin to a sixth sense when it came to the uncanny. And that sixth sense was telling him that he should take Shaw and get the hell out of there, pronto.

"This is a surprise."

Jeremiah twisted around and observed the man coming up on his left with a faint frown.

"Agent Milton," he murmured in greeting.

Milton's eyes twinkled faintly as he observed Jeremiah and Shaw. "Detective Chase. Detective Shaw. I see your commander dragged you here kicking and screaming."

"Oh no," Shaw protested weakly. "It's a great honor to serve the mayor and the city, sir!"

"Your senior appears to think otherwise, detective," Milton said, clearly amused.

Jeremiah bit back a sharp retort. "What brings you here, Agent Milton?" he murmured coolly instead. "This isn't the FBI's usual gig."

"Oh, I had some business to attend to at the courthouse," Milton said with a vague wave of his hand in the direction of the steel and glass high rise to the west of the plaza. "I thought I'd drop by and listen to the mayor's speech."

"I wouldn't have put you down as someone with an interest in politics," Jeremiah said with a grunt.

Milton's smile widened. "Politics is what's gotten me

where I am today, detective. Besides, had I been able to carry out my interviews with Mr. Steele et al as I'd planned to today, I wouldn't be here right now." He raised an eyebrow. "I take it you heard about the explosion at his antique store?"

Jeremiah dipped his chin, his expression carefully neutral. "Yes. It was an unfortunate incident."

"Indeed. Mr. Steele seems to be plagued by bad luck lately." Milton observed him curiously. "You two seem close. How long have you known each other?"

"I met Artemus about a year ago. To be fair, we're not that well acquainted."

Though the FBI agent's expression remained friendly, Jeremiah couldn't help but feel that he'd seen through the barefaced lie Jeremiah had just uttered. A commotion at the front of the plaza drew their gazes. The mayor had arrived.

"It's show time," the task force commander called out briskly.

"I'll catch you later, detectives." Milton flashed a smile at them before turning and strolling into the crowd.

Jeremiah watched him leave with a guarded expression.

"Boss?" Shaw said jumpily. "We better move. The commander looks like she's about to shoot us."

Jeremiah dragged his gaze from Milton's fading figure and glanced at the woman scowling at them from the steps of the command truck. "It's a good thing we're wearing tactical vests then."

They joined the cops supervising the south end of the plaza. Up ahead, Mayor Briggs was crossing the square toward the stage erected in front of the U.S. Post Office building, where he would be making his address. Cheers and claps erupted as he headed onto the podium amidst his security detail.

Though he hadn't voted for the man in the last local election, Jeremiah could not deny Briggs's popularity with the public. In his late fifties and sporting a charismatic face and voice, the man was an ambitious career politician aiming for higher office. Briggs smiled pleasantly at the crowd while a city official made an introductory speech. Further applause broke out when he finally took the stand.

"Strange weather we're having, isn't it?" he drawled, his tone relaxed and his composure seemingly unaffected by the bizarre eclipse overshadowing the plaza.

The crowd laughed nervously.

"I'm not going to pretend to understand what's causing our city to experience, well, *that*." He indicated the overcast heavens. "Hopefully, the clever folks at NASA will enlighten us later today."

And with that, the crowd relaxed. Briggs continued addressing them with ease, his words washing over Jeremiah in a drone. He only paid passing attention to the political statements and promises being made by the man and concentrated on the gathering.

So far, everything was proceeding smoothly. The mayor's speech was supposed to last another fifteen minutes, after which he'd be whisked away to the safety of City Hall. Still, Jeremiah couldn't stop the trepidation drumming an urgent beat through his veins.

He was scanning the plaza for signs of what was putting him on edge when he sensed a faint tremor under his feet.

CHAPTER TWENTY

JEREMIAH STIFFENED. "DID YOU FEEL THAT?"

"Yes," Shaw said, his expression perplexed.

The tremor came again. Briggs paused and frowned faintly where he stood on the podium. Murmurs broke out in the crowd. The mayor smiled reassuringly and resumed talking to his audience. On the opposite side of the plaza, the task force commander had come out onto the steps of the command truck and was observing the area with a guarded expression.

Her gaze met Jeremiah's above the heads of the people separating them.

A flock of birds shot up from the trees behind her, wings rustling wildly and panicked squawks rending the air. The commander's head snapped around to follow their flight. The mayor stopped talking, his gaze matching that of the crowd as everyone turned to stare after the birds.

An eerie stillness descended on the plaza, the silence as abrupt as it was expectant. The primitive part of Jeremiah's brain screamed at him to run. His hand found Shaw's arm just as a violent quake shook the ground.

A low rumble filled the air as the world started to wobble under and around them. The tremors rapidly intensified, causing the granite tiles of the plaza and the facade of the surrounding buildings to vibrate and warp alarmingly. Screams erupted in the eerie twilight as the crowd finally unfroze and started to scatter. People stumbled and crashed into one another as they ran for cover.

Jeremiah saw an old man fall and get crushed under the stampede.

"Shit!"

He'd taken several steps toward the old guy and the frightened mob when a deafening crack ripped the ground asunder five feet to his left. Jeremiah rocked to a stop and followed the fissure with his gaze, his heart slamming erratically against his ribs. It snaked behind him and up the steel-and-bronze-tinted glass facade of the federal building towering over the plaza. His eyes widened.

He twisted on his heels, bolted toward Shaw, and shoved the detective under the recessed colonnade encircling the high rise at street level. They landed on the ground just as giant sheets of glass started coming off the buildings abutting the plaza.

The sound of smashing glass drowned out the terrified shrieks of the crowd trapped inside the plaza. Shards exploded into the air, filling the plaza with lethal pieces of jagged glass and glittering fragments. Jeremiah covered his head and face with his arms and felt tiny slivers slice the backs of his hands.

The tremors started to abate. Shaw murmured a shaky prayer when they finally stopped and pushed up unsteadily onto his hands and knees. Jeremiah followed suit and sat up slowly, his skull ringing from the chaotic din in the plaza. His stomach dropped at the scene of chaos and destruction before him.

The wounded crawled and stumbled across the bloodied bodies of the dead and unconscious scattered across the plaza. Groans and wails echoed toward the sky as people began to grasp what had happened to them. A few were on their feet and walking around dazedly, seemingly oblivious to their injuries.

Jeremiah's ears popped. Goosebumps rushed across his skin. He froze.

He knew this feeling.

Oh God.

Up ahead, a hush descended upon the plaza once more, as if everyone else had also registered the otherworldly pressure rapidly thickening the air.

Jeremiah's gaze gravitated to the stage left of the plaza. Briggs crouched miraculously unharmed next to the stand, his face pale with fear.

The building behind him trembled. It collapsed with sudden violence, the structure caving in on itself, as if the ground beneath it had suddenly subsided.

Jeremiah gasped, the implosive wave pulling at his body and dragging him some three feet across the ground. Briggs yelled out and tumbled off the podium.

The world seemed to stop in the next instant. Jeremiah's ear drums throbbed.

Something smashed out of the center of where the post office building had once stood. Debris detonated in its wake as it rose, the explosive force driving the wreckage in every direction.

A jagged piece of glass the size of Jeremiah's hand sliced the neck of the task force commander where she stood by the command truck. Her expression froze as she met Jeremiah's horrified gaze across the plaza. She raised a hand to the crimson jet spurting from the fatal wound and stared at her bloodied fingers with a puzzled air. Gravity took over. Her head tilted lopsidedly, her partially severed neck sagging to the side. She toppled over and disappeared from view.

Cries split the air as the victims of the quake tried to escape the disaster zone and the terrifying presence now hovering above the plaza, his dark wings thrumming the air with powerful beats.

Jeremiah's stomach dropped as he looked upon the last face he'd expected to see.

Drake Hunter's crimson pupils glowed eerily in the center of his obsidian eyes. Black flames danced along the serrated teeth of his broadsword where he floated some thirty feet above the plaza in his dark angel form, his expression strangely detached.

Jeremiah caught faint movement next to what remained of the stage. His breath froze when he saw Briggs crawl out from under a pile of rubble. The mayor shook his head slightly, his expression stunned. Blood coursed down the side of his face from a cut on his head, tracing a red line over the dirt covering his skin. He pushed himself up slowly to his knees.

The dark angel's gaze found the wounded man beneath him. He dropped down and landed gracefully behind Briggs. The mayor turned as the creature's winged form cast a shadow upon him. Incredulity widened his eyes. Drake extended a hand toward him.

Briggs blinked and reached out automatically.

"*No!*" Jeremiah roared. "*Get away from him!*"

The mayor turned and looked in Jeremiah's direction just as the dark angel grasped his fingers and drew him to his feet. The bewildered look pasted across his face turned to one of horror as Drake extended his wings and shot up into the air, taking him along with him.

His scream reverberated around the plaza as the dark angel climbed some hundred feet. The sound ended on a shocked grunt when Drake rocked to a halt in mid-air.

Incoherent words left Briggs where he dangled helplessly at the end of the dark angel's left arm.

"Oh God!" Shaw mumbled shakily. "*Oh God!*"

Drake started rotating. He twisted round and round, his motion accelerating until his figure blurred, the mayor a shadowy shape at the leading edge of the centrifugal force he was generating.

He stopped abruptly and cast the man in his hold high up above him.

Briggs's body spun wildly, rising some fifty feet or so before gradually decelerating. He froze at the arc of the throw and stayed suspended for an instant. Gravity took over.

Briggs yelled as he started to plummet toward the ground.

Drake watched him fall impassively. He raised his broadsword and swung it once.

Jeremiah choked on a shout of denial as the blade sliced the falling man in half at the waist.

A crimson spray rained down upon the stage and the people on the ground. The bloodied remains of the mayor smashed onto the podium with fleshy thuds.

Drake observed the macabre carcass and the injured crowd with a disinterested air. He extended his wings, flapped them once, and disappeared into the ominous sky.

CHAPTER TWENTY-ONE

THE EXCITED SHOUTS AND LAUGHTER OF CHILDREN peppered the air above the front courtyard of the children's home. Drake watched the kids play from where he crouched atop a water tower in the field across the road, on the outskirts of the small Texas town.

It had been some time since he'd visited the place where he'd grown up.

The children's home had been erected on the grounds of the orphanage that had stood there once. No signs remained of the devastating fire that had ripped through the buildings of the original institution twenty-two years ago, on the night Drake's powers had started to awaken. The townsfolk had taken great pains to rebuild something that would not succumb so easily to another disastrous blaze.

He'd been eighteen when he'd come back here for the first time since the accident. He'd visited the graveyard where the bodies of the nuns and the children who had perished that night had been interred and had mourned their demise all over again, tears falling down his face as he silently begged for their forgiveness.

Though he knew now that he had had no control over what had happened that fateful night, it did not take away from the guilt he would carry with him for the rest of his life.

In time, the graveyard and the children's home had become a place of reflection, one he came to when he had a decision to make. Today was such a day.

A sense of calm filled Drake as he rose into the overcast sky a short time later. He turned and headed back toward Chicago, the wind whipping away at his body oddly refreshing.

He knew what he had to do when the time came for him to face the inescapable fate that awaited him.

The trip home was swift, his supernatural speed eating away hundreds of miles in a matter of minutes. It was when he came in sight of Lake Michigan that the clouds started to clear and he saw the eclipse bathing the land in a half light.

"What the—?!"

Drake jolted to a stop in mid-air, his shocked gaze on the dark circle in the sky. The conversation he'd had with Artemus the night before sprung to his mind.

When Solomon alluded to the unforeseen repercussions of him delaying the opening of his gate, is this what he meant? Could it have resulted in a solar eclipse?!

He stared at the celestial event for a long time before slowly resuming his original course, unease clouding his thoughts. He couldn't help but feel that the eclipse was an omen.

He was on the outskirts of the city when he started to

hear Artemus's voice in his head. His brother sounded tense and anxious.

Drake frowned. *Did he not see the note?*

The bond linking him to his twin and the divine beasts grew stronger as he closed in on the mansion. To his surprise, he soon sensed the other Guardians' agitation too.

Drake slowed when he detected the heavy police presence surrounding the LeBlanc estate from over a mile away.

What the hell is going on?

He stopped and hovered in place for a moment, his disquiet growing. He decided an elevated approach was best, soared high in the air, and headed over to the mansion. He waited until he was directly above the manor house before tucking his wings and dropping like a bird, his descent so fast it would be a flicker to the naked human eye.

He was climbing through the window of his bedroom in his human form when the door slammed open.

Artemus barged in, his face dark with anger. "Where the hell have you been?!"

Drake stopped in his tracks. "I left a note." He glanced at the nightstand. The piece of paper he'd scribbled on was gone. "Oh. Did it fall under the bed?"

Artemus closed the distance to him and grabbed him by the front of his shirt, startling him.

"I got the note!" his brother snarled. "Now, tell me where you really were!"

The dread Drake had experienced when he'd seen the eclipse increased ten-fold as he stared into his twin's accusing glare.

Smokey darted inside the room and skidded to a stop

at their feet. Urgent huffs and grunts escaped him as he attempted to separate them, his head butting their legs.

Jeremiah came in next, Callie, Haruki, Leah, and Elton in his wake. Naomi and Solomon hovered near the doorway, their expressions as troubled as everyone else's.

"What's happening?" Drake said, his pulse now racing with fear.

"Where were you two hours ago?" Artemus said between gritted teeth.

"Like I said in the note, I went to visit the town where I grew up, in Texas."

"That's it?" Callie said, her voice tinged with hope. "That's the only place you went?"

"Yeah." Drake frowned. "Where else would I have gone?"

The doubt clouding Artemus's face faded. His eyes probed Drake's, as if he were searching his soul. A shudder shook him. He let go of Drake and stepped back stiffly.

"He's telling the truth, Dad," Leah mumbled.

"She's right," Haruki said with a confident nod. "Drake isn't lying."

Elton gave the Guardians a dubious glance.

"Why would I be lying?" Irritation stirred inside Drake for the first time that morning. "Will one of you please tell me what the hell is going on?!"

Jeremiah observed Drake with a brooding look.

"Two hours ago, an earthquake similar to the one that destroyed part of Elton's auction house rocked downtown Chicago," the detective said curtly. "The epicenter was the Federal Plaza, where Mayor Briggs was giving a public speech. A man with dark wings and a black broadsword appeared out of the rubble. He killed Briggs in cold blood.

There were other fatalities, including a Chicago PD commander."

Coldness filled Drake as he stared at the detective. "Wait. You think that guy was me?"

"He had your face."

Drake stared at Artemus, confused.

"He had your face, Drake," Artemus repeated in a leaden voice. "The footage is all over the news." He hesitated. "Are you sure you didn't—"

He faltered, his expression miserable.

"You think I lost control and blacked out, like I did in L.A.?"

Although Drake did his best to mask his dismay, Artemus still saw through him.

"I'm sorry," his twin mumbled. "I had to ask."

"It wasn't Drake."

All eyes turned to Solomon.

"The man who killed Briggs looked like him," Elton said uneasily. "We've all seen the news clips."

"And demons can change their appearance," Solomon said calmly. "It's how we spread lies and dissent. Besides, you heard what the Guardians said. If Drake was lying, they'd know."

"But why would someone do this?" Callie murmured, pale-faced. "Why go to such lengths to frame Drake for something he didn't do?"

"To separate him from you." Solomon gazed at Jeremiah. "Just as Detective Chase is proposing to do."

Jeremiah frowned. "I don't really have a choice. Besides, if I don't bring Drake in, the FBI will."

"The Vatican agrees," Elton said guardedly. "I spoke to Archbishop Holmes an hour ago. The church is getting inundated with questions about the appearance of an apparent angel in Chicago. Though most of the public are being led to believe the apparition used some kind of jetpack to fly, the Vatican thinks the best thing to do for now to calm the ruffled feathers of local government officials is to let the authorities take Drake in until we can clear things up."

Artemus frowned. "And how long will that take? If this is a ploy by Ba'al to separate Drake from us, then we'll be playing right into their hands if we let Chicago PD arrest him!"

"I'll go."

A pained expression washed across Artemus's face. He stared at Drake, a muscle jumping in his cheek.

"I'll go," Drake repeated calmly.

CHAPTER TWENTY-TWO

SERENA RUBBED THE DIRT BETWEEN HER GLOVED FINGERS before bringing it close to her face and taking a careful sniff. Had it not been for the nanorobots inhabiting her blood and flesh, she would not have detected the faint odor. She frowned.

It was the same smell she and Nate had picked up in Peru and another quake site they'd visited before this one. They'd been the only ones who had discerned it, the Immortals and the humans' noses nowhere near as refined as theirs. She bagged the soil sample and rose to her feet.

Their investigations into the strange earthquakes had brought them to a remote village in south Albania, the epicenter of the latest disaster.

When Serena and Nate had reported what Artemus and the others had relayed to them about the Nephilim, their proposition that mythical biblical creatures might be behind these incidents had been met with skepticism by the Immortals and humans leading the search. Only the Vatican agents, Gideon, Greene, and Jackson had had faith in their words. The Vatican agents because they'd seen firsthand what Ba'al was capable of and Gideon because he knew Serena and Nate were unlikely to let their emotions get in the way of their analytic minds. As for the two Immortals, Serena suspected they knew more about what was going on than they'd let on, just as she'd surmised a few months ago when she'd crossed paths with Jackson and his wife, and Dimitri Reznak.

However much the Immortal societies and the humans wanted to reject Serena and Nate's crazy hypothesis, two things were undeniable. The earthquakes were increasing in frequency and the bodies of the dead were mounting.

Jackson appeared on the lip of the crater where Serena stood. He slid down the embankment and joined her. "Is it the same as the other sites?"

"Yes. I'm sending a sample to Gideon for analysis."

"Damn." Jackson heaved a heavy sigh, his face full of frustration. "I hope this turns out to be a clue that helps us predict where the next quake is going to be. We'd save a lot of lives if we could do that."

Serena recalled what Artemus and Drake had said about the Nephilim. "I doubt it would make much of a difference."

Jackson's expression grew troubled. "Was the creature those two fought in Chicago that strong?"

"Yes." Serena studied the dark circle in the sky above their heads. "Any news of what's causing this?"

Jackson frowned. "No. According to Alexa, it has the Immortals stumped too." He stared at the obscured sun. "The only parts of the world experiencing a full eclipse are southern Europe and the American Midwest, which is why our retinas aren't burnt to a crisp right now. It's unprecedented, not to mention wholly unexplainable by the laws of astronomy."

"I don't think demons pay terrible attention to those laws."

Jackson stared at her. "You think this is Ba'al's doing?"

Serena shrugged. "Ba'al. A bored archangel. For all we know, this could be Michael's handiwork. He comes across as the kind of guy who'd pull a shitty stunt like this just to annoy his kid."

Jackson grimaced. "Wow. Artemus has it bad."

They climbed out of the crater and headed along a dirt path into the village hugging the side of the mountain. It was a peaceful settlement of some two hundred and fifty souls, most of them elderly folks. Or it had been, until whatever had caused the quake had butchered them.

Blood stained the cobbled streets the villagers had once walked, puddles still congealing here and there in uneven, crimson blotches. The splashes and spatters that had sprayed from the bodies of the living and the dead made macabre patterns on the whitewashed walls of their one-story houses and huts.

Most of the carnage had taken place outside the village hall, where the inhabitants had sought refuge. The building was a slaughterhouse, the scene one of the worst they had come across in their investigations to date.

It was Greene who'd discovered the children under a trap door in the floor of a closet, next to the restrooms. There were twenty of them, ranging from two to fifteen years, huddled together on the warm dirt ground beneath the building. It had taken him half an hour to convince them to climb out of where their grandparents had hidden them. The Immortal had asked the kids to cover their eyes while they were led out of the back door and into waiting vehicles, his tone firm yet gentle.

Some of the older ones had refused to do so, as if they

had wanted to burn the terror they had witnessed the night before into their memories. Their dazed faces rose in Serena's mind.

I wonder if we looked like that when we were rescued in Greenland.

She glanced curiously at Jackson.

"What?" he said.

"Nothing."

Serena swallowed a sigh. She would never have entertained such a notion before she'd met Drake and the others.

I'm turning soft. Pretty soon, I'll be cooing at pictures of kittens, like Callie and Leah.

A commotion drew their attention when they neared the area where they'd set up a temporary command center. Nate, Greene, and some dozen Immortals and Vatican agents were watching something on a laptop sitting on the hood of an SUV.

Nate's distressed gaze found Serena as she and Jackson approached. Greene looked up briefly, a frown on his face. Dread filled her.

Drake.

She didn't know why she'd immediately thought of the dark angel. But her worst fears were borne out when she rounded the SUV and saw what they were looking at. It was a news channel replaying jerky footage that had been filmed on a mobile device.

Serena's stomach clenched as she made out the Federal Plaza in Chicago. It was almost unrecognizable and resembled one of the quake sites they'd been analyzing in the last few days.

Gasps rose around her as the post office imploded in on itself.

A muscle jumped in Jackson's jawline. "Shit."

She was dimly aware of the worried glance he cast at her. Her unblinking eyes remained focused on the otherworldly form that had risen from the debris of the building, black wings stark against pale, rising dust clouds. The figure landed gracefully on the ground, grabbed an injured man Serena thought she recognized by the hand, and rose into the sky, his victim's scream echoing through the speakers.

"Oh God!" one of the Vatican agents mumbled seconds later.

He turned and threw up, his retches drowned out by the shrieks of the panicked crowd being transmitted through the laptop.

Serena stared at the remains of the man the dark angel had just killed. She took a step forward, her heart thudding painfully against her ribs as she came closer to the screen. She raised a hand and laid her fingers lightly on the frozen image of the winged murderer as he rose in the sky, his black blade in hand.

"No." The denial was on her lips before she could stop it. She turned and looked at Nate and the Immortals. "This isn't Drake."

Nate's expression grew anguished. "Serena."

Serena swallowed and shook her head.

"That isn't Drake," she repeated, her tone adamant.

"The evidence is pretty damning," Greene said guardedly. "How can you be so sure that's not Drake Hunter?"

Serena wondered once more how much the Immortals really knew about Artemus and the others.

Now isn't the time for that discussion.

"It's his eyes. Drake's eyes have never looked like that

in his angel form." Serena frowned. "I don't know who or what that thing was, but it wasn't Drake."

For a moment, the words *my Drake* had almost left her lips. She curled her hands into fists.

A call came through on Nate's smartband, the sound loud in the tense silence. He answered it, his eyes still anxious.

Gideon's voice came through. "Are both of you there?"

Serena stiffened at his tone. "Yes, I'm here."

She joined Nate, her misgivings growing. She'd never heard Gideon sound so highly strung before.

"Get your asses back to Chicago." The super soldier scowled at them across the video link. "There's some crazy shit going down in that city and you need to be in the thick of it."

"We just saw the footage." Jackson came up behind Serena, Greene in his wake. "That angel resembled Drake Hunter." He faltered. "Did he really kill the mayor?"

"That's what it looks like."

Serena clenched her jaw.

Gideon blew out a frustrated sigh when he saw her face. "There's no need to glare at me like that. I know it wasn't him."

Greene's expression remained dubious. "Why are you guys so certain this wasn't Drake?" He glanced at Serena. "Bar his eyes, that is?"

Gideon's reply had Serena's stomach twisting with fresh dread.

"Because Artemus and the other Guardians could tell he wasn't lying before the cops arrested him."

CHAPTER TWENTY-THREE

"WHY ARE THE FBI TAKING OVER THIS CASE?" JEREMIAH struggled to keep his tone civil as he addressed the man on the other side of the desk. "They have no jurisdiction here."

His words echoed across the office of the Area 3 Deputy Chief. Shaw stood beside Jeremiah, his face pale but determined.

Jim O'Grady observed them coolly over his steepled hands. It was the second time Jeremiah had spoken to the man in person. The first time had been after Tony Goodman was attacked a few weeks back. O'Grady had visited the wounded detective in the hospital, something that had earned him the respect of the 18th District detectives.

"Because they are the lead federal agency for cases of suspected terrorism," O'Grady replied.

Though the Deputy Chief's voice was detached, Jeremiah could tell he was just as irritated by this latest development as Jeremiah and Shaw were.

"And who said this incident is a terrorist act, sir?" Shaw

asked sharply.

Jeremiah glanced at him. The experience the rookie detective had gone through at the plaza seemed to have given him a second backbone.

"I did," someone drawled behind them.

Jeremiah looked over his shoulder. Milton stood in the doorway of O'Grady's office, his expression as mildly amused as his tone.

Jeremiah scowled. Somehow, he wasn't surprised to see the man. "I could have sworn you were in the thick of things when that earthquake struck. I expected you to be dead or in the hospital."

Jeremiah clocked the warning glance O'Grady aimed at him out of the corner of his eye.

"Your concern for my wellbeing touches me, Detective Chase," Milton said wryly. He waved a hand dismissively. "And I only stayed for the first five minutes of Briggs's speech. I was already a couple of blocks away when the earthquake happened." He strolled inside the office, his steps confident. "It's clear today's incident is related to the disturbance at Elton LeBlanc's auction house two nights ago. Mr. Hunter was present then too."

O'Grady leaned back in his chair and drummed the fingers of one hand on the armrest.

"The FBI is acting pretty blasé about the fact that the main suspect in this affair grew wings on his back and flew away," the Deputy Chief said guardedly. "Last time I checked, terrorists didn't do stuff like that, domestic or otherwise. And, bar the suspect's face bearing a passing resemblance to Mr. Hunter's, I haven't seen much evidence yet to prove he was the man who killed Briggs."

"He has no alibi for his movements at the time," Milton replied. "He claims he was out of town, but there are no witnesses to corroborate his statement. This makes him a prime suspect. As for the wings and the flying, it was obviously a stunt intended to fool us into believing some kind of mystical being was behind the murder." The FBI agent smiled faintly. "The Vatican has made it clear in their statement that Mr. Hunter is not an angel."

Jeremiah swallowed a sigh. *If only they knew.*

Milton glanced at him, as if he'd read his mind. The FBI agent's next words had Jeremiah's spine stiffening.

"Mr. Hunter is being moved to a secure facility as we speak. I'm sure Detectives Chase and Shaw will hand over the evidence they gathered at the scene of the crime without any resistance."

Jeremiah ignored the subtle threat in the agent's voice and crossed the floor to a window in a few brisk steps. He swore at the sight of two patrol vehicles escorting a dark van out of the precinct.

Shit!

He'd promised Artemus and the others that he'd stay close to Drake at all times.

Jeremiah whirled around. "Where are you taking him?"

Milton arched an eyebrow. "I don't believe I need to give you an answer."

Lines wrinkled O'Grady's brow. "Hunter is Chase and Shaw's suspect, Agent Milton. You owe them the courtesy of telling them where you're taking the man they just arrested."

"I'm afraid we'll have to disagree on that matter," Milton said mildly. "Feel free to take it up with my superiors." He eyed Jeremiah and Shaw. "Now, how about you give me what you have on the incident at the plaza."

ARTEMUS TENSED WHERE HE SLOUCHED AT THE KITCHEN table. Solomon, Callie, and Haruki similarly stiffened around him. Leah straightened on the window seat next to Jacob. Smokey raised his head from the boy's lap.

Their gazes gravitated to the back door.

They'd all sensed the divine energy that had just manifested in the rear yard.

The door slammed open seconds later, breaking the morose silence that had befallen them. Serena stormed inside the mansion ahead of Sebastian and Nate. Sebastian had a reserved air about him, while Nate just looked plain harassed.

"Serena, calm down," the super soldier pleaded urgently.

Serena ignored him, marched over to Artemus, and hauled him to his feet by the front of his shirt.

"You asshole!" she hissed in his face. "Why did you let them arrest him?!"

"Nate is right. You need to compose yourself." Sebastian frowned at the super soldier. "Getting worked up about things is not going to help Drake." He headed over to the window and crouched by Smokey. "Are you well, brother?" He stroked the rabbit's head. "I heard what happened."

Smokey let out a low huff. *I am alright. Do not fret so.*

Sebastian's eyes darkened at what he no doubt sensed from the hellhound. He clenched his jaw and looked at Callie.

"His life force feels weaker than usual. Is the poison the Nephil left in his body that strong?"

"Yes," she mumbled. "Solomon held it back for as long as he could."

Nate joined Callie and laid a gentle hand on her shoulder. She grasped his fingers tightly as she fought back tears.

Sebastian's expression grew strained. He dipped his chin at Solomon. "Thank you." His gaze moved to Jacob. "You must be Jacob. It is nice to meet you."

"It's—it's nice to meet you too," Jacob murmured.

Serena glared accusingly at Artemus. "Well? Are you going to answer my question or not?!"

"It's complicated," Artemus said stiffly.

He could understand Serena's fury. He was pretty angry with himself right now.

Serena gritted her teeth. "What the hell is complicated about protecting one of our own?!" She glowered at the other occupants of the room. "Do you even know what Drake must be going through right now? How betrayed he must feel by the very people he—"

"He's the one who turned himself in."

Serena froze. She twisted around mechanically and stared at Callie. "What?"

"Drake turned himself in," Callie repeated. "We couldn't stop him."

The blood drained from Serena's face. She let go of Artemus, her hand falling limply to her side.

"Why?" Her voice trembled as she stared at them. "Why would he do that? It wasn't him!" She shook her head vehemently. "That—that thing?! The angel who killed Briggs? That wasn't Drake! It—"

Artemus took Serena in his arms, stemming the flow of her words.

"I know," he mumbled into her hair as she went rigid in his embrace. "We all know that wasn't Drake, Serena." He felt her heart pound rapidly against his chest, her anguish amplifying his own remorse. "But the authorities need someone to blame for what happened today and for Briggs's murder. The only way they're keeping the city under some kind of control right now is because Drake is in their custody."

Serena sagged in Artemus's hold. Her hands rose to clutch desperately at his back, as if she needed something to anchor her.

"The eclipse and the apparition of an angel have put the people of this city on edge," Solomon explained in the face of Serena and Nate's confused expressions. "That hysteria is slowly spreading not just across this country, but around the world. Not everyone is buying the story that the figure they saw on the footage from the plaza isn't a real angel."

"Though they put out a statement earlier in the day, the Vatican is having a hard time dealing with the thousands of requests for information coming their way from governments and religious organizations around the world," Sebastian confirmed gravely. He was the only one who didn't look surprised by what the demon had just said. "The heads of state who know about Ba'al and who have been assisting the Vatican behind the scenes for the last couple of decades cannot exactly come out and tell their people that Hell has been trying to unleash the Apocalypse for some time now. Persephone is at her wits' end."

"How come the three of you came here together?" Haruki asked in the lull that followed.

"Nate and I were in Albania." Serena stepped out of Artemus's hold, her expression a tad more composed. "Gideon called and told us what happened. The fastest way to get here was via a rift, so we flew to Rome."

Artemus hesitated. Serena, Nate, and Sebastian didn't

know the full details of everything that had happened in the last twenty-four hours.

"There's something we need to tell you." He glanced uneasily at the other Guardians and Solomon. "The antique shop was—"

The shrill ring of Leah's cell cut him short. She fished the phone out of the rear pocket of her jeans and frowned at the screen. "It's my father."

Artemus's stomach churned with sudden apprehension. He knew instinctively that Jeremiah was calling with bad news. From the nervous looks on the others' faces, so did they.

"Hi, Dad." Leah's eyes slowly widened as she listened. "What?! Wait, I'll put you on speaker!"

Jeremiah's voice came through in the next instant. "Like I was just saying to Leah, the FBI has moved Drake to a secure facility somewhere in Chicago. Shaw and I are trying to find out where they've taken him."

Artemus's alarm turned to anger. He frowned. "Was it that Milton guy?"

"Bingo. He turned up thirty minutes ago and laid claim to the case and Drake. His agency has sold the city officials a cock and bull story about this being a terrorist act, like the attack at Elton's place." Jeremiah paused. "Artemus, there's something else. Something I'm only now realizing may be a significant factor in whatever the hell has been happening for the past few days. Milton was at the plaza today, just before the attack."

Solomon straightened in his seat. "He was?"

"Yes. I'm starting to think the guy's not telling us everything he knows."

Artemus clenched his jaw. "You think he's working for Ba'al?"

"I don't know." A heavy sigh traveled over the line. "Was there anything about him that seemed odd to you when you met him at the auction house?"

"No." Artemus scowled. "Then again, the strongest demons are the ones who conceal their auras the best."

"I should be able to locate Drake," Serena said tersely.

Artemus turned to her, puzzled. "What do you mean?"

She started working the screen of her smartband, a frown on her face. "I planted a chip on Drake. Unless he's behind a reinforced, lead-plated wall or the FBI is actively jamming GPS signals, I should be able to pick up his tracer."

"When the heck did you stick a microchip in him?" Haruki asked, his aghast tone mirrored by everyone's expressions. "And why?!"

"We all know he's been struggling to contain the demon inside him," Serena replied in a voice devoid of remorse. "I thought it best to put a tracking device on him in case he lost control and went MIA." She shrugged. "And it was when we were making out. I tied him to the bed and—"

"Hey!" Leah dropped her phone on her lap and clapped her hands over Jacob's ears. "There's a kid in the room!" she hissed, color staining her cheekbones.

Smokey blew out an embarrassed huff.

Sebastian frowned. "How uncouth."

Serena narrowed her eyes at the Englishman. "I don't want to hear that from a guy who looks like he has a serious leather fetish."

"I can't believe she just said that," Jeremiah muttered leadenly over the line while Sebastian choked and spluttered incoherently. "And *that*."

Jacob pulled at Leah's hands, his eyes sparkling with innocent interest. "What's a leather fetish?"

CHAPTER TWENTY-FOUR

DRAKE FINISHED COUNTING THE MARKS ON THE WALLS and started on the floor.

The cell was ten by fifteen feet. It was larger than a standard supermax prison room and featured the obligatory concrete bed and stainless-steel lavatory facilities. There was no desk nor chair, nor any form of entertainment.

It was evident he wasn't going to be there long.

Drake sat cross-legged on the bed. A tired sigh left his lips. He stopped tallying the scratches on the ground, closed his eyes, and dropped his head wearily against the wall. Artemus's face rose in his mind as he did his best to calm his fraught nerves.

His twin's expression when Jeremiah had led Drake from the mansion in cuffs was one that still made his heart twinge with guilt. He knew Artemus and the others presumed he'd given in. That he'd just resigned himself to his fate and the demonic machinations that had resulted in Briggs's murder.

Drake frowned. *Yeah, well, unfortunately, I have no intention of going down that easily.*

He didn't know where Milton had brought him. His only impression of the place when he'd come out of the van that had transported him from the Central Chicago PD precinct in Near South Side was that it had an underground car park and was at least eight stories tall.

He hadn't sensed any other prisoners in the cells he'd passed when they'd come out of the secure elevator he and his silent guards had ridden. His room was located at the far end of a long, brightly lit corridor and he'd clocked at least a dozen cameras from the point he'd stepped out in the basement to when he'd reached it.

This could make his escape challenging. Challenging, but not impossible.

Though he'd been relieved of his knife by Jeremiah upon his arrest, the FBI agents hadn't stripped him of his clothes and watch and put him in an inmate's uniform before they'd brought him here. Which meant he'd been able to slip a ballpoint pen out of an FBI agent's pocket when they were climbing in the back of the van and tuck it in his boot.

Of course, he could transform into his angel form and smash his way out of the building with his bare fists. But he didn't want to do that. Not if it meant Samyaza consuming another part of his soul and causing more panic among the populace.

He was busy contemplating how long it would take to short-circuit the electronic lock on the cell door when he heard the faint whirr of the steel bolts securing it to its hinges retract into their recesses in the wall.

Milton walked in, a tray of food in hand. "I thought

you might be hungry. The meals here are better than at the precinct house, believe it or not."

Drake kept silent while the agent deposited the tray on the bed and retreated to the opposite wall. Milton crossed his arms and ankles and adopted a casual air.

Drake's stomach growled as he inspected the cup of black coffee, and the beef stew and bread. "Thanks." He lifted the tray onto his lap and picked up the spoon next to the bowl before indicating the cell with a vague wave of his hand. "I'm sorry to be a shitty host. I don't have a chair for you to sit on."

"We're planning to transport you out of here at first light, so I didn't see a need for the warden to supply your room with one," Milton drawled. "I hope you don't mind."

"It's no skin off my back." Drake broke off a chunk of bread and dipped it in the stew. "Where are you taking me?"

Milton flashed him a smile and watched him bite down on the food. "You'll understand if I don't answer that question, Mr. Hunter. After all, some walls have ears."

Drake chewed and swallowed. He paused and stared at the food. "I'm impressed. This *is* good, even by normal standards."

"I'm glad you like it."

Drake finished the meal in a matter of minutes. He gulped down the coffee, wiped his mouth with the back of his hand, and sighed.

"Thank you. I needed that."

"No problem." Milton removed something from his jacket and dropped it on the bed. "Here, you're going to need this."

Drake stared. It was his knife.

He leveled a frown at Milton, a thread of unease uncoiling inside him. "What do you mean?"

A smile stretched the FBI agent's lips. It didn't reach his eyes. He took out a small, glass vial that fit in the crater of his palm out of the pocket of his trousers and showed it to Drake.

"See this?" Milton said blithely. "It contained twenty drops of Samyaza's blood. That blood was in the food you just consumed. You should start to feel the effects in about," he pulled back the sleeve of his suit and inspected his watch, "oh, the next sixty seconds."

Fear exploded inside Drake, drenching him in a cold sweat. The pressure inside the chamber dropped. The vile stench of excrement erupted all around him, making him gag. Flies appeared out of thin air and swarmed the cell.

Drake's heart slammed against his ribs at the sight of Milton's eyes flashing red through the living cloud. The agent transformed into a fearsome demon some eight feet tall. Curved, flame-tipped horns sprouted from his temples and deadly spikes erupted along the lengths of his arms and legs.

Drake instinctively grabbed his knife. The item morphed into the black broadsword at the same time he leapt from the bed and changed into his angel form, his watch stretching out into a rune-covered shield that protected his armor-covered arm.

"Perfect," Milton growled.

Confusion danced through Drake. Severe nausea rolled his stomach in the next instant. He bent over and threw up violently.

The dreadful headache that had nearly overwhelmed him when Milton had interviewed him the day before was back with a vengeance.

Shit! Was it him all along?!

Drake wiped his mouth with the back of a metal-gloved hand and glared at the demon. "What the hell did you do to me, asshole?!"

"Oh, nothing much." Milton shrugged. "You see, we had to do *something* to hasten your awakening." He smiled mirthlessly, his eyes glowing a deep vermilion. "As you've just surmised, I'm the reason you started to feel unwell in the interview room. I put the first six drops of Samyaza's blood in the coffee I gave you." He paused, his smile mocking. "You know, everyone was so ready to believe it was you who killed Briggs they never even entertained the idea it was one of my Nephilim made to look like you. That must really stick in your craw."

Something on the floor drew Drake's gaze. The flies were congregating on the mess he'd just regurgitated. A form was starting to take shape amidst them.

No!

The scream of denial echoed through Drake's skull. Terror choked the breath from his lungs.

The amorphous figure rising from the ground took on the appearance of someone he had seen many times before. Someone he loathed with every fiber of his being.

Samyaza's mouth opened on a grin as he towered over Drake. "*Hello, my son.*"

Drake stepped back, unable to suppress his instinct to run.

How?! I thought he was inside me! How is it that he's able to manifest otherwise?!

Samyaza's grin widened, the rictus splitting his demonic face from ear to ear. It was as devoid of amusement as Milton's smile and radiated the utmost evil.

"*How about you and I have a talk?*"

CHAPTER TWENTY-FIVE

"You sure about this?" Artemus said dubiously.

"Yes," Serena replied curtly.

Smokey shifted where he crouched next to Artemus, causing the boat to rock slightly in the water. Though they all would have preferred it if the hellhound were holding the fort with Solomon and Jacob back at the mansion, he'd insisted on tagging along for the rescue mission.

Callie studied the high rise above them. "Drake's really on the eighth floor of that building?"

They were hunkered down in a black Zodiac in the shadows of the trees under an embankment on the South Branch of the Chicago River. Towering above the street level next to them was a twelve-story building. According to the information available on the internet and through the city's administrative website, the place housed the offices of several major international corporations.

Gideon's intel said otherwise.

"It's a CIA black site," the super soldier had told them when Serena had pinpointed Drake's tracer to the building. "I should know. My teams have delivered several international political prisoners there over the years." He'd made a face. "Or, as the U.S. government likes to call them, 'people of interest.'"

"Why would the FBI be using it as a prison to hold Drake?" Artemus had asked back at the mansion.

"Probably because no one else knows it exists? I gather the public is still tense about what went down in the plaza. No one wants to see a lynch mob outside the police precinct where they were holding Drake." Gideon's expression had turned guarded as he'd studied them across the video link on Serena's laptop. "I'm gonna pretend I never told you any of this. And if the Feds come knocking on my door demanding information about how Drake Hunter went missing from that facility, I'll disavow any involvement in your plans."

"Your support is heartwarming," Serena had said darkly. "And I'm pretty sure you sent Nate and me here to do just this."

Though it was past nine p.m., lights were still on across some of the floors of the building. The GPS tracker on Serena's smartband put Drake's current location on the north end of the eighth story.

Haruki's voice came through Serena's earpiece. "We're in position."

"I still think this is a foolish idea," Sebastian murmured across their comms. "There must be another way to free him. Violence only begets violence."

The two Guardians were on the other side of the building, along with Leah and Nate.

"Brother, there are times when a man needs to grow a pair," Callie said firmly.

Smokey huffed in agreement.

"Yes, well, I *have* a pair of testicles and I value them

highly, thank you very much," Sebastian said haughtily. "Besides, you are not the one standing next to a stolen gas tanker waiting for the Nemean Lion to send a lightning bolt through it. May I point out that she looks far too enthused at the prospect."

"Oh, come on!" Leah protested. "What's wrong with being passionate on the job?"

"There is being passionate and there is naked blood-lust," Sebastian retorted. "You are displaying the latter."

"Christ, spare me from amateurs," Serena muttered under her breath.

Artemus gave her a sympathetic look. "Now you know how I feel most of the time."

"I don't want to hear that from you. You're the biggest amateur of them all."

Artemus scowled at the super soldier. Callie bit her lip.

"Are we doing this or not?" Haruki said testily. "I'm starting to get blue balls."

"It's barely autumn," Nate said.

"Yeah, well, you could probably fry an egg on the curbs in L.A. right now, so sue me."

Serena closed her eyes and pinched her brow with her fingers. "Are you guys done?"

"Yes," Nate murmured. "Sorry."

"We go in sixty seconds."

Clouds gathered above them as Leah drew on her elemental powers. Thunder boomed in the distance.

They were thirty seconds into the countdown when a shudder shook Artemus, Callie, and Smokey. Serena stiffened.

She could feel the air pressure plummeting around them.

A glazed expression came over Artemus and the hellhound.

"No!" Callie mumbled, ashen faced. She was staring into space, as if seeing something that wasn't there.

Serena snatched her gun and dagger out of the holsters on her hips and scanned the area for demonic rifts. She saw none.

"What is it?" Her inability to tap into the bond the others shared brought a frustrated scowl to her face. "What's happening, Artemus?!"

An explosion high above had their heads snapping up.

A dark, winged shape with a flaming, black sword shot out of a jagged hole in the side of the building. Another, bigger shape followed, lightning fast. It grabbed the first figure as the latter tried to escape, spun around several times, and sent its victim crashing back inside the building through a fresh hole in the facade.

Artemus transformed into his angel form and shot up wordlessly into the sky.

Dread swamped Serena. "Shit!" She grabbed the rope they'd secured to the top of the embankment and started climbing. "Was that Drake?!"

"Yes!" Callie bounded up the vertical wall in her Chimera form, her claws scoring the surface with ease. "We need to hurry!"

A shadow swooped over them as Smokey cleared the Zodiac in a single, powerful leap. He landed above them with a thud, his back paws scrabbling briefly at the wall of the embankment before he found purchase on the ground.

Lightning lit the sky. It formed a jagged, brilliant line that dropped from the heavens. The tanker detonated on the opposite side of the high rise. Orange light bloomed in the gloom. By then, Serena and Callie were racing toward one of the building's rear exits, the hellhound's dark form bounding ahead of them.

"That other demon!" Serena glanced at Callie as they closed in on the fire escape. "Any idea who that was?!"

Callie shuddered. "From what I can feel from Drake, I think—I think that's his father!"

Serena's stomach dropped. *Wait! Samyaza is* here*?! How?!*

Smokey smashed the door down with his body and leapt up the dimly lit stairs beyond.

CHAPTER TWENTY-SIX

ARTEMUS'S HEART RACED AS HE ROSE IN THE NIGHT, HIS unearthly gaze focused on the jagged openings in the facade of the building.

He could feel Drake's growing darkness and despair even from a distance. It coiled through his consciousness, a band of blackness tinged with crimson. He knew Smokey sensed it as acutely as he did, since they were both Drake's Guardians. So would the others across the divine bond they shared, to a lesser extent.

Something flickered out the corner of Artemus's eye.

He snapped his wings and twisted on himself just as a window exploded on his right. A demon shot out through the flying debris, missing him by a hairbreadth.

A foul stench thickened the air around Artemus, along with a cloud of flies. He batted at the living shroud with his sword. The insects dispersed for an instant before swarming him once more. Artemus frowned.

Sparks erupted as he raised his blade and blocked the near invisible attack aimed at his right flank.

"Bravo." The demon who'd charged him lowered his

dark sword. "Your fighting skills are nearly as good as your father's."

Artemus turned and faced the hulking, red-eyed fiend, tension swirling through him. Though he couldn't detect anything familiar in the demon's face, he could guess who he had been in his human form.

"You're Milton, I presume."

The demon smiled. "You presume correctly, Son of Michael."

"And which demon prince are you meant to be?" Artemus frowned. "You are not Belial, that I can tell."

Milton's smile widened. "You are right, again. You can call me Beel. As in Beelzebub."

Artemus's knuckles whitened on his sword. "The Lord of the Flies."

Milton shrugged at the familiar designation. "Not my favorite of appellations, I must admit. It loses something in translation." His teeth flashed. "I much prefer the Hebrew title, Prince of Demons. It has more...flair." He hefted his serrated blade over his shoulder, the spikes on his arms glinting in the night. "Now, how about we leave your brother to his little tête-à-tête with his father? It would be rude to interrupt their reunion, don't you think?"

Dread formed a leaden pit in Artemus's stomach. *So, it was Samyaza I could feel through my bond with Drake! How the hell did he manifest outside Drake's body?!*

"Nah. I think I'll gatecrash their party," he retorted grimly. "Wouldn't want to miss saying hi to my stepfather now, would I?"

Artemus rushed toward the closest breach in the side of the building. He cursed and rocked to a stop when Milton appeared before him, the demon matching his preternatural speed.

"Now, why do I get the feeling you're not taking me seriously, kid?" Milton said pleasantly.

Something heavy smashed into Artemus's chest. He gasped and looked down in time to see Milton's fist head up toward his face.

Though he pulled away, the blow still caught him on the edge of the chin. Stars exploded in front of his eyes. Artemus blocked the next strike with his armored forearm and felt metal vibrate under the force of the impact. He knew it would have broken his bone had he not been wearing a divine shield.

An inhuman grin distorted Milton's face as he continued his relentless assault, his fist and sword blurring as he pummeled Artemus. Artemus deflected his blows, his frustration gnawing at him. He knew Milton was keeping him away from Drake so Samyaza could accomplish his sick goals, whatever those were.

He warded off another deadly hit to his chest, drew on his powers and that of the ring on his right hand, and brought forth the Flame of God. The fire swept over the ring-turned-gauntlet and engulfed Michael's heavenly blade.

Milton hissed and drew back, irritation making his crimson eyes flare. An angry sound left him.

Artemus looked down. A whip had wrapped around the demon's left ankle, the triple thongs blazing with holy fire.

"I have him," Sebastian said coldly as he rose beside Artemus. "Go to Drake." The Sphinx's golden gaze met Artemus's, as old and as wise as the world. "Your brother needs you."

Artemus dipped his chin and headed for the opening on the eighth floor.

Milton roared behind him. The sound was cut off as Sebastian yanked him into the air and flew toward the sky, the fiend dangling helplessly at the end of Raguel's whip. The Sphinx's words reached Artemus dimly as he darted through the jagged hole in the building.

"How about you and I go smell the ozone, demon?"

Artemus navigated the wreckage of a cell and followed the sounds of intense battle echoing from the south end of the corridor. Smoke filled the passage. The red glow of flames and incandescent bolts of light lit the air as he grew closer.

A shout reached him.

"*Smokey!*"

The hellhound's dark form parted the shadowy pall and hurtled toward him. A grunt escaped Artemus as he caught the beast in mid-air. He cursed and spread his wings to slow their progress, the tips of the feathery appendages raking the ceiling and walls. They crashed through the outer wall of the building and slowed to a stop after traveling some fifty feet.

Smokey's outraged growl made Artemus's armor vibrate. He took them back inside the high rise. Trepidation throbbed through him as he dropped to the ground and carefully lowered the hound.

"You okay?"

Smokey snarled. *We need to hurry! He has Drake!*

The hellhound limped toward the opposite end of the hallway.

Artemus froze at the sight of the nasty claw marks carved down the hound's left foreleg. He blinked when he sensed the other Guardians' pain across their bond. Fury overcame dread. His racing heart slowed. Icy stillness filled him from the inside out.

"Stay here."

I want to—

"Stay here, Cerberus."

Smokey flinched at Artemus's steely tone. He hesitated before stopping in his tracks, his head drooping dejectedly. Artemus touched his flank lightly before rising and winging his way to the other end of the building. The walls blurred on either side of him as he accelerated, his whole being focused on the evil energy ahead.

CHAPTER TWENTY-SEVEN

THE SMELL OF FRESH LIGHTNING TAINTED THE AIR WHEN Artemus entered the place where the battle was unfolding. It was the remains of three holding cells, their walls smashed and their melted concrete and metal furnishings lying amidst the rubble strewn across the ground.

Nate and Serena were climbing to their feet on his left, daggers and liquid-armor suits shimmering with divine light. Their chests heaved, the fresh lacerations on their heads and faces healing rapidly as they scowled at the demon floating above the ground some thirty feet away.

Artemus gritted his teeth when he finally beheld Samyaza's monstrous form. The demon was bigger than Milton. Drake dangled limply under the fiend's left arm, unconscious and bleeding in his human form. Leah struggled in the demon's right grip, choked noises wheezing out of her as she scrabbled frantically at the talons squeezing her throat. Despite her predicament, the Nemean Lion showed no fear, her eyes alight with fury and her golden gaze seeking the spear gleaming on the floor beneath her kicking feet.

Haruki snatched up the weapon and cast it at her before roaring out a jet of white-hot fire, blood streaming from the wounds on his chest and left flank. Callie's scepter hummed as it left her grasp. She stood panting to Artemus's right, one hand staunching the crimson flow oozing out of the terrible gash in her side.

The Dragon's flames washed harmlessly over Samyaza's body. He blocked the spear Leah aimed at his face with his right wing, sent her flying into the nearest wall, and grabbed Callie's scepter an inch from his heart. He hurled the weapon back at the Chimera, a sneer distorting his corrupt features.

The giant snake making up Callie's tail darted over her head and coiled around the scepter before it could bore a hole through her left eye. It hissed savagely as the friction tore some of its scales clean off, exposing raw flesh.

Callie's gaze flashed jade. She inhaled deeply, her rib cage expanding to three times its normal size. The sonic roar she released made Artemus's ear drums vibrate painfully and smashed all the windows on the eighth floor.

The wave pushed Samyaza back a couple of feet.

He lowered his open wings and smirked at Callie. "That barely tickled, Chimera."

Five seconds had elapsed since Artemus had entered the chamber. He narrowed his eyes and charged the demon.

Samyaza's eyes widened slightly as Artemus flickered in front of him. A grunt escaped the demon when he smashed into him shoulder first and carried him to the wall at the back. Concrete and plaster detonated around them as they blasted through the exterior of the building and shot out into the cool night air, the fire from the oil tanker painting their winged shapes with flickering, orange light.

Artemus swung his flaming broadsword at Samyaza's left arm. The demon jerked back instinctively. It was all Artemus needed. He kicked Drake out of the demon's grasp, snapped his wings closed, and dove.

Artemus caught his brother's falling form a hundred feet above the river, saw the demon closing in on them in their reflection in the water, and flicked his wings to the left. Claws raked his flank as Samyaza shot past him. Fire lanced Artemus's flesh as the demon's talons shredded his armor and tore into his skin. He spread his wings and rose, his gaze locked on the ragged opening in the building above them, Drake's body a dull weight under his right arm.

I need to get to the others!

A roar of rage rose below him as Samyaza hurtled to an abrupt stop above the river, the force of his descent causing a twenty-foot-wide depression in the surface of the water before casting violent waves up onto the embankments.

Artemus's pulse thrummed when he reached the ruins of the chamber where the other Guardians and the super soldiers waited. He cast Drake in their midst, gripped his sword in both hands, and blocked Samyaza's blow a hair-breadth from his head.

The others formed a wall in front of Drake's motion-less shape, their faces radiating determination despite their many wounds. Cerberus appeared out of the smoke behind them, fangs dripping acid and his golden gazes spewing pure hatred at Samyaza. He crouched and wrapped his enormous body protectively around Drake, shielding him from view.

Artemus gritted his teeth as Samyaza forced him toward the others inch by slow inch. Desperation throbbed though him.

More! I need more power, dammit!

He focused desperately on the light burning through his soul and seized it with every fiber of his being.

Help me! Please!

For a breathless moment, nothing happened.

Brightness blossomed inside him, silent and powerful. He gasped as an incredible force rushed through his veins and filled his body, a heady combination of the energies he'd inherited from his goddess mother and his archangel father. For the first time, he sensed their presence fleetingly at the back of his consciousness.

They were there, with him. Had always been there.

He just hadn't realized it before.

Their strength hardened Artemus's resolve. He scowled at the demon.

"*You. Will. Not. TOUCH HIM!*" Artemus roared, Michael and Theia's voices underscoring his own faintly.

Samyaza snarled as he was shoved back some five feet. An explosion sounded to Artemus's right, distracting them both. Sebastian crashed through the ceiling and landed heavily amidst the rubble.

The Sphinx shook his head dazedly before raising his angry gaze to the opening through which he'd appeared. He wiped his mouth in disgust and climbed to his feet, a scowl darkening his face and a ball of crackling, white light filling his right hand.

"You foul fiend! That was cheating!"

"Oh, come now. You can hardly expect demons to play by the rules." Beelzebub flew down through the gaping hole and joined Samyaza, a grin on his face. "It seems our time is up, Samy. Let's go."

Samyaza glared at him. "*I told you not to call me that!*"

Beelzebub ignored his protest. "You know Bel will flip his lid if we don't return soon. I don't want to have to wade through the ashes of another thousand dead demons just because he flew into a fit of rage." He glanced in the direction of Cerberus. "Besides, our work here is done, for now."

Fear pierced Artemus at the demon's words.

"What do you mean?" He looked over to where the hellhound still shielded Drake and knew it was his brother they were talking about. He glowered at Beelzebub and Samyaza. "*What have you done to Drake?!*"

Beelzebub smiled. "That's for us to know and for you to find out, little boy."

A crimson rift tore open next to him. He ushered Samyaza into the hellish void and disappeared.

The blare of police sirens and fire engines filled the deafening hush that followed. Artemus landed on the ground and hurried over to Cerberus. The others exchanged worried glances as they gathered around him. The hellhound huffed before finally uncoiling his giant form from around Drake.

"Drake," Artemus mumbled. "Wake up. It's over."

He dropped to his knees, reached out, and touched his brother's shoulder with trembling fingers.

His twin's eyes slammed open. Redness filled his pupils.

Drake opened his mouth and screamed in agony, crimson sigils exploding across his arching body.

CHAPTER TWENTY-EIGHT

JEREMIAH SCOWLED AT SERENA AND HARUKI AND rubbed a spot over his breastbone. "You guys are gonna give me a heart attack one day, you know that, right? I already have severe acid indigestion as it is from your recent shenanigans."

Smoke and steam clouded the air behind the detective where they stood in the mouth of an alley, half a block from the CIA black site. The wind blowing off the lake had scattered the billows across half of downtown.

The city's firefighters had put out most of the blaze that had taken hold of the oil tanker and the row of parked vehicles outside the building. The last ambulance had left a short while back, taking an injured guard who had been on the eighth floor at the time of the attack to the nearest hospital.

There had miraculously been no fatalities among the CIA and FBI staff who had been manning the black site. Serena knew the prime reason for this was because their attention had been drawn to the tanker. It helped that she and Nate had jammed the elevators and blocked the stair-

wells from the fifth to the eighth floors after most of the
agents had gone down to the ground level to investigate
the explosion.

"Where's Drake?" Jeremiah asked gruffly.

Serena shared a guarded look with Haruki. "Somewhere safe."

Jeremiah blew out a tired sigh and raked his hair with a
hand. "Yeah, well, 'somewhere safe' isn't going to satisfy
my bosses or Milton's. They already suspect I'm involved
in this. I'm surprised they haven't asked me for my badge
yet." The detective's expression turned suspicious. "By the
way, did you guys do something to the security cameras in
that building and the nearby streets? They can't retrieve
any of the feed data from the high rise and the street
cameras over a good two-mile radius."

"What a shame," Serena said steadily. "Must have been
a power failure."

Haruki's lips twitched.

Jeremiah narrowed his eyes at them. "It's funny how
that kind of thing keeps happening around you guys." A
grimace twisted his mouth. "So, Milton really is a demon,
huh?"

"The worst kind." Haruki made a face. "He won his
fight with Sebastian with a dirty tactic."

Jeremiah arched an eyebrow. "How so?"

"He kissed him." Serena sighed. "I don't think there's
enough mouthwash in Chicago to satisfy Sebastian."

Jeremiah gaped.

"Solomon said Beelzebub is the joker among the
demon princes," Haruki explained. "Apparently, he did the
same to Satan once and was banished to the lower level of
Hell for a hundred years."

Jeremiah eventually found his voice. "I don't think I've ever seen you guys get such a beating before."

He examined their bloodied clothes with a jaundiced eye.

"Yeah, well, the demons of Hell's Council are evidently invincible," Serena said darkly.

Jeremiah stiffened. "Wait. Does that mean Leah—?"

"Leah is fine," Haruki said. "She's got a few cuts and bruises; nothing that won't heal by tomorrow." He frowned. "I won't let anything happen to her."

Jeremiah looked unconvinced by his words.

"We'd better join the others," Serena said. "We stayed back to let you know what happened and that Leah's okay. Also, we think Ba'al managed to achieve one of their goals tonight, so nothing else should happen in the city imminently."

"And what goal did they accomplish?" Jeremiah asked uneasily.

Lines furrowed Serena's brow. "We don't know, but it's clear everything they've done in the last week has to do with Drake."

They bade the detective goodbye and headed for the back alley where Serena had hidden her sportsbike.

"Are we really sure about that?" Haruki said as he climbed onto the back of the Kawasaki. "That Ba'al has what they want, so they'll leave us alone for now?"

"You heard what Beelzebub said to Samyaza," Serena replied. "Besides, Drake is still with us." Her voice hardened. "We'll find a way to fix whatever they've done to him."

She started the bike and headed off into the night, hoping the words she'd just spoken would not turn out to be a promise none of them could keep.

"I WOULD STRONGLY ADVISE AGAINST DOING THAT."
Solomon frowned. "We have no idea what sealing his sigils
will do to him."

"You weren't there." Artemus glared at the demon.
"You didn't see how much pain he was in!"

Jacob shifted closer to Solomon where they sat on the
couch.

Callie clenched her jaw at the kid's anxious expression.
She walked over to Artemus and laid a hand on his arm,
her expression calm despite the disquiet swirling through
her.

The angel halted his pacing of the floor in front of the
leaded, glass windows in Barbara Nolan's drawing room.
He cast a frustrated glance her way, his hands fisting and
unfisting at his sides.

Callie didn't know if it was her imagination or not, but
Artemus's fury seemed to be thickening the very air
around them.

It might not be him. She masked a frown. *It might be
Drake.*

The dark angel was currently in a guest bedroom on
the second floor of the Nolan mansion. He still hadn't
regained consciousness after what had happened at the
CIA black site, having fainted seconds after his sigils
appeared. It was the second time Callie had seen them and
they were as horrifyingly beautiful as the first time she'd
witnessed them. Nate and Smokey were currently guarding
him while the rest of them debated what to do next.

It was Artemus who'd come up with the idea of asking
the Nolans to seal his twin's sigils. Leah's mother had done
the same to the Nemean Lion when she was a baby,

successfully masking her divine presence from curious eyes for years by hiding her birthmark. It was Naomi who had deliberately broken the seal a few months back, during a demonic attack.

Callie shared a guarded look with Sebastian and Solomon. She knew the same thing was going through all their minds. Artemus was behaving recklessly. It was as if seeing Drake with Samyaza had driven him to the edge of despair and beyond, pushing him to try anything to save his brother, consequences be damned.

The head of the Nolan clan watched Solomon carefully.

"Why are you against sealing Drake's sigils?" Barbara said. "What Artemus is suggesting makes sense."

"Because they are bound to his soul," Solomon retorted. "It is clear to me now that Samyaza never intended to manifest his presence physically through Drake. He only meant to control him through the demon blood that courses through Drake's veins and the runes he bears on his body. Messing with them could do untold damage to who he is."

"Samyaza has already done that!" Artemus snapped. "Whatever he and Beelzebub did tonight changed something inside Drake. I can feel it." He clutched at his heart, his expression wretched. "I can feel it *here*. And it hurts, even across our bond!"

"Still, we have never sealed demonic runes before," Floyd Nolan said in the stilted silence.

Carmen Nolan nodded where she perched on the armrest next to him, her expression similarly reserved.

"Besides, won't our council have something to say if they find out we did something like this?" Naomi murmured uneasily behind her father.

Barbara studied the members of her coven before steepling her hands against her mouth, her expression pensive. "What do the tea leaves say, Esther?"

Esther Nolan looked up from her porcelain cup, her face troubled. "They say nothing." The ginger cat at her feet let out an anxious meow. The witch hesitated. "It's as if the Fates are intentionally hiding what the future may hold."

Barbara was silent for some time. She finally released a sigh.

"I will help you," she told Artemus. "I owe you this much for what you and yours have done for my coven and my granddaughter."

Callie closed her eyes briefly. Relief and dread filled her in equal measure at the witch's words. Although she wanted to give Artemus's desperate plan a chance, she could not ignore Solomon's warning.

"But understand this, Artemus Steele." Barbara's stony voice echoed around the room. "If this backfires. If this unleashes Hell upon the Earth. That responsibility will lie solely at your feet." She paused. "Are you willing to take that risk and accept the consequences of your actions?"

A shudder shook Artemus. He took a shallow breath and squared his shoulders. "Yes."

CHAPTER TWENTY-NINE

Solomon watched wordlessly as Artemus carefully laid Drake on the floor, his heart full of misgivings. Smokey plopped down next to Drake in his rabbit form, the wound on his left foreleg oozing slightly despite Naomi's healing.

The Nephil's poison was getting stronger, draining the hellhound's life force with every passing hour.

Flaming torches crackled and hissed in the iron brackets lining the walls of the Nolan mansion basement. Their flickering, yellow light illuminated the complex, concentric design Barbara and Floyd were tracing out on the ground in white chalk. It consisted of three circles linked by a pattern of lines and symbols.

Solomon swallowed a sigh. He recognized Azazel's handiwork despite not having seen it in eons. There was none who could control the essence of magic that coursed through Heaven and Earth like the Third Leader of the Grigori.

Esther and Naomi finished preparing a concoction in the pot simmering in the hearth at the far end of the chamber. Carmen dipped a ladle in the potion, tasted it, and dipped her chin wordlessly.

"Anyone else think we should be doing this under a full moon, on an exposed hilltop somewhere?" Haruki murmured.

He'd turned up with Serena a short while back.

"I do not think they are *that* kind of witch," Sebastian said. "And this is not exactly a sabbath."

Callie glanced at Sebastian, her green eyes dark with disquiet. The demon could tell she shared his qualms about what was currently unfolding.

"May I suggest something?" Solomon said quietly.

The Guardians and the super soldiers looked at him. For some reason, they appeared to trust his guidance more than their own leader's right now.

"Keep your weapons close at hand."

Serena's gaze moved to Drake's unconscious form. "Why?"

"Because I have a bad feeling." Solomon frowned faintly. "Trust me, when a demon gets a bad feeling, it means a lot more than when a human gets one."

Jacob clutched the key hanging from the makeshift, leather necklace dangling at his throat. Callie tightened her grip on her cane. Haruki and Sebastian danced their fingers across their weapons.

"It might work out." Serena's voice wavered, her words tinged with hope. "This could be exactly what we need to do."

Callie frowned at the super soldier. "Do you really believe that?"

Serena flinched at her tone. Nate frowned at Callie before laying a gentle hand on the super soldier's shoulder.

Callie bit her lip. "I'm sorry. I can only imagine what

kind of hell you, Artemus, and Smokey are going through right now." She looked at the three figures in the center of the magic circles. "No matter how the dice fall, we need to be here for him. For *them*." Determination filled her face. "Artemus has been a rock for each of us, at one time or another in our lives. We may bicker. We may have different opinions on certain matters. But we have always been here for one another, since the day we met." Callie took a shaky breath. "We rise with him—"

"We fall with him," Sebastian murmured. "Well said, sister."

"We are ready."

Barbara's statement had the tension swirling inside the chamber rise a notch.

Leah reluctantly let go of Haruki's hand and joined Naomi, Floyd, Carmen, and Esther as they each assumed a position on the points of the hexagram. Though the Nemean Lion was not strictly a witch, she was descended from a powerful one and carried Azazel's energy within her.

Barbara poured the potion Esther and Naomi had made into six silver chalices, took them on a tray to the center of the magic circles, and knelt beside Artemus and Drake. She took a dagger from her waist, murmured an incantation, and sliced a thin cut on their right thumbs. She dripped a drop of their blood into the cups and did the same with Smokey.

The High Priestess started uttering an arcane spell as she rose and walked outside the outermost circle, passing a chalice each to the other witches and the sorcerer. She took her place between Leah and Naomi, raised her cup, and swallowed a sip. The others did the same and joined in the incantation.

Static started to charge the chamber. Solomon felt the hairs rise on his arms. Jacob clung to his side. He laid a reassuring hand on the child's head.

The magic circles shimmered. Solomon narrowed his eyes.

Here we go.

The witches and the sorcerer continued their low, mesmerizing chanting while they sipped from their chalices, their movements and speech perfectly synchronized. Though Solomon only understood half the words they spoke, he could not deny the power they contained. It echoed through his bones and made his blood shiver.

Hazy, white lines materialized on the ground, above the design Barbara and Floyd had etched out. They rose, forming a circular wall of magic enclosing the two men and the hellhound.

Smokey whimpered as the ethereal pattern scored his body. Artemus sucked in air and clenched his fists.

Callie took a step toward the circle, her face reflecting their pain.

"Don't."

She froze at Solomon's curt order.

Haruki ground his teeth as he gripped the Sword of Camael, his expression similarly tortured. Sebastian touched Callie's arm, a muscle jumping in his cheek. Jacob's fingers dug into Solomon's leg.

The demon swallowed a frustrated sigh.

Whatever this spell was, it came at a clear cost to those bound by it. And there was nothing the rest of the Guardians could do to help them.

A shudder shook Drake. Though he remained unconscious, his sigils flashed into existence, crimson and full of corruption, their glow evident beneath his clothes.

A frown knotted Barbara's brow. She exchanged cautious glances with the sorcerer and the witches gathered around her.

Solomon tensed as the power of the spell soared, causing the fire in the hearth and the flame torches to dance and flicker wildly.

Drake's body slowly levitated off the ground. Artemus climbed to his feet as his brother tilted upright, legs dangling and arms rising as if pinned to a cross.

A sudden blast of energy rippled through the basement and prickled Solomon's skin. Alarm bells sounded in the marrow of his soul. Before he could shout out a warning, Callie transformed into the Chimera next to him, horror leaching the color from her face.

"Solomon was right. We have to stop this!"

The sigils on Drake's body suddenly dimmed. Solomon's heart lurched.

"Wait," Serena mumbled. "Is it—is it working?!"

The red lines scorching Drake's flesh slowly turned a pale gold. Hope brightened Artemus and Smokey's eyes. Relief similarly filled Barbara's face. She nodded encouragingly to the other witches and the sorcerer.

Only Solomon remained wary where he'd taken a defensive position in front of Jacob.

Serena glanced at him. "He's gonna be okay. The sigils are—"

"*No.*"

The word sliced the air like thunder.

Solomon's pulse stuttered as all eyes locked on Drake. He cursed.

Drake's symbols were turning a deep vermilion once more. Dark wings sprouted from his back. Armor coalesced out of thin air and covered his flesh from the neck down, the sigils on his skin translating onto the inky metal as if engraved by an unseen power. Runes exploded across his watch-turned-shield. His fingers twitched.

His knife rose from the table next to the fire and flashed across the basement.

Barbara gasped as the dagger scored a shallow cut on her right cheek before striking the magic wall surrounding the dark angel and his Guardians. The High Priestess's eyes widened when the knife transformed into the dark, demonic, serrated broadsword.

"No!" she gasped.

The witch's blood was sucked from the tip of the blade into the complex design, turning the pale lines crimson in a heartbeat. The magic circle shattered an instant later, the force of the detonation casting the spell wielders to the four corners of the chamber and forcing Solomon and the others back several steps.

The demonic sword found its owner's hand.

Naomi scrambled to her knees. "*Artemus, run!*"

Drake opened his eyes.

Solomon flinched at the hellish glow emanating from them. They had lost all signs of the golden radiance that signaled his divine power.

A frown darkened Drake's face. His expression became icy as his gaze found the frozen man standing beneath him. "*What have you done?*"

The power of the dark angel's voice made Solomon's ears throb.

Samyaza!

Smokey transformed into his dark hellhound form and stepped in front of Artemus, his eyes wary.

Drake moved.

Artemus blocked the black sword an inch from the startled hound's hide.

"Don't," the white angel begged, sparks rising from where he'd countered his twin's attack with his divine blade. "Please, don't do this. *Drake, if you're in there, come to your senses, damn you!*"

An evil smile curved Drake's mouth. "*You're right. My son and I have bigger fish to fry.* She *needs to die first.*"

The air ripped open next to the dark angel. His wicked gaze swept over them before he dove inside a crimson rift.

Artemus lunged after him, Smokey in his wake.

CHAPTER THIRTY

DANIEL KNELT A FEW STEPS BEHIND PERSEPHONE WHERE she prayed at the altar of the Sistine Chapel. Warm silence surrounded them, the guards at the doors having taken their usual position outside the chamber for the Pope's daily invocations. The bright sunlight filtering through the arched windows lining the building lit the colorful frescos adorning its barrel-vaulted ceiling and walls, and cast a pretty haze in the air.

Daniel hadn't realized how much he would miss the beauty of the Holy See until he'd moved to Chicago. His time with Persephone would end when he and Otis left Rome in three days. He did not regret coming to visit her and his friends at the Vatican. Walking the corridors where he had spent most of his adult life had been as refreshing as it had been melancholic.

His thoughts strayed briefly to the latest events in Chicago, bringing a faint frown to his face. Otis had received a call from Sebastian at four a.m. that morning, shortly before Persephone had been contacted by Elton.

Daniel knew the news of Artemus and Drake's

encounter with Beelzebub and Samyaza weighed heavily on his adoptive mother's mind. Though she hadn't said anything to him, he suspected her prayers this morning were directed at the brothers' wellbeing. After all, she was the bastion of the organization tasked with protecting the world from Hell's machinations and it was becoming increasingly clear that Artemus and Drake were very much the focal point of Satanael's schemes.

Otis's consternation at Artemus's proposal that the Nolans seal Drake's sigils was something Daniel had shared. Although neither of them could pinpoint the reason why, they both inherently felt it was a dangerous thing to do. But, from what Sebastian had said, not even Heaven itself could dissuade Artemus from carrying out his insane plan.

Daniel sighed and focused on his prayers. He'd just fallen under the rhythmic lure of the familiar words tumbling silently from his lips when the temperature in the chapel dropped.

Daniel's ears popped at the same time his eyes snapped open. He jumped to his feet, the ring on his left middle finger extending into a gauntlet. The metal brightened as the Flame of God wrapped around it. Fire swept over his body and engulfed the wings sprouting from his back.

"Daniel?!"

Persephone's alarmed voice had Daniel's head snapping around. His eyes widened. He moved.

A lasso of flames shot out in front of Persephone. The weapon wrapped around the black broadsword flying toward her heart, stopping it mere inches from her robes.

The dark angel who held the blade frowned, the crimson portal that had brought him there wavering in the air behind him.

Daniel gritted his teeth as he dropped between Drake and Persephone, his wings extending into a protective wall guarding her. He could feel the demonic blade fighting its holy restraints.

"What's wrong with you?" he snapped. "Why are you doing this?!"

"That's not him."

Daniel glanced over his shoulder at Persephone, startled.

"That's not Drake." Her unblinking gaze was locked on the face of the devil who'd just attacked her. "Not the Drake we know, anyway. Samyaza has his soul."

Dread swelled inside Daniel as he looked at the dark angel. The hateful look in Drake's crimson eyes was one he hadn't seen before. The dark angel's armor was also different and sported symbols similar to the ones that appeared on a Guardian's weapon. Even his face was scorched with unfamiliar runes.

"Why is he trying to kill you?" Daniel said between clenched teeth.

"Because I am one of the most important people who stand in their way," Persephone said shakily, understanding dawning in her voice. "Because I represent the power of humanity against Hell. If they strike me down, it will deal a terrible blow not just to our organization, but to Heaven's forces too."

A savage smile twisted Drake's mouth. "*You are correct, sinner.*"

Daniel's pulse spiked as the corrupt energy swamping the air thickened, making it hard to breathe. He scanned the room, searching for more rifts.

It only took a couple of seconds for him to realize the hellish power he was sensing was coming from Drake.

Daniel's stomach twisted with a fresh wave of fear. The dark angel slowly pulled his arm back. Samyaza's sword screamed as it slipped out of the hold of the Flame of God. Daniel blinked.

Drake had disappeared.

A gasp rose behind him. He twisted around and froze.

Persephone met his stunned gaze. Her eyes darkened to a sea green. A single tear spilled over and coursed down her left cheek.

"I'm sorry." A shaky smile tilted her lips. "I love you, Daniel. You are my son and always will be."

Daniel stared at the bloodied blade that had ripped through her back and out her stomach. His roar of denial thundered around the chapel as he moved toward the grinning devil behind her, rage fanning his flames and filling his vision with a red haze.

The chapel doors opened, distracting him. The guards rushed in.

Drake withdrew his sword and swung it at Persephone's neck.

Two blurry shapes slammed into the dark angel and carried him across the chamber. The south half of the marble screen dividing the chapel exploded as they crashed into it.

The guards staggered to a stop near the entrance, their shouts of alarm rending the air as Artemus and Smokey rolled across the floor toward them. The white angel and the hellhound leapt to their feet and looked frantically in Persephone and Daniel's direction.

In their eyes, Daniel read remorse and an apology he was unsure he could ever accept.

"Stop the bleeding!" Artemus shouted. "We can still save her!"

His words jolted Daniel into action. He swooped down next to Persephone, lifted her onto his lap, and clamped a hand on her wound, his flames wrapping her in a warm embrace.

"Hang in there," he mumbled desperately. "Don't you dare die!"

Persephone nodded, perspiration dotting her brow.

A golden rift tore the air next to where the crimson portal had been. Sebastian shot out of it ahead of the others.

ARTEMUS GRUNTED AS HE PARRIED DRAKE'S STRIKE, THE blow making his teeth vibrate. He knew the strength he sensed was not all Drake's.

Smokey leapt and closed his jaws on Drake's left calf where they hovered above the floor. Furious growls rumbled out of him as he shook his head savagely and tried to bring the dark angel down.

Drake sneered and kicked him straight across the chapel.

The hellhound crashed into Rosselli's 'Descent from Mount Sinai' with a whimper of pain. Bright-colored plaster peppered the air as he thudded to the ground.

"*You bastard!*" Artemus snarled.

He renewed his attacks on Drake, outrage overcoming the guilt clawing at his insides.

Callie rushed across the chapel and dropped next to Smokey's still form, her face pale with fear.

"Callie?!" Artemus yelled as he blocked Drake's sword an inch from his neck.

"He's okay!" She cast a wild glance at him, her shoulders sagging with relief. "Just stunned!"

Artemus's knuckles whitened on his sword. "Stay with him!" His gaze swept over the others, self-reproach giving way to iron resolve. "I was wrong. We need to stop Drake. Here! Together!"

Solomon dipped his chin and morphed into his demonic shape. Haruki, Leah, Sebastian, and Nate nodded. Serena clenched her teeth before bobbing her head in agreement, her expression resolute.

Only Callie, Jacob, and Daniel stayed where they were with Smokey and Persephone, Jacob darting across the chamber to join the Chimera and the hellhound.

The dark angel observed the ring of challengers surrounding him, his expression full of disdain. His crimson gaze landed on Solomon.

"Why do you stand with them, blood of my blood?" he asked the demon, his gravelly voice echoing to the vaulted ceiling. *"These sinners deserve to die."*

"They are not sinners, Samyaza." Solomon frowned. "We are. We have strayed from the path for too long, Brother. I, for one, have been repenting my past mistakes. You should too."

Drake stared. A low chuckle left him with his next breath. It grew into maniacal laughter that set Artemus's teeth on edge. In that moment, Artemus wanted nothing more than to punch his twin senseless.

A gasp tore from his lips as something smashed into his solar plexus.

Artemus flew backward some twenty feet and glimpsed Sebastian slamming into the north wall of the chapel out of the corner of his eye. Haruki fell to his knees with a grunt, a fresh wound carved across his abdomen in a livid, red line. Leah cursed colorfully as she sailed across the chamber and smashed into the other half of the marble screen, sending pale fragments flying over the ashen faced guards crouched near the entrance.

Drake's figure blurred between them, his attacks so fast even Artemus couldn't follow them with his preternatural eyes.

How?! How is he—?!

A growl rumbled out of Solomon as he blocked Drake's blade with his hands. Inky blood spilled thickly from his palms. He bared his teeth and snarled at the dark angel.

"*Father!*" Jacob yelled.

Drake's head snapped around, his scarlet gaze finding the terrified, young Guardian. He grinned.

"*No!*" Solomon roared, his scream full of rage and panic.

Artemus's stomach plummeted. Though he moved, he knew he would not reach Drake in time. His wings parted the air like treacle as he headed for the boy his brother would soon kill.

Jacob's eyes flashed gold. His fingers rose in slow motion to snatch the key suspended from his neck, the divine beast he harbored reacting to protect her host.

A figure darted between Drake's blade and the boy.

The softest of gasps parted Serena's lips.

Artemus rocked to a standstill, as did everyone else in the chapel.

"*Serena!*" Nate shouted.

Drake blinked. The crimson light in his eyes flared before gradually fading. He lowered his gaze to the sword in his hands and followed it to where it had pierced the body of the super soldier.

Artemus's heart shattered into a million pieces as he watched awareness slowly return to his twin's face.

Horror widened Drake's eyes. The sigils faded from his skin and armor as he shifted to his human form.

A sliver of blood burst from Serena's mouth and dripped onto her chin as Drake's knife exited her flesh, the blade clinking noisily onto the ground.

"No," he mumbled hoarsely. "No! No! *No!*"

His rising shout of denial rang in their ears. He stumbled forward and caught the super soldier in his arms as she fell to her knees.

A familiar energy rippled across Artemus's skin.

Otis appeared beside him and dropped a shimmering barrier around Drake and Serena. The seraph's third eye and the four-pointed star on his right hand blazed with the white light of Heaven as he frowned at the dark angel.

"I didn't—that wasn't—" Drake stammered incoherently while he stemmed the blood pulsing out of Serena's wound with his hands.

"I know." A gentle smile curved her lips. She lifted crimson-stained fingers to Drake's cheek, her eyes roaming his features with hungry tenderness. "Will you kiss me?"

Drake choked on a breath. Tears fell from his eyes as he leaned down and took the super soldier's mouth fiercely.

Serena returned the kiss just as passionately.

"I love you," she whispered against his lips.

Her hand gradually went limp before falling from Drake's face, leaving red trails on his flesh. Her eyes fluttered closed and her body sagged in his hold.

Drake went deathly still. "Serena?"

A sob left Callie in the shocked silence.

Drake's face crunched up. He threw his head back and screamed, the agonizing sound tearing through their minds and wrenching their hearts asunder.

CHAPTER THIRTY-ONE

DANIEL'S KNUCKLES WHITENED BY HIS SIDES AS HE PACED the floor of Persephone's bedroom, his gaze glued to the hands of the man who was tending to her.

The Aesculapian snake mark on Conrad Greene's left forearm shimmered faintly while he poured his healing powers into Persephone's broken body.

Daniel could feel a divine energy not dissimilar to his and the other Guardians' coursing through the Immortal. In fact, it was identical to the one he'd sensed from Alexa King, the Immortal who had crossed their path a few months back and who had helped him and the others battle Paimon.

He knew now that the Immortals had been gifted Uriel's essence. Though Solomon had been deliberately vague about the circumstances under which the archangel had bestowed his powers upon the humans who would give rise to the Immortal race several thousand years past.

Greene had turned up shortly after the battle in the Sistine Chapel had ended, as if brought there by the hands of Fate itself. The fact that Archbishop Holmes and Persephone's attendants had given in to his demands and followed his orders without so much as a protest told Daniel the man had some kind of history with the Vatican and with Persephone. It was also clear that Greene was used to taking charge in a crisis.

"That should do it."

Daniel startled. Greene had lifted his hands from Persephone's stomach.

Relief flooded Daniel. The color was slowly returning to Persephone's cheeks.

"Is she—" he paused and swallowed, "—is she going to be okay?"

"Yes. She's just sleeping." Greene rose from the bed. "She should be right as rain after a couple of days."

"Will there be any lasting damage from Samyaza's sword?" Daniel hesitated. "The Nephil who injured Smokey left a poison inside his body through his blade."

Greene shook his head. "I didn't detect anything like that in Persephone's wound." He turned and headed for the door. "Now, if you'll excuse me, I'll go see to my other patients."

"Wait." Daniel glanced at Persephone. "I'll come with you. She'll pop a fuse if she wakes up and sees me wearing a tread in the carpet."

Greene smiled faintly.

They exited the heavily-guarded chamber and crossed the corridor to another room. An irate voice sounded as they entered.

"Look, I'm telling you I'm fine," Serena grumbled.

"No, you're not!" Nate glared at her as she attempted to sit up. He pushed her back down on the bed by the shoulders. "Your heart stopped beating, damn it!"

"You sure are lively for a chick who died an hour ago,"

Haruki told Serena acerbically. A grimace twisted his face. "Ouch!"

"Stop being a baby," Leah murmured, dabbing at the cut on Haruki's chest with some antiseptic.

"Listen to Nate," Callie admonished Serena.

Greene scowled. "I thought I told you guys to stay put until I could heal you."

Guilt danced across the Guardians' and super soldiers' faces.

Callie's hopeful gaze swung between Greene and Daniel. "How's Persephone?"

"She's gonna be fine," Greene replied gruffly.

The occupants of the room visibly brightened.

"Unlike you guys, she'll do as she's told," Greene added, crossing the room.

Nate frowned at Serena. "Yeah, tell her she needs to rest too, doc."

"I told you, I'm not a doctor," Greene grumbled. "A doctor would have jabbed your stubborn asses with a strong sedative to knock some sense into you."

"I think we've upset him," Haruki told the others.

Greene narrowed his eyes at Serena. "The only reason you're alive is because *she*," he cocked a thumb at Leah, "stabbed a lightning bolt through your heart and put your nanorobots in stasis."

Leah shrugged. "To be fair, it was Solomon's idea."

Jacob stirred where he sat next to Callie, shoulders drooping and knees against his chest. The boy still hadn't recovered from what had happened in the Sistine Chapel.

Daniel swallowed a sigh. *Drake did try to kill him too, after all.*

The anger he'd borne toward Drake had faded as rapidly as it had appeared. Daniel could not blame the man. Not when it was clear he had not been in control of his actions and after seeing him break down when he'd realized what he'd inadvertently done to Serena.

Drake's only sin was that Samyaza had sired him—another thing he'd had no power over.

"Well, I'm fine now," Serena said defiantly.

"No, you're not," Greene retorted. "I only had time to partly heal you before I had to attend to Persephone. Now, let me finish the job."

The super soldier opened her mouth to voice another protest, saw the look on Nate's face, and capitulated. Greene tended to her and Nate's injuries before eyeing the Guardians.

"Alright, who's next?"

Callie, Haruki, and Leah exchanged surprised glances.

"Wait. You can heal us too?" Callie said dubiously.

"I didn't come to Rome for my health," Greene said irritably.

Daniel hovered anxiously while Greene ministered to the divine beasts' hosts.

"Wow." Haruki climbed off the bed a short while later and twisted sideways before trailing light fingers over his chest and flank. "I feel as good as new."

The wounds he'd sustained in the past day were gone, the skin over the areas unblemished.

Leah's eyes glinted as she stared. "Yeah."

"I'd put some clothes on if I were you," Serena told Haruki. "The Lion's looking at you like she's about to pounce."

"I am not!" Leah protested, flushing.

"You're practically drooling," Callie said.

Haruki muttered something under his breath and shrugged into a T-shirt.

Greene blinked when Callie transformed into the Chimera after he'd healed her. She stroked the head of the giant snake sprouting from the base of her spine, her lips curving in a smile.

"Thank you. You even fixed Toby."

The reptile made a contented sound, scales intact once more and eyes shrinking to slits of pleasure at her petting.

Haruki stared. "You named your tail Toby?"

"He's not just a tail." The snakes making up Callie's golden mane writhed and hissed in outcry. "He has a mind and a will of his own." She paused and frowned. "We can hear the Dragon laughing."

Daniel bit back a sigh as the Phoenix and the Lion similarly tittered across their bond. Only Jacob's beast stayed silent. Somehow, Daniel couldn't help but sense that she was observing them with haughty disdain.

Toby spotted the snake birthmark on Greene's forearm and bobbed his head closer. To the Immortal's credit, he didn't flinch when the giant snake tasted his skin inquisitively with a forked tongue.

"I think Toby's in love," Leah said.

"Thanks for the nightmares, kid," Greene muttered.

"I—I have a snake birthmark too," Jacob mumbled in the silence.

The other Guardians studied him with faint surprise. It was the first time he'd admitted to having a mark similar to theirs.

"You do?" Callie said curiously.

"Ah-huh." Jacob hesitated before pulling up the hem of his jeans and revealing the dark tail of a serpent wrapped around his left ankle. "It goes all the way up my leg and body."

Daniel stared. *I wonder who his beast is?*

"That's pretty cool," Greene murmured.

Jacob flushed at the compliment. Callie's snake flicked his tongue at the inky lines on the boy's skin.

He giggled. "That tickles!"

Greene smiled faintly before scanning the chamber. "Where's the pooch? He needs fixing too."

The Guardians exchanged guilty glances.

A defiant huff came from beneath Callie's bed. She pursed her lips and poked her head under the edge.

"I swear, it doesn't hurt one bit, brother. There are no needles involved."

Greene raised an eyebrow. "The hellhound is scared of needles?"

"He nearly mauled the vet at his last check-up," Daniel admitted awkwardly.

Greene frowned, went over to the bed, and crouched on his haunches.

Gasps erupted around the room as he dragged the outraged rabbit out by a hindleg. He ignored Smokey's crimson glare and the growl rumbling from his throat and held him up under the armpits.

"You know, my dog is braver than you," the Immortal told the hellhound in a chiding tone.

Smokey stilled. The red light in his eyes dimmed. He turned his head and sniffed curiously at Greene's hands.

"That's Rocky you're smelling. He's a German Shepherd mongrel and the only Immortal dog in the world."

Greene sat on Callie's bed, plopped the rabbit on his lap, and started examining his injuries.

Jacob's eyes brightened. "You have an Immortal dog?"

He shuffled closer to Greene.

"Indeed I do."

"Does he, like, eat bad guys and stuff?" Haruki asked.

Greene made a face as he drove his healing powers into the rabbit. "I'm afraid not. His special abilities are long naps and chasing his tail."

The Immortal's expression soon turned thoughtful.

"What is it?" Callie said anxiously.

"The Nephil's poison is...interesting."

"Can you get rid of it?" Leah asked, her words imbued with hope. "I mean, you managed to heal us."

Greene hesitated. "Not all of it." He narrowed his eyes. "I suspect Solomon is correct. I've staved off the worst of its effects for now, but killing the source is likely the only solution to the problem."

Greene lifted his hands off Smokey. The rabbit shook himself and bumped the Immortal's chest with his head in a show of affection, his fur and eyes bright and healthy once more.

He hopped onto the floor, scampered over to the door, and scratched at it anxiously.

Sadness clouded Callie's face. "He'll be back soon."

CHAPTER THIRTY-TWO

Artemus hesitated when he turned the corner and spied the iron-plated door at the end of the passage.

Sebastian stopped and looked at him. "Are you okay?"

Artemus swallowed. "No."

Otis laid a hand on Artemus's shoulder. "You need to do this."

Though he had assumed his human form once more, Otis's words retained the musical twang of the seraph's powerful voice.

Artemus faltered before dipping his chin, his heart in turmoil.

He followed Sebastian and Otis as they headed toward the smithy located deep beneath the Apostolic Palace. Few people ever came down here. Most of the current residents of the Holy See had long since forgotten it even existed.

Otis removed the keys Archbishop Holmes had given him and unlocked the heavy, metal door. He crossed a stone landing and started down a flight of stairs.

Artemus's steps slowed as he beheld the ancient

arsenal lining the shadowy space beneath them. His gaze
drifted to the giant hearth at the far end of the cavern. It
was the only one still alight out of the dozens of forges
occupying the Vatican's original foundry.

A sick feeling clenched his belly as he stared at the
grille-covered pits dotting the floor between the furnaces
and water wells.

Drake is in one of those. In the dark. All alone.

Artemus's nails dug into his palms. With everything
that had happened in the last twenty-four hours, he
couldn't blame Drake for surrendering his soul to Samyaza.
There was only one person responsible for the chaos that
had been unleashed inside the Vatican today and that
person was him.

He caught the guarded looks Otis and Sebastian gave
him and hurried his steps. Otis navigated the smithy and
stopped in front of an alcove in the west wall. He pressed a
knot in the rock surface to his left.

The floor of the recess sunk into the ground with faint
puffs of dust. Murky steps appeared below.

Otis's eyes gleamed with a flash of divine light. The
four-pointed star on his right palm started to glow. He led
the way down into the darkness.

Artemus's heart thudded dully in his chest when they
reached the bottom of the stairs. They started along a
narrow, winding corridor dotted with the doors of the
oubliettes that had once held prisoners beneath the
Vatican.

An orange glow flickered in the gloom ahead. It grew
as they approached a prison.

Artemus inhaled shakily at the sight of Drake sitting
on the ground inside, under a flaming torch. There was a

pallet and a blanket on the floor next to him, as well as a tray of food and some books.

Artemus glanced at Otis and Sebastian, gratitude surging through him. "Thank you."

"It was the least we could do," Sebastian murmured.

"Besides, Persephone would want this too," Otis added.

Artemus steeled himself before meeting Drake's forlorn gaze.

"I'm sorry," his twin mumbled for what felt like the thousandth time.

Artemus sighed before sitting cross-legged on the ground in front of the cell. "I know. And I'm sorry too. For what I did to you. It's my fault this happened."

He felt Sebastian and Otis shift behind him.

"That is not strictly true," the Sphinx murmured.

"The ones at fault are Beelzebub and Samyaza," Otis said firmly.

"And I just played right into their hands, didn't I?" Artemus said bitterly. "If it wasn't for me, Samyaza might not have succeeded in taking over Drake's soul."

Drake frowned and straightened his legs. Metal clinked in the gloom.

Artemus's eyes widened. He studied the manacle around his brother's left ankle and frowned at Sebastian and Otis. "Is that strictly necessary? There's enough iron in this place to deaden his inner demon."

"I was the one who asked for it," Drake said.

Surprise shot through Artemus. He stared at his brother.

"I asked them to chain me up," Drake affirmed. "Just as I asked them to put me down here. It's the only place in Rome with enough iron to keep my dark side at bay." A mirthless chuckle left him. "In fact, I'm in two minds about asking Persephone to keep me here forever."

Artemus scowled. "Don't joke about stuff like that! I—I don't know what I'd do if that actually happened!"

A tormented look danced across Drake's face. His expression hardened the next instant. "I would expect you to forget about me and get on with your life, Artemus. You need to face the truth. I cannot be saved."

Drake's words scorched fiery lines through Artemus's soul as they echoed around the oubliette.

"No," Artemus grated out. "I refuse to believe that. There must be a way. There has to be!"

Drake moved with a speed that startled Artemus. He reached through the iron bars holding him prisoner and yanked Artemus close by the front of his shirt.

"*And that's why Samyaza will win!*" he hissed in Artemus's face. "Because you don't know when to give up!"

Artemus's face crumpled. He grabbed Drake's wrist with his hands, his vision blurring.

"You're asking me to let you die!" His voice shook uncontrollably and his breath hitched in his throat as he gazed beseechingly at his brother. "You're the other half of me. The other half of Smokey. How can you ask us to do that? How can you—?!"

Drake tugged him forward and pressed a kiss to his forehead through the iron door, his own tears falling hotly on Artemus's face.

"Because I don't want to hurt you. Any of you. I—"

"Persephone and Serena are both alive!" Artemus protested brokenly. "Greene is healing them as we—"

"It doesn't matter, Artemus. I tried to kill them. And Jacob." Drake swallowed convulsively. "I would have killed all of you had Serena not stopped me."

Artemus trembled in the silence, his heart breaking all over again.

There has to be a way to save him. There has to be!

SOLOMON WATCHED THE CROWDS IN ST. PETER'S SQUARE from where he sat atop one of the bell towers of the Basilica. A pair of shadowy shapes soon dropped out of the sky and landed beside him.

"Hey," Solomon murmured.

Michael flashed a smile at him as he settled in a comfortable position on Solomon's left. "Hey, yourself."

Solomon looked to his right.

"I see he's still as disgustingly cheerful as ever," he told Arael drily.

The Angel of Crows shrugged. "It's a genetic condition."

Solomon smiled.

"What?" Arael murmured.

"The goth look suits you."

Arael looked down at his outfit. "Thanks."

"Are you guys ignoring me?" Michael whined.

"No, you big wuss," Solomon said with a sigh. "By the way, I think your son would appreciate a visit from his father."

Michael made a face. "He yelled at me the last time I dropped by."

"That's because you wanted to scrub his back in the shower," Arael said.

"What's wrong with spending some quality time with my kid?" Michael frowned. "Will the two of you stop looking at me like I'm some kind of pervert?"

Solomon shook his head. "You haven't changed. I still don't get how you led an army against Satanael. You're the most laidback of all Heaven's archangels."

"It's because I'm insanely strong," Michael said smugly.

"So are rocks and they are less dense than you."

A comfortable silence descended between them.

"I've missed this," Michael said.

"What, the bickering?" Solomon said.

"Talking to you." Michael turned a solemn gaze on the demon. "I miss all of you. We all do."

Solomon clenched his hands. He knew what the archangel meant.

Despite the fact that they were technically enemies, they had once all been brothers.

"You know I should be driving a sword through your heart right now, right?" Michael said conversationally.

"Your sword is with Artemus," Solomon said, unfazed.

"There are other swords," Michael protested.

Arael rolled his eyes. They lapsed into silence.

"Are you ready for what's coming?" Michael finally said, his tone serious.

Solomon raised his head to the sky. "Not really."

"You're afraid to die?"

"No." A sad smile tilted Solomon's mouth. "I'm afraid to leave him."

"You mean Jacob?"

"Yes."

"He will be alright," Arael said. "He has Artemus and the divine beasts."

"Still, he's my son."

Michael and Arael gazed at him and said nothing.

"It's funny, isn't it?" Solomon said quietly. "All this time, we have always thought of humanity as one of His weakest creations. They are fragile, their life spans ephemeral compared to ours, their bodies frail, and their minds easy to corrupt. Yet, they can make our hearts soar with the most incredible happiness and our souls cry with the darkest despair. Maybe that's why He created them. To teach us a lesson in humility."

"It would be arrogant to presume mankind was created for us," Michael said. "We know not the reasons behind His designs. But one thing I am certain of, above all."

"What is that?" Solomon said after a short silence.

"Despite the challenges He continues to cast in our path, He truly wishes for our happiness and salvation."

CHAPTER THIRTY-THREE

ARTEMUS DRAGGED HIS FEET AS HE HEADED BACK UP into the Apostolic Palace with Sebastian and Otis, his heart and mind still heavy.

"Did you find anything else concerning your symbols while I was gone?" Sebastian asked Otis where they strolled a short distance ahead of him.

"Yes. I came across a brief mention of the Seal of God in a two-thousand-year-old manuscript unearthed in Egypt by the Immortals. It was written by a saint who'd had several visions of the Apocalypse."

"And?"

Otis frowned. "Apparently, the full manifestation of the Seal involves two four-pointed stars on the hands of the seraph who wields the power to stop and destroy Hell's gates, as well as the third eye."

Sebastian stared. "But you only have one four-pointed star."

"I know." Otis looked at his left palm. "Which means the other one has yet to manifest itself."

Artemus's ears pricked up at that. He caught up with

them, his curiosity piqued. "Why the delay? Shouldn't all your powers have revealed themselves by now?"

Otis hesitated. "I don't know. But there has to be a reason behind it."

"Right place, right time." Sebastian shrugged at Artemus and Otis's expressions. "I am just saying it is likely to happen when it is—" He stopped and narrowed his eyes at Artemus. "What's wrong?"

Artemus had rocked to a standstill in the middle of the palace courtyard. The hairs rose on his arms. His gaze gravitated to a third-story window on the southwest facade.

He'd just sensed something. Something eerily familiar.

Yet, however much he tried to focus on it, it remained a distant, indecipherable whisper fluttering at the edges of his consciousness, like waves sighing on a deserted beach.

Otis and Sebastian followed his stare.

"What is it?" the seraph murmured.

"I—" Artemus paused. The feeling had gone. He shook his head, puzzled. "I don't know."

CONRAD ENTERED THE OFFICE AND CLOSED THE DOOR behind him. The woman standing behind the curtains of the window facing the courtyard of the Apostolic Palace glanced over her shoulder at him.

Conrad joined her and watched three men disappear under an arched doorway on the first floor.

"You sure you don't want to say hi?"

She hesitated before shaking her head, her chestnut locks dancing around her face. "It isn't time."

She bit her lip. Conrad sighed. He could see the

longing darkening her blue eyes. He wrapped an arm around her shoulders and gave them a light squeeze.

She inhaled shakily before dropping her head on his shoulder. "Is love supposed to be this painful?"

"I'm the last person you should be asking that question," Conrad said with a dry smile. "My romantic history isn't exactly one others should aspire to emulate."

"I think your and Aunt Laura's love affair is wonderful."

Conrad rolled his eyes. "Has Mila been stuffing your head with angsty romance novels again?"

The woman smiled. "No. Caspian found her manuscripts and threatened to make them public if she didn't help him with his studies."

Conrad sighed again. "That kid is a menace. Between him and Will, I don't know who's worse."

The woman chuckled.

~

LIGHT RIPPLED ACROSS PERSEPHONE'S INNER VISION IN warm, hazy waves. She sighed and slowly blinked her eyes open. The canopy of her bed came into focus above her.

Memory returned in a rush of images and sounds. She gasped and sat up.

"Take it easy," someone said lightly.

Persephone groaned. Her body felt heavy and achy, as if she'd run a marathon. She scanned the room and found the man who'd spoken.

Michael sat in a red leather Chesterfield chair by the fireplace, a book in hand. He turned a page, raised his head, and met her gaze.

"I know Uriel's child has healed you, but you're not exactly a spring chicken," he said wryly.

"You're the last person I want to hear that from."

Persephone swung her legs over the edge of the bed and sat still for a moment, a wave of dizziness washing over her.

"I told you," Michael said smugly.

Persephone ignored him.

"What happened?" she mumbled once she could speak.

"Samyaza took over Drake's soul and tried to kill you." Michael shrugged. "I reckon he thought getting rid of you would make a perfect opening salvo for the Apocalypse."

Persephone pulled a face. "I'm flattered." She frowned at the sight of the darkness gathered outside the windows of her bedroom. "How long was I out for?"

"A day. It's just gone ten o'clock."

Disquiet stirred inside Persephone. She rose from the bed, shrugged into her dressing gown, and came over to the fire. A tea set appeared on the coffee table as she sank into the armchair opposite Michael.

The archangel poured their drinks and passed her a porcelain cup.

"Thank you." She took a sip of hot tea and studied him over the rim of the cup. "What else happened?"

Michael gave her an abridged version of what had transpired in the Sistine Chapel earlier that day, his tone steady. Persephone's heart sank as she absorbed it all.

"Serena and the other Guardians are okay?"

Michael dipped his chin. "Yes. Since we know they will need all their strength for what is to come, Uriel's child intervened."

Persephone digested this statement with a frown. "I thought Uriel and the Immortals were specifically instructed not to interfere with Artemus and the Guardians."

A faint smile curved Michael's lips. "Technically, they haven't. Their actions won't change Artemus and Drake's fates. They only...assisted their future allies."

"And you?"

Michael raised an eyebrow.

"You could stop all this, if you wanted to," Persephone said quietly. "You could stop this Apocalypse before it can even begin. And the one destined to take place at the End of Days."

Michael looked down into his cup. "You think too highly of my abilities."

"You drove Satanael and his brethren to Hell once." Persephone frowned. "You can do it again."

"Much has changed since that time, in Heaven and on Earth." Michael's eyes gleamed with a flash of gold as he raised his head and met Persephone's gaze. "Besides, I cannot deny them their chance of salvation."

Persephone stared at the archangel, puzzled. "Who?"

Michael's expression turned sad. "The End of Days isn't just about mankind's redemption, Persephone. It is also about the absolution of my fallen brothers."

CHAPTER THIRTY-FOUR

SERENA TURNED ON THE TAP, FILLED THE SINK, AND splashed cold water on her face. She looked in the mirror and grimaced. Though Greene had healed her wounds, nothing could erase the haunted look in her eyes.

She'd masked her anguish in front of the others as best she could all day. Only Nate had seen behind her facade. Like him, she couldn't stop reliving what had happened in the Sistine Chapel that morning.

That Samyaza would be successful in taking control of Drake's soul was something all of them had dreaded for a while. However much Drake fought the power of the one who had sired him. However strong the prison Theia had helped build inside his body. All of it had been destined to fail.

All they had achieved in their battles with Ba'al to date was to delay the inevitable. Drake's fall to Hell was fated. And nothing she or Artemus and the others did could stop it.

She studied her reflection for a moment longer before drying her face and heading back into the chamber Persephone had assigned her and the Guardians. Nate had stayed back to wait for her while the others went ahead to get some food. He had a visitor.

Serena's heart stuttered at the sight of the man standing next to the window. "Father?!"

Ivan Vlašic turned and smiled at her gently. "Hello, Serena."

"What—?" She stopped and glanced at a flushed Nate, not sure what to make of the Immortal's sudden appearance at the Vatican. "What are you doing here?!"

"Conrad told me what happened." The former head of the Order of Crovir Hunters and leader of the Crovir First Council rubbed the back of his neck awkwardly. "I know you and Nate don't want to have anything to do with me, but I was too worried to—"

Serena crossed the room and hugged the Immortal fiercely, overcome with emotion. Vlašic rocked back on his heels. He froze for a moment before wrapping his arms around her and returning her embrace just as fervently.

Serena shuddered and buried her face in the Immortal's chest. His scent was as warm and as comforting as she remembered it.

"I've missed you." She raised her chin and gazed miserably at the man who had helped rescue her and hundreds of super soldier children all those years ago, in Greenland. "I'm sorry. I'm sorry we ran away from home. I didn't know what to do! You were—"

"Hush now." Vlašic's hand found the back of her head and pressed her face against his chest once more. "I know why you left." He sighed. "And even though it pained me, I knew I had to let you go."

"Because of your work?" Serena murmured.

"No."

Vlašic stepped back slightly and extended an arm to Nate. The giant super soldier hesitated before joining them, his throat working convulsively.

Vlašic clasped them both to his chest. "I didn't let you go because of my work." He pressed a kiss to their foreheads. "The moment I took your hands in Greenland was one of the scariest and happiest of my life. I knew while I waited for death on that icy ridge and held the three of you in my arms that if we were to survive that day, you would be mine to cherish and watch over." A gentle smile stretched his lips and his eyes gleamed with affection. "You were a gift I never expected and didn't deserve. And I will treasure the time we had together forever more."

Nate sniffed. Serena's vision blurred.

Vlašic's next words made her stomach twist with fresh guilt. Nate stiffened with remorse.

"To say I nearly lost my mind with worry when I found out you'd left the estate would be an understatement. I was going crazy trying to find you. I spent the entire day and night pacing the mansion, hoping and praying to hear word of your whereabouts. The next morning, someone came to me. Someone you both know, actually. She told me something extraordinary. Something that shocked and awed me in equal measure."

Serena and Nate exchanged a startled glance before staring at their father.

"This, right here." Vlašic indicated the room around them and what was visible of the Vatican through the window. "This is where you are meant to be. With them. That's why I had to let you go."

Serena's pulse spiked. "Wait. Do you mean Artemus and—"

"Yes. You are part of their fate." Vlašic caressed their

cheeks gently. "What they've been through? The Apocalypse they are trying to prevent? You were always destined to be at their side. Not just as accidental associates, but as fully participating actors in their fight against Ba'al." Their father's expression slowly hardened as he observed them. "So, stay strong, my children. Believe in yourselves and the ones you are bonded to. Because your hardest battles are still to come."

"Do you want to go for a walk?" Solomon said.

Jacob put his spoon down and stared at him before nodding and climbing down from his chair.

"We'll catch up with you guys later," the demon told Artemus and the other Guardians, who were having seconds.

Greene had advised them to eat plenty to recover from their injuries and the effects of his healing. The hellhound was already demolishing his third roast chicken where he crouched under the table, oblivious to the anxious stares of the Apostolic Palace cooks peeking out at him from the kitchen.

"Don't go too far," Artemus said.

Jacob clasped Solomon's hand as they headed out of the dining hall. Solomon smiled at him and squeezed his fingers lightly, his heart growing heavy.

A cool breeze danced across the demon when he escorted Jacob out onto the rooftop of the Apostolic Palace a moment later. Jacob's eyes widened. He let go of Solomon's hand and rushed up a flight of steps to a parapet.

"It's so pretty!"

Solomon joined him and gazed out over the brightly lit Basilica and Rome beyond. The cupola of the church was covered with scaffolding, the renovation work addressing the damage it had sustained from the Guardians' battle with Paimon a few months ago still in progress.

"That it is."

He saw Jacob shiver, removed his long coat, and dropped it on the boy's shoulders.

Jacob made a face. "It's too big for me, Father."

"You'll soon grow into it."

Jacob stilled at his words. He turned his back to the beautiful views of the city and looked up anxiously at the demon.

"What does that mean?" The boy swallowed. "Are you —are you leaving?"

Solomon dropped down on his haunches until he was eye level with Jacob.

"Yes," he said quietly.

Jacob's gaze darkened. His lower lip wobbled. "I don't want that." He launched himself at Solomon and sent him tumbling back onto the ground. "I don't want you to go anywhere! I want you to stay with me, forever!"

Solomon swallowed and wrapped his arms around the boy. Although he'd prepared for this moment for years, he hadn't foreseen how agonizing it would be or how much his dark heart would ache at the prospect of parting with the child he had watched over for so long.

"Even when I am gone," he whispered into Jacob's hair, "even when I have left this world, I will still be with you." He pulled back slightly and pressed a hand to Jacob's chest. "Right here."

Hot tears fell from the boy's eyes and dripped onto the demon's knuckles.

"So, you need to be strong, Jacob." Solomon pressed a tender kiss to the child's forehead, his own breath choking in his throat. "For me. For them."

Jacob shuddered in his embrace. He stayed quiet for the longest time.

"Okay," he finally mumbled. "I will do it for you, Father. I will be strong. For you."

Solomon closed his eyes and inhaled the achingly familiar scent of the boy he considered his son. Something in the sky drew his gaze. He tensed.

Jacob pulled away slightly and wiped his eyes with the back of his hand. "What is it?"

"The eclipse." Dread stirred inside Solomon. Though he couldn't see the sun right now, he could sense what was happening. "It will soon end."

Horror filled Jacob's face. "The gate! It's going to—"

Solomon nodded. "Yes."

A sudden stillness fell around them.

Solomon frowned and climbed to his feet. He looked out over Rome. He couldn't hear the sound of traffic coming from St. Peter's Square or the city. It was as if someone had muted the world.

Jacob's hand found his. Surprise shot through Solomon. The child's skin was hot to the touch.

"*It is starting,*" the boy's host said through his mouth.

A violent tremor shook the ground beneath their feet.

CHAPTER THIRTY-FIVE

MILTON SMILED WHERE HE STOOD IN THE SHADOW OF the statue of Michael, atop the roof of the Castel Sant'Angelo. Distant screams echoed across Rome as the holy city shuddered and trembled from a series of powerful earthquakes. The chaos escalated as lights started to go out in vast swathes across the capital, the power grid faltering and failing under the violent seismic activity. Milton's demonic heart fluttered with excitement as terror thickened the air.

He liked nothing more than hearing humans cry in fear.

The demon looked along the Tiber River and the Via della Conciliazione to the towering bastions of the Holy See. The scaffolding around the Basilica started to come apart even as he watched. His grin widened.

"Hey! You there! What are you doing up here?!"

Milton looked over his shoulder. Two guards were coming up the steps of the rooftop terrace, their hands on the pistols strapped to their waists.

"Oh my." The demon turned and raised his arms, his tone mild. "I'm sorry, officers. I appear to be lost."

The two men stopped and glanced at one another before studying Milton warily, likely wondering how he'd gotten past them.

"You shouldn't be here, sir," the first guard said gruffly while the other one looked out anxiously over the city. "Please, come with us."

Milton didn't move.

The guard who'd spoken frowned. "I said, come with—"

He stopped and gasped.

His companion stared with wide eyes at the bloodied claws that had ripped through the man's back and out his chest. An incoherent mumble fell from the second guard's lips. It turned into a bellow of horror and pain as the demons who'd appeared out of the rift behind him pounced.

Milton ignored the grisly sounds of the two men being ripped to pieces and eaten alive and turned to survey the landscape once more. He shifted to his demon form, called upon the dark powers swirling through his corrupt soul, and focused them on the army of Nephilim converging on Rome from where they'd been lying in wait, deep beneath the ground.

"*Rise, my children!*"

The tremors shaking the city intensified. A giant crack appeared at the mouth of the bridge opposite the castle. The marble statues spanning its length toppled into the turbulent waters as it collapsed, their fall slow and graceful. Violent waves surged through the middle of the river and crashed over the steep embankment.

The fissure widened and snaked along the Via della Conciliazione toward St. Peter's Square.

"S HIT!"

Artemus jumped up from the table and staggered across the unsteady floor with the others. The overhead lights flickered and went out as they stumbled out of the dining hall and into the corridor overlooking the court-yard. They gazed out over a rooftop toward St. Peter's Square and Rome, panicked shouts ringing through the palace around them.

Darkness was falling rapidly across the capital.

Artemus's heart raced with trepidation as he watched the lights blink out. He couldn't help but feel the gathering night was some kind of omen.

A frown marred Sebastian's brow. "This does not feel like a normal earthquake."

"What do you mean?" Leah asked.

Footsteps sounded on their left. Serena and Nate appeared out of the shadows at a dead run.

"Is this—?" Artemus started.

"Yes! It's the Nephilim!" Serena dipped her chin sharply. "I just checked the Immortals' seismic data on the way here. These tremors bear all the hallmarks of the ones associated with the Nephilim!"

Dread twisted Artemus's belly as the super soldier confirmed his worst fears. "Where's the epicenter?"

"There is no one epicenter," Serena said grimly. "These quakes are happening across the entire city."

A breach split the wall next to them. Chandeliers and

windows exploded along the passage, peppering them with glittering, crystal and glass shards.

"We need to get everyone out of here and somewhere safe." Artemus scowled and changed into his angel form. "Daniel, go to Persephone! Smokey and I will fetch Drake!"

Smokey shifted into the dark hellhound at the same time the other Guardians transformed.

"No!" someone shouted. "You need to come with me! All of you! *Now!*"

Artemus whirled around, his broadsword in hand.

Archbishop Holmes was lurching up the corridor toward them, his face pale. He clung to the shuddering walls, blood coursing down his left temple from a fresh cut.

Artemus landed next to the man and guided him to their group. "What do you mean?"

"The gates! The ones belonging to the Chimera and the Dragon," Holmes said shakily. "The barriers guarding them are coming apart! Persephone and Otis are already there!"

Callie and Haruki froze at the archbishop's words.

"Wait!" Sebastian stared at Holmes, aghast. "You mean the gates of Hell are here? In the Vatican itself?!"

Holmes swallowed and nodded unflinchingly in the face of their accusing stares.

"It was the safest place to keep them, what with the divine barrier surrounding the Holy See," he explained hurriedly. "The Immortals created a wall around the iron dungeon where we've been studying them, deep underground. Those barriers are breaking down. If we don't secure the gates, Ba'al could open them and unleash Hell right beneath the Vatican!"

"Damn it!" Artemus cursed.

He faltered, torn between his urge to rescue his brother and the necessity to follow Holmes. The decision was taken out of his hands a second later.

A draft washed across them as Solomon descended from the rooftop of the palace in his demon form, his black wings stark against the starlit skies and Jacob held securely in his embrace. He flew through a broken window and deposited the young Guardian amidst them.

His crimson gaze found Artemus. "We have to go to those gates. Now!"

Artemus clenched his jaw. His every instinct was screaming at him to go to Drake. Yet, he could not deny the urgency in Solomon's voice.

Sebastian and Daniel joined him as he took flight and joined the demon.

"Go! We'll be right behind you!" Holmes shouted.

Solomon led the way into the night, his black wings sweeping the air with powerful beats. A familiar energy rippled across Artemus's skin as they soared past the Basilica. Though he couldn't see them, he sensed Solomon's demons close by.

They were halfway across the Vatican gardens when he realized where they were headed.

"The monastery?" Artemus stared at the dilapidated building looming at them from a shallow dip in the land. "That's where the gates are?!"

"Yes. Now that the barriers surrounding them are falling, I can sense them deep beneath the ground." Solomon frowned. "We must hurry!"

A wave of bittersweet memories rushed through Artemus as they closed in on the abandoned structure. It was where he and Drake had met their mothers a few months back.

They'd just landed in the garden fronting the building when a shape dropped from the sky and alighted before them.

"You're gonna need your blade." Michael folded his wings and closed the distance to Artemus. "Go to the gates," he instructed Solomon and Daniel curtly. "There's a trapdoor in the basement." He turned to Sebastian. "Please, stay."

Surprise danced across the Sphinx's face. He dipped his chin wordlessly.

Solomon and Daniel hesitated before heading inside the building, their troubled gazes moving between Michael and Artemus before they melted into the gloom, the Phoenix's flames leaving an orange afterglow in the night.

"What are you talking about?" Artemus stared at his father. "I already have your sword."

"I mean the other blade. The one you made for Karl."

Artemus blinked. Understanding flared inside him. He frowned at his father and wondered how much of what was happening had already been foretold.

"It's not set in stone, son."

Artemus's stomach lurched. In that moment, he sensed Michael had read his mind.

Something that looked like sadness darkened the archangel's crystal-blue gaze. He laid a hand on Artemus's shoulder.

"There is always hope, Artemus," he said quietly. "As long as you believe. As long as you don't give up. There will *always* be hope."

Artemus startled as the archangel hugged him before

vanishing into the night. He gazed blindly at his father's disappearing form.

It was the first time he'd felt Michael's embrace. It had been as warm and as loving as his and Drake's mothers' had been.

"Artemus?" Sebastian murmured.

Artemus took a shuddering breath, Michael's mystifying words still ringing in his ears. He knew what he had to do for now.

"Can you rift us to Chicago?"

CHAPTER THIRTY-SIX

TREPIDATION CHURNED PERSEPHONE'S BLOOD AS SHE studied the giant, iron cage enclosing the stone arch and the gilded mirror in the center of the dungeon from where she stood in one of the recessed observation bays in the rock wall.

The steel-and-electromagnetic-reinforced concrete barrier the Immortals had erected around the prison had just collapsed. Only the iron bars remained, although even those were starting to crack, the metal warping and bending under the effect of the tremors rippling across Rome.

Persephone was conscious the phenomenon the capital was currently witnessing was not natural. She could feel the corruption soaking the air and the steadily falling pressure that heralded the impending appearance of demons. So could the hundreds of Vatican agents crowding the floor of the dungeon, their faces resolute and their weapons aimed steadily at the two gates despite the trembling ground beneath their feet.

She suspected the main reason they showed no fear

was the seraph who hovered in the air before them, his white wings still and his expression calm beneath his blazing third eye.

Otis and the Vatican agents would stand their ground, whatever happened. Still, they would not be enough to stop the forces of Hell if Satanael were to appear with his army. Persephone frowned.

Where in blazes is Holmes?! We could really do with Artemus and the Guardians right now!

Her silent prayers were partly answered when the metal doors behind her slid open. Solomon and Daniel rushed inside the bay.

Persephone glanced over their shoulders. "Where's Artemus?"

"On his way." Daniel crossed the floor and embraced Persephone. "Are you okay?!"

Relief surged through Persephone as the Phoenix's flames engulfed her in a warm hold. "Yes."

Solomon's crimson gaze shifted to the glass wall and the iron prison beyond. "The Nephilim are close."

Persephone's anxiety skyrocketed at his words.

"Wait," she mumbled. "Do you mean to say that these earthquakes are the work of—?"

A muffled shout drew their attention to the dungeon. Persephone inhaled sharply.

A giant crack was splitting the east wall of the cavern.

She turned and pressed a hand against the window, her heart slamming against her ribs. "*No!*"

"Watch out!"

Daniel yanked Persephone back and folded his wings around her just as the glass exploded into a thousand glistening pieces.

The rumbles tearing through the dungeon washed over

them with a thunderous roar as the fissure snaked across the floor and under the iron bars, cleaving the cavern in half.

A sudden stillness fell around them.

Persephone's pulse stuttered as the silence rang in her ears. Her breath misted in front of her mouth with her next exhale. The pressure inside the observation bay plummeted, along with the ambient temperature.

"Here they come," Solomon said grimly.

A pale rift tore open beside him. The demon reached inside with a clawed hand and withdrew a pale, serrated broadsword brimming with divine flames.

The floor of the prison started to cave into a widening abyss.

Dozens of gray, winged figures shot up from the chasm.

The snakes making up Callie's mane hissed in alarm as pale sigils exploded along the Scepter of Gabriel. She stiffened and stared at the weapon where it lay on her lap.

It was growing warm in her grip.

Leah drew a sharp breath. "Haruki?!"

The Dragon frowned as runes materialized on his holy blade. Horror widened Jacob's eyes where he huddled between him and Callie.

Nate scowled at them over his shoulder before flooring the gas. The van shot down the tunnel, its headlights carving the inky darkness. Dust motes spiraled in the bright beams as the passage shook violently around them, sending dirt drifting down in a fine shower.

Holmes had brought them to a network of secret passages that ran deep beneath the Holy See. Heavily used during the World Wars, the tunnels had fallen into disrepair over the latter half of the previous century. Persephone had ordered their restoration and further expanded them for use by the organization fighting Ba'al when she had become Head of Church.

Haruki met Callie's troubled gaze above Jacob's head, a muscle jumping in his jawline. "Our gates. They're about to open."

Callie bit her lip. She knew he was feeling the same rising dread she was experiencing. It was as if a dark hole were opening inside her mind and soul, drawing her inexorably in. The whine of the engine and the roar of tremors echoed loudly in her ears as she fisted her hands in frustration.

"I'm afraid I have more bad news!" Serena said next to Nate, her fingers flying across the touchscreen of her smartband. "Remember how I said there was no epicenter to these quakes?"

"Yeah?" Haruki said tensely.

"There is now!" Serena frowned as she stared through the windshield. "You're not gonna believe this, but all the earthquakes are converging on a single location."

"Where?" Leah asked worriedly.

"Up ahead. Exactly where we're headed."

The van lurched. Nate swore and spun the steering wheel to the right. The vehicle shot off a low, jagged outcrop that had appeared out of nowhere and landed on the tunnel floor with a violent judder.

"What was that?!" Holmes shouted.

Serena stared unblinkingly to her left as the van accelerated once more. "You guys might want to look out the window."

Callie gazed into the gloom. Her eyes widened, the Chimera's vision piercing the darkness.

A large fissure was racing along the floor of the tunnel next to them, matching their speed.

Haruki peered over Jacob's head. "Shit."

Smokey growled where he occupied the rear footwells. Callie scowled. She could sense Daniel across their bond. The Phoenix was roaring in anger somewhere up ahead.

"Archbishop Holmes, what's at the end of this passage?" Haruki said stiffly.

He'd followed the path of the crack with his gaze and was staring into the shadows ahead, his pupils narrowing to vertical, orange slits that enhanced his vision ten-fold.

"A pair of giant, steel doors. They lead into the dungeon where the gates are being kept. We used this tunnel to bring them down here."

Haruki clenched his jaw. "Those doors are coming apart!"

A distant detonation ripped the air in the wake of his words. Fire bloomed in the darkness some three hundred feet in front of them. The flames outlined the enormous, metal panels being wrenched off their hinges.

"Everyone, brace!" Serena slammed her hands against the roof of the vehicle and the dashboard. She glanced wildly at Nate. "Do it!"

"Hang on!"

Nate slammed on the brakes and sent the van careening on its axis, his knuckles whitening on the steering wheel.

The world spun dizzyingly around Callie as they twisted and slid across the tunnel, the vehicle tilting precariously on its suspension as it went through several stomach-lurching revolutions. Her heart thundered against her breastbone when they screeched to a stop sideways across the passage seconds later.

The steel doors at the end of the tunnel finally tore from the walls and shot toward them on a river of roaring flames.

"Oh God!" Holmes mumbled.

Callie cursed.

There was no way they could avoid the explosion or the metal panels about to plow into them.

A sibilant voice rose beside her. *"If we cannot escape them, we have to carve a path through them."*

Callie turned and stared at Jacob. The boy's eyes glowed gold, his gaze alight with the presence of his beast.

"How?!"

Jacob glanced at the Scepter of Gabriel. *"That is not a matchstick you are wielding, Chimera."*

Callie drew a sharp breath. She yanked the vehicle door open and leapt out into the tunnel. "Leah!"

Leah stepped out beside her, her spear in hand and understanding dawning on her face.

"Together," Callie said, her pulse racing. "We need to blast them apart!"

Sparks fizzed through the air as the Nemean Lion gathered her power. Even this far underground, Callie tasted the scent of lightning gathering around them. Static enveloped the Spear of Ramiel.

"Everyone else, behind the van!" Haruki barked.

Callie took a deep breath. Heat bloomed inside her. Power flooded her veins and limbs, thickening her muscles. She drew her arm back and threw the scepter with a mighty roar at the same time Leah's lightning-wreathed spear left her hand.

The two weapons whined along the tunnel before

twisting around one another in a bright burst of golden light, their divine powers resonating as they accelerated.

Haruki grabbed Callie and Leah and yanked them under the cover of the van. "Get down!"

Callie glanced over her shoulder in time to see the scepter and the spear blow the steel doors into pieces. The resulting shockwave carved a ten-foot-wide hole through the blaze racing toward them. Then she was on the ground with the others, Smokey and Jacob in her arms and Haruki crouched protectively above all of them, his eyes glowing with power and his heat-resistant scales brightening as the fire roared inexorably closer.

CHAPTER THIRTY-SEVEN

DRAKE CURSED AS ROCKS PELTED DOWN AROUND HIM. The tremors rocking the oubliette were getting worse.

Great! At this rate, I'm going to be stuck down here under a pile of rubble!

He scowled and tugged on the chain holding him to the wall.

"Well, shit," he muttered under his breath. "They really knew how to make these last, huh?"

He could feel Samyaza's fury and vexation deep within him. The demon was trying to take over his soul but couldn't because of the metal around them.

"I would swallow a bar of iron if it meant keeping you quiet, asshole."

He grinned as the devil roared inside him.

A powerful judder made the ceiling groan. Drake's eyes widened as a web of cracks tore across the bare rockface. He dropped onto one knee and raised his left arm defensively as his prison collapsed.

Debris slammed and clanged heavily against metal, raising clouds of dust and dirt.

Drake blinked.

His stomach dropped when he realized he'd instinctively changed into his angel form, his watch transforming into his shield to protect him from the brunt of the wreckage.

Drake's heart raced as he steeled himself against Samyaza's possession, knowing the demon would take over his soul within seconds. But the devil stayed strangely quiet where he lurked inside him.

What the——? Why isn't he——?!

A chunk of stone clattered against his armor and fell by his feet.

Something clinked in the gloom. Drake's gaze dropped to the iron manacle around his left ankle. The shackle had broken from its anchor and was secured snugly to his leg.

SPARKS ERUPTED AS SOLOMON BLOCKED A STRIKE FROM A Nephil, the flames on his sword roaring brightly against the monster's pale blade. A grunt left him when another Nephil punched him in the flank and thigh with an armored fist, breaking his skin.

Gunshots echoed across the dungeon as the Vatican agents valiantly fought the army of gray figures swarming them. Many lay bloodied and dead, their bullets futile against their all too powerful enemy.

Solomon's demons fought alongside them, silent and bright-eyed, their will as strong as his own. A fresh wave of determination surged through him as he felt the bond that connected him to the fallen brethren he commanded strengthen. He bared his teeth and pushed back against the Nephil.

Violent flashes lit the air out of the corner of his eye.

Floating in the middle of the cavern, seemingly oblivious to the Nephilim battering away at the shimmering barrier surrounding him, the seraph held the gates of Hell at bay, the symbols on his palms blazing and a faint frown enveloping his third eye as he concentrated on controlling the throbbing shadows threatening to engulf the arch and the mirror.

An explosion rocked the dungeon, the shockwave clapping against the demon's eardrums. Fire bloomed at the mouth of a tunnel in the east face of the cave.

One of the Vatican agents' bullets had pierced a fuel line.

Daniel dove down from where he'd been battling two Nephilim and raised a giant, fiery wall to shield the agents in the path of the flames.

Something resonated with Solomon as he resumed his deadly fight against the monsters surrounding him. He turned and stared beyond Daniel's conflagration to the tunnel.

Jacob!

∼

HOLMES MURMURED A PRAYER AS HE STUMBLED OVER THE threshold of the underground passage.

Serena guided the archbishop gently to the ground. "Stay here."

She straightened and gazed in the direction of the fierce battle they could hear on the far side of the fire ahead of them.

Haruki had protected them from the brunt of the

blaze that had scorched the tunnel. Bar some crisp hair-ends, they were all miraculously unharmed.

Callie started up the rock corridor, her scepter brimming with divine energy and her face resolute as she broke into a run. "We must hurry!"

Smokey morphed into his ultimate shape and loped beside her, his eyes glowing with a savage light and a low growl rumbling from his throats. Leah clenched the Spear of Ramiel and headed after them, Haruki matching her speed.

Jacob slowly followed, his face pale with apprehension.

"You gonna be okay, kid?" Serena said as she and Nate fell in step on either side of him.

Jacob hesitated before nodding. "My father is up there. I need to go to him."

Serena tightened her hold on her gun and blade before exchanging a guarded glance with Nate over the boy's head. "I don't think we're a match for those Nephilim."

Nate's mouth tilted up slightly at her words. "Since when has something like that ever stopped us?"

Serena returned his smile. "Since never."

"Serena?" Nate said as they closed in on the battleground.

"Yeah?"

"I'm glad you're my sister."

"And I'm glad you're my brother, Nate."

They steeled themselves and walked out into Hell, their skin and combat suits shimmering with a pale, golden light.

~

"You think you can rift us to the place where the gates are?!" Artemus yelled as they flew through the golden portal.

Sebastian shook his head. "Since I have never been there before, no."

They'd just left the mansion in Chicago.

A circle of darkness grew in the center of the shimmering light ahead. They exited the rift and emerged in the Vatican gardens, the cool night air wrenching the warmth of the heavenly doorway from their flesh.

Sebastian landed beside Artemus and followed him as he raced toward the abandoned monastery. "That weapon. Why did you not tell us about it?"

Artemus flashed him a guilty look. "I—I just never found the right time."

Although Sebastian had yet to see the sword Artemus had retrieved from his bedroom in action, he knew it was all powerful. Divine essence practically dripped from the sheer, thin blade.

He tensed when they reached the open trapdoor in the basement of the building. He could feel the power of the other Guardians rising from somewhere deep beneath the winding staircase spiraling down into the gloom. The Sphinx snarled behind his eyes when he sensed his brethren's pain. Fury brought a scowl to Sebastian's brow.

The Guardians were fighting for their lives.

Artemus folded his wings and swooped down the curving steps, his face dark with anger. "Let's go!"

CHAPTER THIRTY-EIGHT

CALLIE GLARED INTO THE PINPOINT, CRIMSON PUPILS opposite, her arms trembling and her scepter scraping against the gray broadsword trying to cleave her head from her neck. The Nephil's face remained expressionless as he met her furious gaze, the monster as devoid of emotion as the one who had attacked them in Chicago.

A giant shape slammed into the gray angel and took him to the ground. Smokey jumped to his feet, closed his enormous jaws on the creature's head and shoulders, and bit down, his eyes ablaze with loathing. The Nephil punched him blindly in the breastbone, right where he'd been wounded a few days ago. A whimper escaped the hellhound. He clung on with grim determination.

"*You bastard!*" Callie snarled.

She pinned the Nephil to the floor with a clawed foot and drove her scepter through his heart. The creature froze.

Smokey let go and stepped away, his chest heaving with his labored breaths. The poison inside him was taking hold once more, draining the brightness from his eyes and hide.

Inky blood pooled around the Nephil's wound. He studied Callie blankly before opening his mouth.

Shit!

She dug her heels in the ground a second before the monster's lips stretched inhumanly wide. The sonic scream he released shoved her back several feet, the Chimera projecting a golden barrier across her flesh to protect her body from the destructive power of the attack. Smokey's claws raised sparks on the dungeon floor as he was similarly forced backward, the pressure wave gouging fresh wounds into his faces and flanks.

"Brother!"

I am alright. Smokey panted heavily, blood dripping from the gashes scoring his body and pain darkening his golden gazes. *I can still fight.*

Trepidation swamped Callie as the Nephil removed the scepter from his body and dropped it on the ground, leaving a gaping hole where his heart should have been. The weapon levitated in the air and returned to her grip.

He should have died! Why is this bastard still moving?!

Her frustration was echoed by the other Guardians across their bond. However much they attacked the Nephilim, the monsters did not fall.

Callie moved in front of Smokey as the Nephil climbed to his feet. He picked up his blade and focused his attention on them once more.

His figure flickered as he moved.

Callie clenched her jaw and twisted the scepter in rapid revolutions in front of her, creating a fast-spinning, defensive wall that she knew would only last seconds.

Black blood sprayed across her weapon in the next instant.

Callie blinked.

A blade had sliced into the side of the Nephil's neck, partly severing his head. It moved again and again in lightning-quick slashes, shearing the tendons in the monster's limbs. The Nephil dropped to his knees, his sword falling from his limp grasp.

Callie's stomach plummeted when Drake rose from behind the monster.

He was in his dark angel form, his serrated broadsword alive with red flames and his eyes burning crimson and gold. The sigils that marked him as a key glowed brightly on his armor and shield.

"Drake?" she mumbled.

The dark angel smiled. "You missed me?"

Relief had Callie's shoulders sagging at his familiar, teasing tone. "It's you." She stared. "How? I thought Samyaza could control you in this form!"

Drake indicated the manacle dangling from his left ankle. "This is probably the oldest and purest iron in the world. Apparently, the asshole really hates that."

Someone shouted out his name. The dark angel turned.

Serena bolted into his arms and sent him rocking back on his heels, her expression fierce as she hugged him.

"Hey." Drake stiffened before squeezing his arms tightly around the super soldier. Relief and remorse clouded his eyes as he pulled back slightly. "I'm sorry about before. That wasn't me—"

Serena clutched his face in her hands and kissed him.

Half a minute passed. Smokey huffed impatiently.

"Not that your reunion isn't heartwarming, but could you guys maybe give us a hand?!" Daniel yelled from across the dungeon.

Leah scowled. "Yeah! Stop making out and kill something!"

Serena slowly let go of Drake.

"Don't go far," she whispered against his lips.

"I won't," the dark angel breathed.

The hairs rose on Callie's arms. Her snakes stilled. Her pulse thrummed rapidly as she and the serpents stared up at the ceiling. Drake and the other Guardians followed their gazes.

They could all feel the powerful presence coming toward them.

"Artemus," Solomon murmured.

Something bright smashed through the ceiling and flashed through the air ahead of a wave of exploding debris.

By the time he landed on the ground, the white angel had disposed of five Nephilim. The monsters' disintegrating bodies rained crimson ash around him as he straightened, his eyes and armor aglow with golden power.

Callie's gaze locked on the narrow, blood-stained, gossamer blade in his left hand. *What the hell is that?!*

She could sense an immense energy pulsing from the sword, more so than coming from any other divine weapon.

Sebastian drifted down beside Artemus, a scowl on his face.

"What was wrong with the stairs?" the Sphinx grumbled.

"It was taking too long," Artemus said.

Sebastian flicked a hand irritably at his cravat and waistcoat. "Well, now I have dust all over me."

Solomon landed next to them with a thud, his expression curious. "Is that the sword Michael referred to?"

"Yeah. I made it three weeks ago, when Karl was around."

"That's one hell of a blade," Drake muttered as he approached the white angel.

Artemus froze as he registered his brother's presence.

"Drake!" He closed the distance to his twin and embraced him, his face full of emotion. "How did you—?"

"The earthquakes caused my prison to collapse. Luckily, the iron shackle I'd asked for stuck to my armor. That's why Samyaza can't take over my soul right now." Drake grimaced. "Although that bastard's voice is really starting to annoy me."

Artemus looked over Drake's shoulder at Smokey. Concern filled his eyes. "You're hurt."

They went over to the hellhound. Smokey met them halfway and huffed as they gently touched his flanks.

It is nothing I cannot recover from.

Surprise jolted Callie. She stared. "Brother. Your injuries. They're healing!"

Oh. Smokey blinked and gazed at the closing wounds on his hide. *I can feel my energy returning.*

"The Nephil who injured Cerberus must have been among the creatures Artemus just killed," Solomon explained in the face of their shocked expressions. The demon frowned. "Your new blade is the only weapon that can kill them. We'll support you."

Artemus dipped his chin.

The air shook with a sudden wave of intense corruption. They froze, their gazes gravitating to the middle of the dungeon.

Darkness was slowly spreading across the twin gates of Hell levitating above the floor. Otis hovered in front of the portals, a scowl wrinkling his brow as he attempted to curb them with his outstretched right hand. A globe of heavenly light throbbed in his left palm.

It was blocking the demonic swords that had pierced his divine barrier and were attempting to cut into his flesh.

Callie's eyes rounded as she beheld the two demon princes who had appeared in their midst.

"Samyaza," Drake growled.

"Beelzebub," Artemus spat out.

The brothers rose toward the fiends.

Dozens of crimson rifts tore open around the cavern. Hordes of demons shot out of them, their ochre eyes shining with hate.

CHAPTER THIRTY-NINE

JACOB CLUTCHED THE KEY DANGLING FROM HIS NECK and stared wide-eyed at the fearsome battle unfolding before him. He was crouched near the north wall of the dungeon, his small body hidden by some fallen Vatican agents.

His limbs shook and his teeth chattered as he watched the angels and the Guardians fight a legion of demons and Nephilim, the fear throbbing through him so strong it made him feel ill.

He had never felt as helpless as he did in that moment.

It is time, child.

The voice of the beast echoed loudly inside his mind.

Jacob had felt her presence for some time now but had deliberately ignored her. He shook his head in denial and clamped his hands over his ears, knowing the motion would be futile but doing it nonetheless. An incoherent mumble tumbled from his lips.

The creature sighed. *We either do this together or I force our awakening. It is your choice.*

Terror twisted Jacob's belly at the beast's threat. "No! Please! I'm—I'm too scared! I don't belong here!"

Heat flared inside his chest. The beast's words tore through his consciousness the next instant, a sibilant cry that made his eardrums ring.

I chose you for a reason, boy. You are the only human in this world who can bear my soul and my powers!

Tears blurred Jacob's eyes as his gaze found Solomon's dark form. "But—but we will lose him if we awaken! We'll lose Father!"

The divine beast blew out another sigh, this one gentler than the previous. *It is his fate. One he has come to terms with. The demon repented for his sins and shed his tears eons ago. It is time for you to quench yours and assume the mantle you were born to bear. You are my Guardian, child. And, together, we will form a terrifying union. One that can fell the monsters born of the Fallen Ones and their human consorts.*

"What?!" Jacob blinked rapidly. "Wait. Do you mean—we can kill *the Nephilim?!*"

Indeed. The Son of Michael currently holds the only weapon that can defeat them. Our venom and our breath can do this too. We must help him.

Jacob swallowed convulsively. He gasped as a Nephil slashed Solomon's back with a blade. An uncommon burst of anger flared through him.

"How dare they?!"

He scowled and climbed unsteadily to his feet. Determination slowly filled him. Truth be told, he was still petrified. And he knew the beast inside him sensed this too. He was conscious she had shown him more patience and leniency than he deserved, as had Solomon over the years. He knew it was because they both loved him.

His gaze found the Guardians and the angels who shared his fate.

He could feel them across the tenuous bond that had formed when he first came into contact with them. Feel their fury and passion. Feel the strength their ties afforded them. Feel the glory of their cause.

For the first time in his life, Jacob wanted something other than just to stay by Solomon's side. He wanted to belong with Artemus and the other Guardians. He wanted the affection that existed between them and the fierce loyalty they showed one another.

In that moment, Jacob wanted nothing more than to be their kin.

He yanked the key from his neck.

"I am ready," he said in a hard voice.

~

SOLOMON SHUDDERED.

The solar eclipse he had brought about had finally ended.

He twisted in the air and stared across the battleground to where Jacob stood, his eyes finding the boy unerringly. He could feel it rising inside him. The darkness that heralded the opening of the gate within his soul.

"Sebastian! Daniel!"

The two Guardians looked over at him from where they fought a horde of demons and a Nephil.

"Come with me!" Solomon commanded. "You must moor me to this plane of existence while Jacob awakens!"

Surprise widened the Sphinx and the Phoenix's eyes at the urgency in his voice. They glanced at Jacob before following him wordlessly.

Solomon felt Artemus and Drake's eyes on him briefly before they returned their full attention to their fight against Beelzebub and Samyaza. He landed in front of the boy a moment later, the Sphinx and the Phoenix at his side.

Jacob's eyes had glazed over, his pupils shimmering with the heavenly light that heralded his awakening. The key in his hand had morphed into a tall, silver staff. Pale runes materialized along its length even as they watched. The boy opened his lips and started murmuring a holy incantation, a low hiss underscoring the archaic words.

Solomon gasped and dropped his blade, his hands rising to clutch at his chest.

Heat enclosed him as Sebastian and Daniel wound their divine weapons around his body, the bright lassos shimmering against his dark skin. He gritted his teeth as the heavenly weapons sliced into his flesh.

Sebastian clenched his jaw.

"How long must we hold you?" Daniel said, clearly torn as he too sensed the demon's pain.

"Until the seraph destroys me." A stoic smile tilted Solomon's mouth at the sight of their frowns. "Do not feel sorry for me. I have waited for this moment for a long time." His gaze moved to the face of the awakening beast before him, his crimson eyes roaming the boy's features to engrave them in his mind forevermore. "I will finally witness whom he was born to be."

~

Fire filled Jacob as the sigils on the staff slowly flashed from gold to scarlet.

The beast's shape rose in his mind as they prepared to

assume their ultimate form, her eyes bright circles of power that bore into his consciousness. He sensed his entire being shatter and remake itself with every forceful thump of their hearts.

It felt like a lifetime before the final symbol shifted to red.

Jacob took a shuddering breath.

The beast appeared before him, her growl of satisfaction underscoring his own as their souls merged. Power blasted through Jacob's core, filling him with heavenly brilliance. Sight and sound disappeared. In that moment, Jacob finally recognized the identity of the creature who had been with him since the day he'd been born into this realm.

His body swelled, gaining height and width to match the largest demon in the room as he was fully roused. Six serpentine heads sprouted from his torso, forming a defensive halo around him. Thick, dark scales covered his skin in an impenetrable armor and a long, sinuous, spiky tail grew from his tailbone.

Heat filled his lungs and came out of his mouth in a purple miasma. The weapon in his hands doubled in size. Violet tendrils swarmed down his arms and engulfed the surface of the staff.

The white haze filling his world slowly lifted.

Solomon's face materialized before him. Pride and affection filled the demon's eyes as he gazed at him.

"Hydra," Solomon whispered shakily.

CHAPTER FORTY

"Whoa." Artemus stared at the monstrous beast towering before Solomon and the two Guardians. "Who had dibs on the kid being the Lernaean Hydra?"

"Not me," Drake muttered over his shoulder.

They blocked the blades arcing toward their hearts where they hovered back to back in mid-air.

Samyaza scowled at Drake.

Beelzebub smiled savagely where he faced Artemus. "*It's a bit rude to ignore two Princes of Hell. We shall have to teach you young ones a lesson.*"

Artemus narrowed his eyes. "Oh yeah? Well, you guys can piss right off! I was having a nice life until you freaks and that senile bastard Belial decided to bring forward the Apocalypse. You have no idea how much debt I'm in because of you douchebags!"

Drake made a face. "We pay you rent."

"Will you two stop squabbling up there and focus on the problem at hand?!" Haruki yelled from below.

"Yeah, less bitching and more slashing!" Leah grunted, blocking a Nephil's blade.

Callie clicked her tongue and pierced several fiends with her scepter. "You sure are bloodthirsty."

"Hey! I'm not the one whose weapon and horns are dripping with demon blood, lady!" Leah protested.

Serena eyed the Guardians darkly from where she stood some twenty feet to their left. "Let's just shoot them. They're practically immortal. They won't die."

"Hmm," a Vatican agent mumbled with a sickly grimace. "I don't think that's such a great—*oh shit!*"

Nate absentmindedly sliced the neck of the demon who'd been about to gouge the man's stomach and sighed. Smokey lifted a giant paw from a pile of dead fiends and rolled his eyes.

A group of Nephilim surrounded the two super soldiers, the hellhound, and some ten Vatican agents.

Artemus scowled.

One of the monsters opened his mouth to unleash a sonic attack.

"Watch out!" Drake yelled as he parried a strike from Samyaza.

A silver staff throbbing with purple lines pierced the back of the Nephil's head before he could utter a sound. It exited his forehead and zigzagged through the air, stabbing the other monsters through their hearts with deadly accuracy.

Dark veins exploded across the creatures' gray bodies from their wounds. They let go of their blades and clutched at their throats, air wheezing from their lungs.

"What the hell?" Serena muttered as the monsters fell to their knees and started to convulse.

"It's poison." Callie's awed gaze found the serpentine beast who had cast the weapon from the other side of the cavern and who was exhaling a cloud of violet miasma onto the Nephilim converging on him. "Jacob's Hydra. Her venom and her breath are poison to the Nephilim!"

～

THREE NEPHILIM DARTED THROUGH THE AIR AND slashed at Jacob's back.

The snakes framing his body blocked their strikes before spitting purple toxin into their faces. The creatures dropped their swords and clawed at their tainted flesh.

More Nephilim fell around Jacob when his breath reached them, their crimson pupils dimming as the Hydra's poison seeped into their lungs and bodies and consumed them from the inside out. His staff returned to his hand while they disintegrated into crimson ash.

Pain echoed through Jacob as he fought the army of red-eyed monsters closing in on him, his weapon and claws and tail injecting their bodies with venom while he exhaled poison at their faces. His gaze found the demon who stood bound by chains of fire behind him.

A scowl of determination clouded Solomon's face as he fought the darkness growing inside him, his fingers clutching the black circle in the middle of his chest despite the agony tearing him apart.

Father!

Solomon met Jacob's tortured eyes. The demon's mouth tilted in a faint smile. "Do not worry about me, my son."

Jacob swallowed and nodded. He turned and faced the enemy, his beast roaring inside him.

Let us finish this, child!

～

Artemus parried a strike from Beelzebub inches from his head.

The demon grinned. *"Did you think you'd defeat me so easily, Son of Michael?"*

Artemus observed him steadily. "I'll admit that you're strong."

Samyaza hissed as Drake drove him back several feet. They fought to Artemus's left, their blades sparking and scraping violently.

Artemus bared his teeth as he felt his twin's powers resonate with his own. "But we're stronger!"

He slashed Beelzebub's flanks with his swords and kicked him in the chest.

Surprise flared on the demon's face as he shot backward some two hundred feet. He smashed into the wall of the cavern with a thunderous boom. The rockface beside him caved into a crater as Samyaza crash-landed next to him an instant later.

Drake's father roared in outrage as he pushed away from the wall, his fury making the very air tremble. Beelzebub scowled and joined him.

Artemus kept pace with his brother as they accelerated toward the demon princes heading for them. "How does it feel to kick your old man's ass?"

"Deeply satisfying," Drake growled.

Metal clanged violently as they clashed blades with the two demons, the shockwave of the impact reverberating across the cavern. The brothers moved again and again, their attacks growing faster and stronger as their energies synchronized across their bond and their connection with Cerberus.

Artemus swooped beneath Beelzebub's sword and glanced at the battlefield.

Jacob and his Hydra had disposed of over half the Nephilim and showed no signs of fatigue. The other Guardians and the super soldiers were steadily overcoming Ba'al's fiends, Solomon's blue demons and the remaining Vatican agents at their side.

Floating in the center of the cave, his expression serene once more, the seraph was closing the gates of Hell.

Hope surged inside Artemus. *We're winning!*

Beelzebub's eyes flared opposite him. A thrilled look lit his face as he stared at the abyss beneath them. "*He's coming.*"

The hairs rose on the back of Artemus's neck. A suffocating wave of corruption flooded the air. Shadows exploded across the cavern, leaching the light out of the chamber.

Artemus's stomach plummeted as he followed Beelzebub's gaze. It wasn't demonic rifts he was sensing. A crimson point was rising from the void below.

Though the creature seemed far away, Artemus knew the demon would soon be upon them.

"Shit!" Drake exchanged an alarmed glance with Artemus. "We need to close that chasm!"

A low chuckle left Beelzebub at the same time a savage expression brightened Samyaza's monstrous features.

"*If you think we are powerful, you have seen nothing yet, you insolent fools,*" Drake's father growled.

"*Yup,*" Beelzebub said. "*I believe the Masterless One is pretty pissed with you two.*"

In that moment, Artemus knew who was headed toward them.

Heat flared inside him. He felt Michael and Theia behind his eyes as his power multiplied exponentially, just as it had done that time in Chicago, when he'd rescued Drake from Samyaza and Beelzebub.

We have to end this. Now!

Drake gasped as Artemus's explosive energy filtered across their bond. His eyes flashed gold.

Surprise dawned on Samyaza and Beelzebub's faces.

CHAPTER FORTY-ONE

THE LIGHT SWELLING WITHIN DRAKE FROM THE TIES
that bound him to his twin tempered the darkness that
always dwelled inside his soul. In that breathless moment
of synchrony, he tasted his brother's supreme power and
that of their goddess mother. He understood then the
reason why Artemus's new sword could never be bested.

His brother had forged a weapon equal to a god's.

As they soared through the air in the timeless seconds
that followed, their movements too fast for anyone but
each other to discern, their attacks overcoming the two
shocked demon princes and driving them toward the
yawning abyss below, Drake reveled in the righteousness
that was his brother's ultimate strength.

Beelzebub and Samyaza raged as they were pushed
relentlessly into the shadowy chasm. High above the
dungeon, the seraph closed his hands on the shrinking
globes of darkness that were all that remained of Callie
and Haruki's gates. Light flared between his palms and in
his third eye.

The demon princes and the remaining fiends roared as the portals crumbled into gold dust.

"Drake!"

Drake looked over and saw Artemus indicate the ceiling. He nodded and rose rapidly alongside him. He knew what his brother intended.

"Otis! Sebastian! We're gonna need a barrier!" Artemus warned as they neared the roof of the cave.

The seraph dipped his chin wordlessly. Drake's eardrums throbbed as he gently beat his wings and moved. He landed beside Sebastian and raised a hand along with the Sphinx.

Surprise jolted Drake at the sight of the two new symbols on the seraph's left palm. Before he had time to make sense of them, a golden haze exploded across the cave. It coalesced into a protective bubble that enclosed the Guardians, the super soldiers, and their human and demon allies.

A voice full of wrath reverberated across the dungeon as Belial rose from the depths of the Earth.

Artemus scowled. "Not today, asshole!"

He swung his blades at the same time Drake wielded his.

Their swords struck the roof of the cavern with powerful clangs. Cracks exploded across the uneven dome. It trembled before collapsing with a thunderous rumble.

A barrier shielded Drake and Artemus's bodies a heartbeat before several thousand tons of dirt and rock rained down upon them in a deafening roar.

The noise went on for what felt like a lifetime.

Drake's blood pounded dully in his ears as an eerie silence descended in the wake of the cave-in. The dust clouding the air slowly cleared. He stared.

A giant pile of rubble occupied the floor of the cave, where the abyss once stood. The remains of the abandoned monastery peeked out here and there through the debris. He looked up and gazed dazedly along a giant shaft to distant stars and an inky night sky.

"We did it," he mumbled, stunned.

"Yeah, we did."

Drake sighed at the look on his brother's face. "Do you have to look so smug?"

Artemus's grin faded. "What? I mean, *come on*! We just thrashed Beelzebub and Samyaza's asses, not to mention their scumbag of a boss!"

His twin's grumbles continued as they headed toward the floor of the cave.

"What's he bitching about now?" Serena asked Drake.

Otis and Sebastian had lowered the divine shield protecting her and the others.

The dark angel landed beside her and took her in his arms. "His ego just swelled to the size of Mount Rushmore."

Serena grimaced. "What else is new?"

SOLOMON BLINKED SWEAT FROM HIS EYES AS HE WATCHED Artemus head over to where he stood imprisoned by the Sphinx and the Phoenix's powers.

"How is he doing?" Artemus asked Otis, his expression sober.

Sadness filled the seraph's gaze.

Tears rolled down Jacob's cheeks. He hugged Solomon, his body that of a boy once more.

He looked beseechingly at Otis. "Can we not save him?!"

"Hush, child," Solomon chided gently before the seraph could respond.

The disk of darkness over his heart throbbed and pulsed as he fought to control it.

Artemus clenched his jaw and met the demon's gaze. "What happens now?"

Solomon's dark heart thudded steadily as he looked to the seraph. "The Seal of God has to destroy me."

"*No!*" Jacob protested with a desperate cry.

Grief swamped Solomon when he felt Jacob's thin, hot arms tighten around him.

He'd thought he'd prepared himself for this moment. That he would be ready when the end came. Yet, he found himself not wanting to let go of the child who had claimed his heart and soul.

"*It will be alright, Sariel.*"

Solomon blinked as a different kind of warmth engulfed him.

The Voice of God reverberated across the dungeon, driving the Vatican agents and Solomon's demons to cover their ears. Even the super soldiers and the Guardians winced as Otis's quiet words washed across them.

"*He has not forsaken you.*"

Solomon stared into the seraph's eyes and understood his meaning. Remorse filled him a thousand times over as he felt a divine blessing fill his corrupt soul. He took a shuddering breath, the darkness inside him subsiding, replaced by the light he had once harbored.

"Jacob?"

"Yes?" the boy sniffed.

"We will meet again."

Jacob's eyes widened as he stared up at him, the golden light that exploded around Solomon's body reflected in his pupils.

Solomon's vision blurred as his tears fell upon his son's face, his skin and wings brightening to their original colors.

"We will meet...at the End of Days."

His voice faded to a whisper, the seraph's power finally consuming him.

Brightness filled his world.

ARTEMUS'S NAILS BIT INTO HIS PALMS AS HE WATCHED the archangel's gold and silver body and his white wings dissipate to a cloud of sparkling dust.

The Prince of God's true form was breathtakingly beautiful.

Jacob fell to his knees, his sobs wrenching all their hearts across the bond that connected them.

A sigh echoed across the cavern. Solomon's demons were fading to glittering ash, relief pasted across their faces as they followed their commander. Artemus's soul grew heavy when he sensed the thousands of years of grief that tainted the air in the wake of their passage.

Then, there was only silence and sorrow.

A sound came from behind them. Persephone appeared at the mouth of a tunnel, Holmes at her side.

"Is it—is it over?" she mumbled.

Daniel went over to her. "Yes."

Artemus inhaled shakily. His breath froze in his throat in the next instant. He twisted mechanically, his gaze moving to a spot by Drake's left foot.

Time slowed.

Artemus's head moved like treacle as he raised his chin and met his twin's widening eyes. They had both sensed the evil rising toward them. Artemus moved just as the rubble detonated in a powerful, explosive wave that sent everyone but him, Serena, Drake, and Otis flying through the air.

A giant, clawed hand ripped through the debris and closed around Drake's ankle. The demon wrenched the iron manacle from the dark angel's armor before dragging him into a widening chasm.

Serena gasped and fell backward as Drake was jerked violently from her arms.

"*Noooo!*" Artemus screamed.

He lunged over the jagged edge of the abyss and grabbed his twin's wrist. Horror twisted his gut at the sight of the enormous, crimson rift below and the demon pulling his brother into Hell.

Belial's red eyes were two bright circles of loathing beneath Drake. Terror flared on the dark angel's face as he gazed helplessly up at Artemus.

Artemus gritted his teeth and tightened his grip on his brother, his body slipping inexorably over the rim of the chasm. Heat wrapped around him from behind, yanking him back from the void. He glanced at the fiery whip and the flaming lasso around his waist and right thigh and followed them to the two Guardians closing in on him.

"Let him go, Artemus!" Sebastian shouted.

"No!" Artemus glared at the Sphinx and the Phoenix. "I can save him!"

Daniel scowled. "We cannot allow you to fall to Hell!"

Smokey's giant paws slipped on rubble as he bounded

across the cave toward them, his golden gazes full of panic and the other Guardians in his wake.

Serena scrambled onto her knees next to Artemus, her face ashen.

She reached out blindly to the dark angel. "*Drake!*"

A powerful presence drifted over Artemus as he resisted the shackles pulling him from his brother. He felt the seraph's hand on his shoulder.

"I have to save him!" Artemus raged at Otis. "*I have to!*"

"No."

Artemus's heart stuttered. It wasn't Otis who had spoken. He shuddered as he looked down into Drake's face.

The fear had faded from his brother's eyes. In its stead was a bone-deep resolve.

"I can't," Artemus mumbled. "Please, don't ask me—"

"Yes, you can," Drake said calmly. "Let me go. We both knew this would happen. I came to terms with my fate a long time ago."

Artemus shook his head, his entire soul flinching in denial.

"*Let me go, brother!*" Drake roared.

Smokey whimpered where he crouched next to Artemus.

Artemus's fingers twitched around his brother's wrist.

"I can't!" he cried. "I just—"

Pain twisted Drake's face. "Then, you leave me no choice."

He clenched his jaw and swung his dark blade. The broadsword hummed through the air and cleaved Artemus's right wing clear from his body.

Artemus recoiled, more in shock than in pain. Hot

blood dripped down his arm. Drake's wrist slipped through his hands.

"No! *Nooooo!*" Artemus bellowed.

The world faded around him as he lost his hold on his brother.

Drake's gaze locked on his one final time as he fell into the void with Belial, his body drifting through a cloud of white feathers, Artemus's tears and blood landing on his face like a blessing.

He mouthed two words before he vanished into the darkness, Artemus's scream following him long after he was gone.

THE END

AFTERWORD

Thank you for reading HEIR! The next and final book in the LEGION series is LEGION.

If you enjoyed HEIR, please consider leaving a review on your favorite book site. Reviews help readers find books! Join my VIP Facebook Group for exclusive sneak peeks at my upcoming books and sign up to my newsletter for new release alerts, exclusive bonus content, and giveaways.

Turn the page to read an extract from LEGION now!

LEGION EXTRACT

I am darkness.
I am wrath.
I am destruction.
I am oppressor.
I belong to Hell.
~ Drake Hunter

SERENA BLAKE STOPPED IN FRONT OF THE DOOR, RAISED a hand, and hesitated.

Heavy silence filtered through from the room on the other side, the stillness echoed by the oppressive hush shrouding the LeBlanc estate. Serena knew what awaited her beyond the door. She steeled herself, rapped her knuckles on the wood, and called out a warning.

"I'm coming in."

Stale, muggy air washed over her when she crossed the threshold, carrying with it the faint odor of human sweat.

Artemus Steele's bedroom was dark, the curtains at the

windows pulled closed against the daylight. She navigated the floor and stopped when her foot knocked against something. She looked down, the nanorobots in her retina adjusting to the dim lighting.

The tray of food Callie had brought that morning lay untouched, as she'd suspected it would be.

Serena sighed and walked around the bed.

Artemus was a shadow where he sat on the hardwood floor, his back against the foot of the four poster and his legs stretched out before him. Jacob Schroeder slept with his head on the angel's lap, his body curved into a tight ball and Smokey clutched snugly in his thin arms. The rabbit opened a heavy eye and looked at her blearily before closing it once more.

Artemus continued staring into space, as if he hadn't registered her presence.

"You need to eat."

Her command got no reaction. Serena stayed still for a moment before making a frustrated sound and raking a hand through her hair. As a super soldier, she shouldn't have felt exhausted. Except she did.

She had never experienced the bone deep tiredness that came with having her heart shattered into a million pieces and sharing that grief with so many others.

"You aren't the only one who lost Drake, Artemus. I did too. And so did everyone else." Her voice remained steady despite the knot twisting her stomach.

She couldn't give in to her emotions. Not again. It wouldn't bring Drake back and it only made Nate feel helpless in the face of her anguish.

Artemus stiffened at her words. Faint lines marred his brow.

"He was my twin," he said stonily. "My blood."

"And he was my lover!" Serena snapped.

"Did you love him?"

His question made her eyes widen and drew a sharp breath from her lips.

Artemus had raised his head and was glaring at her accusingly.

Serena swallowed. She knew it wasn't her he was angry at.

"Yes."

"Did you ever tell him?"

Artemus's words shot through her like bullets tearing into her broken, bleeding heart.

Her reply came out a whisper. "Once."

"I never did," Artemus muttered. "It's too late for me to say it now and for you to repeat it."

Anger quickened Serena's pulse at his callous words. She would have closed the distance between them and punched Artemus in the face had it not been for the sleeping child in his arms.

"That's it!" she grated out. "It's been two weeks since we got back from Rome. You need to quit being a mopey asshole and talk to us!"

She strode over to the windows, grabbed the edges of the curtains, and pulled them open with a brisk motion. Blinding light flooded the room, exposing the dust motes filling the air and covering the furnishings.

Artemus swore and raised a hand to shield his face. Dark stubble covered his jawline and upper lip, and his golden hair was dull and greasy.

Jacob squinted before blinking at the brightness, his face swollen and his eyes red and puffy from crying. He sat up slowly, his expression numb and his arms tightening around the limp rabbit.

Drake wasn't the only one they'd lost in Rome.

Solomon Weiss, Jacob's adoptive father and the fallen archangel Sariel turned demon, had sacrificed his life as Jacob's gate during their last battle.

Serena hardened her heart against the young Guardian's forlorn look.

"The three of you stink," she said in a hard voice. "Go have a shower and come downstairs." She grabbed the tray of uneaten food and stormed toward the exit.

"Don't wanna," Artemus mumbled, his tone low and petulant.

The rabbit's eyes flashed with a crimson glow of defiance.

Jacob clutched Artemus's arm, his face similarly sullen.

Serena stopped on the threshold and arched an eyebrow at the angel and the Guardians clinging to him. "You either shower and get dressed on your own, or we're coming up here to do it for you. It's your choice."

Artemus's outraged snarl followed her out of the bedroom.

"How the hell is that a choice?!"

Serena's mouth stretched in a flinty smile as she navigated the corridors of the mansion. That was the first hint of genuine emotion Artemus had shown since their return from Europe. She sobered as she went downstairs and put the cold food away.

What had happened in the cave deep under the Vatican gardens and the monastery where Artemus and Drake's mothers had once sought refuge was something none of them had gotten over yet.

It was thanks to Jacob's divine beast and Artemus's new sword that they'd managed to defeat the army of inde-structible Nephilims Beelzebub had raised to tear open

Jacob's gate and capture Drake. Having twarted Beelzebub and Samyaza's efforts to drag Drake to Hell, they'd tasted victory for the briefest of moments before everything was ripped from their grasp.

Belial's appearance had shocked all of them and none more than Artemus.

Though they knew Ba'al's leader to be one of the most powerful demons in existence, they hadn't anticipated that he'd turn up personally to complete the task his associates had failed to execute.

They would have lost Artemus too that day had Sebastian, Daniel, and Otis not intervened to stop him from following his brother into Hell. But it was Drake who had ultimately saved his twin by cutting off his right wing and forcing him to let go.

Artemus's blood had grown cold and congealed to thick puddles beneath him before they'd managed to drag his body from the edge of the chasm where Drake had disappeared, his voice raw from screaming and his face streaked with tear marks.

He'd fallen into a state of shock shortly after, his body growing cold as ice and his gaze vacant. It was in that condition that they'd maneuvered him onto the private jet that had borne them to Chicago, their senses too raw still from their latest encounter with Ba'al to wish to travel through one of Sebastian's rifts.

The Vatican was still in the midst of dealing with the aftermath of the battle. They'd blamed the destruction the rise of the Nephilims had wreaked on the capital and the Holy See on the earthquake that had rocked the region that night. So far, the world continued to believe that false claim.

As for the giant sinkhole that now occupied a significant portion of the Vatican gardens, not even Persephone had been able to stop the media from getting their hands on the shocking images of the jagged chasm and broadcasting them to all seven continents.

No one but they and the Vatican agents who had fought beside them knew the borehole was a result of Artemus and Drake bringing down the roof of the cave onto their enemy.

Serena was still frowning when she strolled inside the TV room a short while later. She stopped and studied the figures slouched and draped on various pieces of furniture.

"Seriously, you guys are almost as bad as him."

Callie Stone sniffed as she huddled next to Nate Conway on the couch, her eyes suspiciously red. Leah Chase bit her lip and glared out into the garden, her gaze glistening and her fingers white around Haruki Kuroda's hand on the window seat.

Daniel Lenton stared blindly at the open bible in his hands where he leaned against the wall beside them, his face miserable. Sebastian Lancaster and Otis Boone were attempting to play a game of chess at a low table to the left, without much success.

"Did they eat?" Nate said quietly.

"No. The three of them are being stubborn."

"That is nothing new." A muscle jumped in Sebastian's cheek. "But the child at least should be made to consume some food. He is still young and he used a lot of divine energy during the battle."

"I suspect he might bite us if we do that," Serena drawled. "And Smokey will have something to say about it too."

"That pup is too obstinate for his own good," Sebastian grumbled.

Gravel crunched faintly out the front of the mansion.

Serena tensed.

"It's only Elton and Barbara," Haruki murmured. "They said they'd drop by again today."

"There are more than two people out there," Otis said morosely, his gaze on the chess pieces before him.

GET LEGION NOW!

ABOUT A.D. STARRLING

Want to know about AD Starrling's upcoming releases?
Sign up to her newsletter for new release alerts, sneak
peeks, giveaways, and get a free boxset and exclusive
freebies.

Join AD's reader group on Facebook:
The Seventeen Club

Like AD's Author Page

Check out AD's website for extras and more:
www.adstarrling.com

BOOKS BY A.D. STARRLING

SEVENTEEN NOVELS

Hunted - 1

Warrior - 2

Empire - 3

Legacy - 4

Origins - 5

Destiny - 6

SEVENTEEN NOVEL BOXSETS

The Seventeen Collection 1 - Books 1-3

The Seventeen Collection 2 - Books 4-6

SEVENTEEN SHORT STORIES

First Death - 1

Dancing Blades - 2

The Meeting - 3

The Warrior Monk - 4

LEGION

DIVISION EIGHT

MISCELLANEOUS

Void - A Sci-fi Horror Short Story

The Other Side of the Wall - A Horror Short Story

AUDIOBOOKS

Go to Authors Direct for a range of options where you can get AD's audiobooks.